Praise for Ellie Ale...

"..." ...ew

...T Book Reviews

...es to make your
...ader to Reader

WITHDRAWN

"This debut culinary mystery is a light soufflé of a book (with recipes) that makes a perfect mix for fans of Jenn McKinlay, Leslie Budewitz, or Jessica Beck."
        —*Library Journal* on *Meet Your Baker*

"Marvelous."   —*Fresh Fiction*

"Scrumptious . . . will delight fans of cozy mysteries with culinary delights."   —*Night Owl Reviews*

"Clever plots, likable characters, and good food . . . Still hungry? Not to worry, because desserts abound in . . . this delectable series."
        —*Mystery Scene* on *A Batter of Life and Death*

"[With] *Meet Your Baker,* Alexander weaves a tasty tale of deceit, family ties, delicious pastries, and murder."
        —Edith Maxwell, author of *A Tine to Live,*
                                          A Tine to Die

"Sure to satisfy both dedicated foodies and ardent mystery lovers alike."
        —Jessie Crockett, author of *Drizzled with Death*

Also
by Ellie Alexander

Meet Your Baker

A Batter of Life and Death

On Thin Icing

Caught Bread Handed

Fudge and Jury

A Crime of Passion Fruit

Another One Bites the Crust

Till Death Do Us Tart

Ellie Alexander

St. Martin's Paperbacks

This is a work of fiction. All of the characters, organizations, and events portrayed in this novel are either products of the author's imagination or are used fictitiously.

TILL DEATH DO US TART

For information address St. Martin's Press, 175 Fifth Avenue, New York, NY 10010.

ISBN: 978-1-250-15937-3

Our books may be purchased in bulk for promotional, educational, or business use. Please contact your local bookseller or the Macmillan Corporate and Premium Sales Department at 1-800-221-7945, ext. 5442, or by e-mail at MacmillanSpecialMarkets@macmillan.com.

Printed in the United States of America

St. Martin's Paperbacks edition / July 2018

St. Martin's Paperbacks are published by St. Martin's Press, 175 Fifth Avenue, New York, NY 10010.

10 9 8 7 6 5 4 3 2 1

Till Death Do Us Tart

Chapter One

They say that love makes the world go round. Given the contagious feeling of love in the air in my warmhearted town of Ashland, Oregon, I suspected that the saying might be true. Ashland's amorous tendencies were heightened with preparations for what locals were calling "the wedding of the century." My mom and her longtime beau, the Professor, had finally decided to tie the knot and everyone was humming with eager anticipation. Torte, our family bakeshop, was no exception. For the past few weeks, we had been hand-pressing dainty lemon tarts with mounds of fluffy whipping cream, testing new recipes for strawberry sponge cake, and finalizing the menu for the wedding feast. Mom and the Professor had agreed on an inclusive guest list. That meant that anyone in our little hamlet who wanted to come to the wedding was invited. That also meant that my team and I were going to be baking around the clock to ensure that we had enough food to feed the masses.

To complicate matters, Mom and the Professor each had a trick up their sleeve. They had wanted to surprise one another with a Midsummer Night's Dream wedding on the summer solstice. But the ruse was on them. Neither of them had been able to secure a venue, since Ashland was a prime destination for summer weddings. After I'd had dozens of conversations with each of them, they had both come to the same conclusion—the wedding would have to wait. Only, it wouldn't. We were one step ahead of them. Wedding plans had been going on underground for the past month, and the entire town was in on the secret. We had created an elaborate decoy party, the grand reopening of Uva, a gorgeous hillside vineyard that I was now a one-third owner in. We had sent invitations for a reopening bash, asking guests to come in Elizabethan attire for a celebratory Midsummer's Eve dinner under the stars. At last count, we had over two hundred and fifty RSVPs, and (fingers crossed) hopefully Mom and the Professor were none the wiser.

Keeping the real reason for the festivities a secret from Ashland's lead detective and my very astute mom was going to be no small feat. After tossing around several white lies, we decided our best bet was to host a party. That way we wouldn't have to try to hide vats of artichoke dip and hundreds of peach cobbler cupcakes. I had roped my friend Thomas in to help keep the Professor occupied. Thomas was Ashland's deputy, and the Professor's right-hand man. As of late, the Professor had talked openly about retiring, or at least scaling back, after the wedding. Thomas used the opportunity to distract the Professor by pummeling him with questions about police procedures. Throwing Mom off the scent wasn't as easy. Her sharp walnut eyes seemed to pierce through me when she would ask if I was going overboard on the food for the launch party. I had fumbled through a lie, claiming that the frenzy of preparation around Torte was also due to trying to stockpile product for any temporary closures we might incur during our basement renovation. I'm not sure she bought my story, but she was distracted with trying to find a venue for the wedding and didn't press further.

If we could make it through the next few days without spilling the beans, we should be in the clear. The wedding was on Saturday night—less than a week away.

Time to get baking, Jules, I thought as I unwrapped sheets of filo dough and glanced at Torte's steamy kitchen windows. The sun had yet to fully rise. It cast a purplish glow on the plaza. There was something calming and almost magical about baking in the quiet predawn hours. I loved the idea that while I was kneading bread dough my friends and neighbors were fast asleep. It was as if mornings were exclusively mine. Not many people ever witnessed the sun's slow ascent, the way the sky shifted from deep purple to pink and how light drifted across the treetops. Every sunrise was slightly different. Some days the bricks on the plaza across the street glowed a burning orange, like the sun was begging villagers out of their beds. While other days it lagged behind wispy clouds, encouraging a lazy lie-in.

Sunrises were like pastry. No two scones or turnovers ever came out exactly the same. Sure, the average connoisseur might not notice the nuance of a slightly thinner crust or browning of crystallized sugar, but each sweet and savory treat that I pulled from our ovens had its own unique signature.

I patted the cool dough and stole another look outside.

Antique street lamps cast soft halos on the sidewalk. A maroon banner with Shakespeare's bust flapped in a hint of wind. The new season of the Oregon Shakespeare Festival had kicked off last month, bringing tourists and theater lovers to our small southern Oregon town. From now through the end of summer the bakeshop would see a steady stream of customers. This was our busy season, so of course we were adding in a wedding, launching a new winery, and finishing our basement expansion. No one ever claimed that I strayed away from a challenge. I just hoped that I wasn't in over my head.

Dusting my hands with flour, I set to work placing thin layers of the filo dough on the kitchen island. Then I brushed them with melted butter. I planned to create a stacked strawberry pastry with honey, a touch of salt, and toasted almonds. If it went according to my vision we would feature it as our breakfast special for the morning rush, and potentially add it to the ever-growing list of desserts for the wedding. Once I had brushed the sheets of dough with butter, I layered fresh sliced strawberries, drizzled them with honey, and sprinkled them with toasted almonds and coarse sea salt. I repeated the layers until I had a four-inch stack. I finished the pastry with a final coat of golden butter and then slid it into the oven.

With my test pastry in the oven, I turned my attention to our daily bread and specialty cake orders. About thirty percent of our business came from wholesale accounts. We delivered bread and pastries to several restaurants on the plaza and throughout Ashland, like the Green Goblin on the opposite end of the Calle Guanajuato. They used our breads for pub-style sandwiches and offered their customers custom cake slices. It was beneficial for both of us. The Green Goblin was primarily a bar, but maintained a basic menu. Our partnership allowed them to feature locally made baked goods at a discounted rate and gave us consistent weekly income and some word-of-mouth marketing. As I kneaded sourdough starter and flour on the island, I thought about how lucky I was to live and work in such a supportive community.

Soon, the kitchen was alive with the scent of sweet bread. I was so lost in the process of twisting braids of challah dough that I didn't even realize that the sky had lightened until I heard Stephanie and Andy come inside.

"Morning, boss," Andy called in his usual chipper tone. He wore a Southern Oregon University T-shirt, cargo shorts, and flip-flops. "It's already warm out there. I think it's going to be a cold brew kind of day."

"Sounds delish," I replied with a wave.

Stephanie trudged in after him. Even though they both attended SOU, their styles couldn't have been more different. Her violet hair had been dyed black at the tips. She wore a pair of skinny jeans and a black tank top that matched her surly attempt at a smile. "Hey." She gave me a nod and headed to grab an apron.

Andy stared at the racks of bread. "Dude, how long have you been here?"

"I don't know. A couple of hours, maybe." I glanced at the clock on the wall behind me and gave him a sheepish look. "I couldn't sleep. Too much to do." That was true, but there was more to my lack of sleep than just our bakery production. As excited as I was about Mom's wedding, I had a lot on my mind. My estranged husband, Carlos, was arriving with his son Ramiro in two days. I had never met Ramiro, and while I was confident that we would get along, I couldn't silence a small, nagging fear that he might not like me. I hadn't even known that Carlos had a son until I found a stack of letters in our tiny room on the ship. Learning that Carlos had a son had been a shock, but what made it painful and confusing was the fact that he had kept it from me. I left without giving him a chance to explain. Maybe it hadn't been my most rational moment, but returning to Ashland and cocooning myself among longtime friends had given me space and distance. I had had to come to terms with Carlos's decision. Not that I entirely understood it, but I had forgiven him. It didn't serve either of us for me to hold on to my anger. And, the truth was that I was excited about meeting Ramiro. The way Carlos spoke of his son had opened a desire for a family within me that I hadn't even realized existed. Hopefully, meeting Ramiro in real life would live up to the expectation I had created in my head.

One thing I was worried about was trying to find some time to talk to Carlos alone. He hadn't told me about purchasing a share in Uva. Apparently, keeping things secret was a pattern. I wasn't sure what that meant for his long-term plans, and quite honestly what that meant for me. After a quick return to the *Amour of the Seas,* the cruise ship where we had met and eventually married, I had come home resolved that it was time for me to leave that life behind. Did buying into Uva mean that Carlos also had different plans? Was he thinking of leaving the vagabond lifestyle of the sea too?

Then there was the issue of Richard Lord. Richard owned the Merry Windsor hotel across the plaza from Torte. He'd been a thorn in my side ever since I returned home. It had started when I discovered that he was trying to swindle Mom out of her ownership of Torte. His business practices were shady at best. Normally, I went out of my way to avoid any interactions with the pompous Mr. Lord. Alas, that wasn't going to be possible any longer. Richard was also a one-third partner in the winery and had made it crystal clear that he would do whatever it took to buy us out. For some reason, Richard had been extremely accommodating with Mom's wedding plans. That should have given me peace of mind, but instead it had me on edge. I didn't trust Richard's motivation. Maybe there was a small chance that he had changed his ways, but I suspected his recent sickening sweetness was part of a bigger plan. The question was, what?

Finally, most of my insomnia was due to worry over my friend Lance. Lance was the artistic director at the Oregon Shakespeare Festival. His plays had won multiple awards and had become revered throughout the theater community as cutting-edge. OSF bent gender roles, casting women as the lead in many of Shakespeare's classics and producing works by underrepresented artists. Thanks to Lance's visionary spirit, OSF had become more than just the charming outdoor Elizabethan theater that attracted traditional theater lovers and Shakespeare enthusiasts. Sure, the company was committed to working its way through the bard's canon, but it was also willing to take risks and showcase plays written and staged to challenge personal beliefs and leave the audience with questions.

Lance had recently been accused of murder. Fortunately, it turned out that he wasn't a killer, but he had been struggling with the board of directors at the theater and had taken off for an unknown locale right as the new season had commenced. That wasn't like him. Nor was his erratic behavior and his crazy spending habits. We had been out of touch for two weeks. During the time he'd been gone I'd taken it upon myself to ask around to see if I could come up with any clues to explain the sudden and dramatic shift in his personality. Thus far, nothing had come to light.

The sound of Andy firing up the espresso machine shook me from my thoughts.

He adjusted his well-worn baseball cap. "Okay, if you've been here for hours you need a cold brew—stat. I brewed a batch last night that's chilling in the walk-in. I'll have it ready for you in less than two secs." He flashed me two fingers and sprinted to the fridge.

"You know that I'll never turn down your coffee," I called after him, brushing my hands on my bright red Torte apron. Our current space included the kitchen, which opened to the espresso bar and pastry counter. The front of the bakeshop housed a variety of bistro tables and window booths. My parents had painted the dining area in teal and red—royal colors—in honor of my dad's love of the bard and all things Shakespeare. Short of freshening up the paint and modernizing our ovens, Torte hadn't changed much since the day my parents first opened the front doors. I liked it that way and intended to keep the same welcoming vibe in the newly renovated basement. Mom and I had discussed the possibility of an expansion someday. Neither of us had expected that our dreams would come to fruition so quickly. The basement space became available at the same time that the city announced an incentive program and low-interest loans for small-business owners. One afternoon I was touring the soggy basement and the next thing I knew I was signing a contract for a major remodel.

Progress had sped up over the past few days. The electrician was due later in the afternoon for the final inspection. After that it would be a matter of paint, trim, and then the fun stuff—like arranging furniture and artwork. Our goal was to move wholesale baking operations downstairs within the week. Once we had the new kitchen up and running we could tear through the current kitchen to create stairs between the spaces. The dining room, espresso bar, and pastry counter would expand and customers would have additional seating options downstairs with a view of the brick pizza oven and our bakers at work. Our architect, Roger, had found a way to add a woodstove in the seating area so that customers could cozy up with a latte and pastry on cold winter afternoons. I felt like a kid at Christmas every time I went downstairs to check on progress. We were so close I could hardly wait.

"What do you want me to start on? It looks like you're almost done with the wholesale orders." Stephanie stared at the whiteboard, which had the day's tasks outlined, and then back to the racks of bread. "Weren't you just lecturing me about not getting enough sleep?"

She had a fair point. Mom, the team, and I had almost had to stage an intervention because Stephanie had been so sleep-deprived, thanks to a neighbor with a love of show tunes keeping her awake every night. Her lack of sleep had impacted her personal well-being and her baking. Thankfully, a good set of earplugs was all it took to get her back on track. Was I in the same position? Typically, I thrive on little to no sleep. It comes with the territory—bakers' hours. In my line of work sleeping in is unheard of. Bakers rise with their bread in the wee hours of the night.

I didn't feel rusty or sluggish, but then again, I also felt like I was operating on autopilot. "True," I replied with a chuckle. "But I'm the boss so the rules don't apply, right?"

Stephanie scowled. "Ha!"

"Promise me that if I start acting loopy, you guys will keep me in check?"

"Oh, we'll keep you in check," Andy replied before Stephanie had a chance. He handed us glasses of iced coffee with a lovely layer of something creamy on the top. "You don't have to worry though. This is my toasted-coconut cold brew. One glass of this will have you revved up and ready to bake for days."

Stephanie dunked a spoon into her coffee and swirled the thick coconut milk together with the dark brew. "I don't know about the coffee, but we've got your back, Jules."

I fought a tightness in my throat. Stephanie's outward appearance and aloof attitude sometimes gave the impression that she didn't care. Nothing could be further from the truth. I don't know how Mom and I had lucked out with such a stellar young staff, or what we would do without them.

"Thanks," I said, taking a sip of the coffee. The

rich espresso and bright coconut flavor were a perfect pairing.

Andy returned to his post while Stephanie and I reviewed what I had already completed and what needed to be tackled next. Desserts had begun to outshine the cake at many weddings that we had recently catered and Mom's nuptials would be no exception. We had sketched out a tablescape for the reception with a combination of whimsical and elegant dessert offerings sure to please every palate. I tasked Stephanie with working on the dough for what would become milk and cookie shots.

"How am I supposed to make the dough into cups?" Stephanie asked, washing her hands with lavender soap.

I pulled out my notebook and flipped it open to my sketches and recipes. The milk and cookie shots were a nod to childhood nostalgia. We would make three kinds of cookie dough—chocolate chip, oatmeal raisin, and snickerdoodle—but reduce the butter to create a crumbly, pliable dough. Then we would mold the dough in a popover pan. Once the cookies had baked we would have adorable cups that we would fill with melted dark chocolate, milk chocolate, and caramel to create a seal. Right before serving the shots we would fill the cookie molds with milk infused with vanilla, almond, and cinnamon. I had a feeling that the rich and fun cookie shots were going to be a hit among the guests.

Stephanie added butter, eggs, and sugar into the mixer while I gathered ingredients for a test batch of another fanciful dessert, pie fries. For the sweet fries, I began by cutting butter and flour together for a pie crust. I added a splash of my favorite secret pie-crust ingredient—vodka (which ensures a tender, flaky crust)—and rolled up my sleeves to knead the dough. Soon I had a lovely round ball of dough that I rolled into a thin sheet. Next, I cut the crust into half-inch strips and brushed each side with melted butter. To finish them, I sprinkled them with a healthy dose of cinnamon and sugar and popped the strips into the oven to bake for ten to twelve minutes. The scent of the spicy sticks soon filled the kitchen.

Andy and Stephanie concentrated on their work. One of the many things that I appreciated about our team was everyone's ability to take initiative. I didn't have to remind Andy to wipe down the espresso machine at the start of his shift, or ask Stephanie to whip buttercream for our specialty cakes; they jumped in and helped with whatever was needed.

Once my timer dinged, I removed the golden-brown fries from the oven and arranged a half dozen of them in a red and white striped cardboard fry box. "Who wants a taste?" I called to Stephanie and Andy, setting the fries next to a ramekin of raspberry "ketchup" for dipping.

"Did someone say taste?" Andy practically hurdled the espresso counter.

"Careful," I cautioned. "They might be hot."

Sterling and Bethany, the two other members of our small but mighty staff, arrived. Sterling had been taking on a bigger role as kitchen supervisor. He didn't have formal chef training, but was a quick study and had an innate ability to know what flavors worked well together. Finding Bethany had been serendipitous. We met at Ashland's annual Chocolate Festival where she debuted her droolworthy brownies. Mom and I asked her to help out while we were on the cruise. She was such a natural fit that we ended up inviting her to stay on permanently. To my surprise and equal delight, she and Stephanie hit it off instantly. They had teamed up to expand Torte's social media presence with daily contests and gorgeously styled pictures of our culinary creations.

I knew that we were going to have to hire more staff with the expansion. The thought of interviewing potential candidates made my head swim. That could wait, at least a little while longer.

Bethany squealed when she saw my pie fries. "These are the cutest things I've ever seen." She reached for a fry. "Let me put my stuff down and get my phone. I can see the hashtags now. #PieFries and #PlayWithYour-Food."

"Aren't these the absolute best?" she said to Sterling who joined us in the kitchen.

"Sure." He grabbed a fry. "What's on the lunch menu today?" He folded his apron in half and tied it around his waist. Even with the warming summer temperatures he wore his standard black hoodie and skinny jeans.

"How does an Italian sub sound?" I pointed to the walk-in fridge. "I ordered extra salami. You could use the baguettes that are coming out of the oven next."

"Works for me." He reached for a spiral notebook. "What do you want on them?"

"Maybe start with an Italian dressing with fresh parsley and basil. Salami, black olives, roasted red peppers, spinach, and mozzarella cheese."

"I'll take two of those," Andy shouted above the sound of foaming milk. He had a stash of fries sitting next to the espresso machine.

"Do you want them grilled or cold?" Sterling jotted down my list of ingredients.

I thought about it for a minute. Grilled baguettes brushed with olive oil and served slightly charred sounded delicious, but it was supposed to warm up as the day progressed. "Cold," I said. "In fact, if you make a few dozen now you can chill them so that they'll be nice and cool by the lunch rush."

"On it." Sterling headed for the fridge.

Bethany clicked a dozen shots of the pie fries and Stephanie's cooling cookie cups. She offered to tackle muffins and croissants. That left me to deliver our wholesale orders. I enjoyed getting a chance to pop into neighboring businesses along the plaza, especially as the theater season ramped up. It would become harder and harder to find a spare minute once the summer crowds descended. I packaged buttery loaves of sweet bread and crusty sourdough into a box and headed outside. Flowers spilled from window boxes along the plaza. Empty galvanized tubs were secured with a bike lock on the side of A Rose by Any Other Name, the flower shop owned by my friend Thomas's parents. Soon they would be bursting with colorful, fragrant blooms. The tree-lined sidewalk looked sleepy, but I knew that wouldn't last long. By noon the outdoor bistro tables would be packed with diners and the shops would be bustling with tourists. Each building along Main Street had been de-signed to resemble Elizabethan architecture. Walking this route never got old. I felt like I saw something new each time, like the scalloped iron gate on the terrace above the bookstore or the curved brick archway that opened into a hidden alleyway.

I passed Puck's Pub where a bartender was sweeping up the remains of last night's revelry. He tipped his cap. I waved and continued on to the Green Goblin at the far end of the plaza. The pub and restaurant sat across the street from Lithia Park, Ashland's crown jewel with acres of hiking trails and lush grassy areas perfect for an impromptu summer picnic or to watch herds of black-tailed deer. I was tempted to take a quick spin through the lush grounds before returning to the bakeshop to calm my mind. Instead, I dropped off the Green Goblin's order and crossed Main Street to finish the delivery route. By the time I made it back to Torte, Andy was chatting with a line of customers waiting for lattes and Bethany was packaging up boxes of croissants and sticky buns.

"Are you Juliet?" A woman waiting for her drink order stopped me. She wore a tailored black suit jacket and trim white pants. Most Ashlanders rolled into Torte wearing khaki shorts and sandals or flowy peasant skirts, especially during the morning rush. Evening hours brought a more sophisticated style to the plaza as theatergoers meandered through the shops or stopped for a bite before a show.

"Yes." I didn't recognize her.

She extended a manicured hand with a diamond so huge it devoured half her ring finger. "Clarissa." She didn't exactly smile.

"Nice to meet you. Did you need something?" I nodded to the pastry counter.

"No. This young gentleman is making me a nonfat latte. I wanted to introduce myself, because I believe you're working with my husband?"

"Really?" I placed the delivery box on the counter, and pushed a loose strand of hair back into my pony-tail.

Her penciled lips turned downward. "Yes, Roger. Your architect."

"Oh, Roger. Of course. We love Roger. He's done an incredible job." I suddenly felt self-conscious about my jeans and tennis shoes.

"I know that he's the best," she snapped. "He's not the best architect in Ashland. He's the best architect in the entire Rogue Valley." She twisted the brilliant diamond. "You're lucky that he agreed to take on a project . . ." She paused and glanced around the bakeshop. "Of this size. Typically, he prefers to focus his efforts on larger, more profitable endeavors."

The way she spoke made me feel like we were a char-ity case. "He never mentioned that."

Andy put Clarissa's drink on the bar. "Nonfat latte is up." He glanced at me and rolled his eyes.

"I'm meeting Roger shortly." I tried to keep my tone upbeat. "Have you had a chance to see what he's done with the basement?"

Clarissa shook her head. "No."

"You should come say hello and take a look. He added a woodstove that is going to be the centerpiece of the seating area downstairs. I can't wait to arrange cozy couches and pillows around it." My excitement spilled through in my tone, which seemed to irritate Clarissa.

"I'm sure it will be charming." Somehow, she made the word sound loathsome.

"It's such a quaint space you have here." She paused and turned her attention to the front door and motioned to a woman in her mid-thirties with bleached blond hair and black leather biker jacket. "I must go. I'm meeting someone." Clarissa dismissed me.

She and the woman in the leather jacket made their way to one of the booths in the front. They were an odd pair.

I got the sense that Clarissa wasn't impressed that her husband was designing a bakeshop. She obviously wanted him working on more prestigious projects than our *quaint* bakery. Roger had never seemed disinterested during the time we'd spent working on the redesign. If anything, he'd been enthusiastic and was constantly bringing Mom and me new ideas and suggestions. Oh well, I sighed and returned to the kitchen. Clarissa could turn her nose down on Torte. I knew how lucky I was to get to spend my days in such a comfortable and welcoming space.

Chapter Two

By the time I went to meet Roger to check on progress I had almost forgotten about bumping into his wife. However, the strange conversation flashed through my head when I went outside and found the woman Clarissa had been meeting hanging around one of the picnic tables in front of Torte when I went downstairs. She intentionally turned her back on me, pretending to examine a leaf on the oak tree, as I passed by. I almost got the sense that she was waiting for me. She flipped up the collar on her leather jacket and plucked a leaf from the tree.

Odd. But I'd seen stranger things on the plaza.

I ignored her and descended the brick steps that led to the basement. The steps, handrail, and landing had been cleaned and resurfaced as part of the renovation. After years of neglect, they had been covered in a thick layer of moss and slime, which had made traversing them dangerous. I felt much more confident walking down the new steps than I had a few weeks ago.

Roger was waiting downstairs with the contractor. "Good morning, Jules. I have some good news for you."

Boxes of mud, trowels, and rolls of drywall tape were piled by the front door.

"I'll take any morning that starts with good news." I reached to shake both of their hands.

Roger flipped through his clipboard and removed a sheet of paper from it. "Turns out the electrical inspector came out before close of day yesterday. He signed off. That means we are officially in the home stretch."

"That is good news." I studied the inspector's report.

"The guys are going to finish the trim and molding this morning. We're painting this afternoon, so I'm going to need your final approval of the paint swatches." He unclipped a selection of paint samples from his clipboard.

Mom and I had decided on a bright, creamy white with touches of red and teal accents. Since there were only three small windows in the basement we wanted the space to feel as light and open as possible.

"These still look good?" Roger asked, holding up the paint samples.

"Yep. We're really taking a risk on colors, aren't we?" I joked.

He smiled, revealing deep crevasses around his mouth and eyes. I would guess him to be in his sixties with thinning silver hair and a mustache. "You're being smart. I would do the same thing if I was in your shoes. Color palettes are more my wife's domain, but continuing a color is always a better idea in my opinion than creating two radically different spaces. This should blend quite nicely with the space upstairs."

"That reminds me, I met your wife earlier this morning. She stopped in for a latte."

"Clarissa?" He frowned. "She told me she had an appointment this morning."

"Yes, she was meeting someone, but she stopped to introduce herself."

"Hmm." Roger looked confused. He shrugged. "Anyway, back to plans. If we can knock out the trim and finish painting tomorrow we should be ready to move ovens and equipment in the next day or two."

"Wow." I couldn't believe how quickly things had progressed. When Mom and I had first started the expansion, I had heard horror stories of renovations taking months and months longer than expected and businesses struggling to stay afloat in the process. That hadn't been the case with Torte. Roger and his crew had been meticulous about meeting (and often beating) their deadlines.

"Will you be ready to transfer baking down here? Is there anything else that you need done before we begin that transition?" Roger asked.

"I don't think so, but I'll check with Mom." I surveyed the space. It looked nothing like it had only a few months ago. "How long will it take to build the new stairs?" The next phase of construction would involve building the internal stairs and then redesigning the space above. Our goal was to avoid disrupting service as much as possible.

"Not long. I would anticipate a couple of weeks. Could be more if the city is backed up. The building inspector will have to come out and make sure the structure is up to code before we can actually build out the stairs."

"After that you'll begin to repurpose the old kitchen, right?"

He nodded. "Yep. I have the new set of plans for you

and your mom to review. They include those minor changes we discussed, like adding in the bar along the back window."

"Great." I took the plans from him. "And how much will this disturb our customers?"

"It shouldn't be too bad. We're going to do the bulk of the demo at night and in the early-morning hours. That will minimize the impact on your business. The teardown is going to be the worst part. It shouldn't change anything you do in terms of your baking since you'll be down here. You might have to put up a few signs that say something like PLEASE EXCUSE OUR DUST, but otherwise we'll get moving and have you up and running like new in no time."

I hoped he was right. "What about the espresso bar? When you get to that stage, any suggestions on where we should set up a temporary coffee counter?" Since the second phase of construction involved reworking the upstairs floor plan I was nervous about losing revenue during our busiest time of the year. Too many beloved Ashland restaurants had succumbed to the city's seasonality—flush with cash during the height of the summer, only to lose everything in the bank come the slower winter months. Fortunately our loyal customer base had kept us bustling through the slow season, but I didn't want Torte to become another statistic.

Roger motioned me to the half wall that divided the seating area from the wood-fired pizza oven. He ripped a piece of paper from his clipboard and sketched out a layout of the kitchen. "The espresso bar is basically going to flip," he said, pointing to the paper. "Instead of running horizontally here, it's going to run vertically along this wall with space for customers at either end to place their order or wait for their drinks. The window here will have a counter-depth bar and seating. Your pastry cases will be at this far end next to the stairs going down. That's going to open up this entire area in the front for seating."

He was right. Torte looked three times the size in his rough sketch. "My thought is that we set up a temporary coffee station and pastry section right here where the dining room currently starts. That will allow us to demo and rebuild everything in the current kitchen and still allow you to stay open. What do you think?"

It was going to be tight, but hopefully it would only be a few weeks. "I think we can make it work," I said to Roger with a nod. Andy's creativity would definitely be put to the test, because if the sketch was to scale it looked like he would only have about four—maybe five—feet to move around in.

We finished our walk-through and I headed to the bakeshop to give the team the good news that we had passed our final inspection. As I crested the stairs, I heard a familiar voice. "Juliet, darling! You're just who I wanted to see." Lance stood with one lanky arm propped up against the exterior brick wall. He looked different. His angular face was clean-shaven, his dark hair cut short, and his face was tanned. Instead of his standard three-piece suit he wore a pair of indigo jeans rolled up at the ankles and a casual linen shirt with the top two buttons unbuttoned.

"Lance! You're back." I hurried to hug him.

He smelled like sunscreen. I noticed a pair of expensive sunglasses tucked into the breast pocket of his crisp, white linen shirt.

"Where did you go? Bermuda? You look tan."

A slow smile spread across his thin cheekbones. "There's so much to tell. Where do I start?" He linked his arm through mine. "I believe a pastry is in order."

We headed inside. I left Lance at one of the window booths to grab us coffees and a plate of Bethany's blueberry cornmeal muffins.

"Tell me everything," I said, returning to the booth with two gorgeous golden muffins bursting with juicy berries.

Lance helped himself to a muffin. He tore off a bite and stared pensively onto the plaza. "She looks different."

"Who?" I followed his gaze.

"Ashland. She's changed in my absence."

That was a stretch. I took a sip of the medium roast and waited for Lance to expand on his theory.

He dabbed a crumb from his lip with a paper napkin. "She looks lonely, doesn't she? Like she needs a pick-me-up."

I stared at the bright, sunny plaza where tourists had begun to gather. Ashland's resident poet troubadour had taken up his usual spot next to the Lithia bubblers. He was famous for his ability to wordsmith a poem for anyone who happened to pass by. His setup was a simple card table and folding chair with an old-fashioned typewriter and a stack of creamy paper.

"Where did you go?" I ignored his observation. "I want to hear about your vacation."

"Vacation?" Lance scoffed. "I wouldn't say vacation. Let's say I've been around."

"Around where?" I pressed.

Lance raised his eyebrows in unison. "Medford," he whispered.

"Medford? As in ten miles away from here, Medford?"

"Shhhh. Darling, keep your voice down."

"I don't understand. I thought you were going on vacation. You've been in *Medford* for three weeks?" Medford was the nearest town with ample big-box stores and a large hospital. Ashlanders experienced the best of both worlds with a small, walkable city with tons of family-owned shops and businesses. But when you needed to stock up on supplies or bulk groceries a quick trip to Medford gave you access to any amenity or product found in a big city.

"It was a vacation of sorts. Perhaps the better terminology would be a trip down memory lane."

"What?" I leaned my elbows on the table. "Why Medford?"

Lance polished off his muffin. He took his time brushing crumbs from his fingers before he continued. "Juliet, I have a confession to make, but you have to promise that this little secret will stay between the two of us."

"Of course. You know me, Lance. I never give up anyone's confidence."

"Unless it has to do with murder." He smirked.

"That's different."

"I know, darling, and that's why I'm entrusting you with this highly sensitive information. It just might involve a murder." His dark eyes narrowed.

I was used to Lance's tendency to create drama in any situation, no matter how benign. My jaw tightened. How long was he going to stretch this out?

He must have noticed my frustration, because he reached across the table and tapped my chin. "Chin up. You don't want to clench those pearly whites and risk cracking a tooth."

"Lance, will you please stop with the pomp and circumstance and just get to the point?"

"Moi? Pomp and circumstance? Please." He threw his hand over his forehead. Then he smiled, but there was a sadness—or was it fear?—behind his eyes. "Okay, okay. Relax. I'm getting to the good part." He did a quick glance around the dining room before continuing.

I had to lean closer to hear him as he barely spoke above a whisper. "The truth is that I've been with my family for the last three weeks."

Lance had never mentioned family. Not that I didn't believe he had a family, but I guess I had always assumed that he didn't want to talk about his past.

"Your family came to Medford?" I asked. "Why wouldn't they visit you here in Ashland? See one of your shows?"

He rolled his eyes. "No, darling. My family lives in Medford. They don't ever come to Ashland. You might even say that my family *is* Medford."

"What?" I couldn't believe what I was hearing. Medford was a ten-minute drive from Ashland. In all the time that I had known Lance he had never said a word about his family living close by. "Your family lives in Medford? For how long?"

"Forever."

"Wait." I held up my hands. "Are you telling me that you grew up here? In southern Oregon? In Medford?"

Lance pursed his lips and nodded. "Yes."

Chapter Three

"Why didn't you say anything?" I asked.

Lance shrugged. "It's not something I wanted to admit. You have the honor of returning to your charming hometown. I've spent years trying to bury my past."

"I can't believe you're a Southern Oregon native. We might have known each other growing up."

"Ha! Don't I wish." Lance threw his head back and laughed. "Juliet, think about it. How many times did your path cross with the Medford kids when you were growing up?"

"Probably not very often," I admitted. "Although there was a group who used to come help out with shows and hang around the bakeshop. That could have been you."

"No. The theater wasn't something my father wanted me involved in. The theater was for 'wimps' and 'pansies,' not for our family. He wouldn't let me anywhere near a stage, even though it was evident from the time I was two that I was destined for the spotlight." His voice was thick with emotion.

I reached my hand out to console him. "I'm so sorry." The theater was Lance's life. I couldn't imagine what it must have been like to grow up in a family who didn't support your dreams. My parents had always encouraged me to follow my heart wherever it led me. Even when that meant traveling to far corners of the globe and leaving Ashland behind.

He took a sip of his coffee. Then he squared his shoulders and cleared his throat. "It will be easier if I start from the beginning."

"Okay." I leaned back into the cushy booth.

"As I mentioned, my family is synonymous with Medford. The day I graduated from high school I left for Juilliard and never imagined coming back within a three-hundred-mile radius. Let's just say that my memories from my youth are not exactly fond. I couldn't wait to get out of Southern Oregon. That was until OSF came calling. They offered me my dream job and my first shot at artistic director for a major company. I'd been an assistant artistic director in France for a tiny theater and then again in Amsterdam for a bigger theater."

I nodded. Lance had told me that he had gotten his start in Europe.

"The irony is that when I applied to universities I used my mother's maiden name—Rousseau. First and foremost, it's a fabulous name, don't you agree?" He winked, offering the briefest glimpse of his typical flippant personality.

"It fits you." I broke off a piece of muffin. The crunchy cornmeal paired with the tangy juicy blueberries was a superb balance of textures.

"Exactly. And changing my name to Lance Rousseau ensured that no one would connect me to my Dreadford roots."

"Dreadford? Come on, Lance. You know as well as I do that Medford is a great city with a thriving new downtown."

"Emphasis on 'new.' When I was in school it was Dreadford, trust me. I mean, honestly, how can you call a bunch of boys chasing each other up and down the football field entertainment?" He shuddered.

I didn't try to argue with him, although I've always been a football fan. Ashland was an artistic oasis among a variety of more traditional Southern Oregon towns that had deep roots in agriculture. As more and more people moved into the region the culture had shifted, but for a long time Ashland had been one of the only cities around that attracted writers, musicians, actors, and playwrights. Lance's flair for style and obsession with the arts might not have blended in well with his peers.

Andy appeared at our booth with a carafe of coffee. "I was about to see if you needed a refill, but forget it." He pulled the carafe to his chest and cradled it like a baby. "No refills if you're going to dis Ashland football. You should know that Ashland has had more state titles than Medford. The last time Medford won state was in the 1940s. Ashland's brought home four state titles since the nineties and we've come in second three times." With that he moved on to the next table with his coveted brew.

I knew that Andy took his football seriously.

"Fine. I stand corrected, but you catch my drift." Lance smoothed his berry-stained napkin. "In any event, I adopted Rousseau as my name of choice and never looked back."

"What's your dad's last name?" I took another bite of muffin.

"Brown." Lance folded his arms across his chest.

"Brown?"

"Brown." He stared at me with an annoyed expression. "Think about it, Jules. Medford—Brown."

"Wait, as in the Brown Group?" My mouth dropped open.

"Ding, ding, ding." Lance tapped his index finger in the air.

"Your family owns the Brown Group?"

"My family *is* the Brown Group."

Suddenly, I understood why Lance hadn't been worried about money. The Brown Group practically owned Medford. They were one of the oldest and biggest lumber companies in the state. It was impossible to go anywhere in the Rogue Valley without seeing a Brown Group billboard, TV commercial, or logging truck. They sponsored the Jackson State Fair and dozens of local baseball teams. "Don't you own half the state of Oregon?"

Lance drummed his fingers on the table. "We did at one point. Today, the land holdings are smaller, but we manage acres and acres of timberland and develop property throughout the state."

I took a minute to let what he was saying sink in. I couldn't believe that Lance was a member of the Brown family. And that he had never told me.

He cradled his coffee mug in his hands. "My family's logging roots date back to the early 1900s when timber supplies began dwindling in the Midwest. Industrialists, like my great-grandfather, began looking west. Oregon and Washington were ripe with virgin land. My great-grandfather started with a single sawmill. By the time he died, and the company was handed over to my grand-father, he owned over a million acres of land."

"Wow."

Lance nodded. "Yeah, it's a lot of land. Did you know that the U.S. is still the world's largest exporter of wood?"

I shook my head.

"It's true. We do things differently these days when it comes to preservation of course. Even when I was a kid clear-cutting was still the norm. I remember fighting with my father about destroying so much green space." He sighed. "Then again, I fought with my father about everything. He intended for me to continue the family legacy. My brother and I were destined for a life man-aging a logging empire. I had other ideas that involved silly costumes and men in tights."

I could tell by Lance's tone that he held a longstand-ing hurt.

"I used to put on shows when we were out in the for-est. It made my father fume. I loved it." His eyes had a faraway look. "So did the crews in the field. I would test new magic tricks and my physical comedy on them. One summer I roped a huge, burly bear of a logger into play-ing Friar Tuck and staged a production of *Robin Hood* in the forest, with yours truly as the Sheriff of Notting-ham. You should have seen it, Juliet—sweaty, bearded men, who earned an honest living grinding away gnarly stumps in hundred-degree heat, sitting around watching a gangly kid do his thing. They applauded the produc-tion by firing up their chain saws. Of course, the min-ute my father caught wind of my antics I wasn't allowed on-site again."

I wasn't sure how to respond, so I simply held the space for him to continue.

"My mother used to beg him to open up to me. She didn't know that I would listen to their fights at night. How they ended up together I'll never know." He smoothed his napkin and didn't make eye contact. "She reminds me of Helen, actually. Petite, French, with a penchant for the arts, a champion for the needy. She was a delicate flower who married a lumberjack."

"They say that opposites attract."

Lance's eyes shot up. "You would know."

I flinched.

"Sorry." Lance picked up the napkin and crumpled it into a tight ball. "She championed everything that my father mocked."

"She sounds wonderful."

"She was." Lance swallowed hard. "She died when I was twelve."

"Oh, Lance, I'm so sorry." I reached for his hand again and squeezed it tight. "I know what it's like to lose a parent young. Why have you never mentioned this before?"

He crushed my hand. "I have found it more tolerable to bury those memories."

My heart broke for him.

"She was a smart woman. She knew that my father and I would likely never see eye-to-eye so she set up a trust. When I turned eighteen I began getting payments. Without her foresight, I don't know how I would have paid for college. My father cut me off and cut me out of the family when I told him I was going to Juilliard."

No wonder he had tried to disconnect from his memories. "That must have been terrible."

Lance moved his head from side to side. "It is what it is. My father had my brother to carry on the family legacy so he was happy."

"Tell me about your brother."

"My baby brother, Leo." He picked up his coffee. "Hmm. What can I say?"

Lance and Leo, matching names, I thought to myself. "Is he in Medford, too?"

"He's running the Brown Group."

"Are you two close?"

Lance nearly spit coffee all over the table. "No, not even remotely." He rubbed his temples. "Leo struggled in school. He preferred the football field where he could knock people around. He was never a good student. I, on the other hand, was an excellent student. That deepened the divide between us. You know, I've wondered as an adult whether Leo might have had a real learning disability. He could never read. His grammar is appalling." Lance rolled his eyes. "But I do wonder if he has dyslexia."

"Have you ever asked him?"

"Good Lord, no. Leo and I are the products of our upbringing for better and worse. It's a shame that he didn't get help for his academic challenges, but then again for all I know he would have turned out exactly the same even if things had been different. He's not the sharpest tool in the shed. To be honest, I'm surprised that he hasn't run the Brown Family Group into the ground."

I rested my elbows on the table. "I'm so glad that

you've trusted me with this, but if you're not close with your dad or brother why were you in Medford with them?"

He set down his coffee mug and rubbed his temples. "My father is failing. He's in hospice and doesn't have much time."

"Oh, I'm sorry."

"Thank you, but it's fine. He's lived a full life."

"Did you have a chance to talk to him? To come to some kind of understanding?" I watched as Bethany delivered a tray of salted chocolate caramel tarts and pear bread puddings to the front counter. Nearly every table was now filled with happy customers chatting over steaming mugs of espresso. The smell of Sterling's soup wafted toward us. I didn't want to rush Lance, but soon I should go check in with my staff.

Lance waved to a group of women holding playbills in their hands, but didn't encourage them to come join us. He lowered his voice. "Actually, we did. That's part of why I need your help."

"Anything."

He scoffed. "You might want to wait until you hear the rest of this before committing."

"Okay."

"My father has suffered several stokes that have left him incapacitated. He's in and out of consciousness right now. The nurses are keeping his morphine level consistent so that he's not in any kind of pain. I spent most of my time at the family compound sitting by his bed and relaying stories from my life. It was strangely cathartic. It gave me a chance to explain my choices and tell him about my adventures and accolades. At first, I wasn't sure whether he heard me or understood. In some ways it didn't matter. I didn't think he even knew I was there or who I was." He ran a finger along the rim of the coffee mug. "Then two nights ago it was just me and him. His night nurse had taken a break and the strangest thing happened. He sat up. I panicked. I was about to run find the nurse, but he reached for my arm, and called me by name. He was lucid. He apologized. He cried."

"Lance, what a gift." I felt breathless.

"Exactly. It was healing for both of us. He told me that he had followed my career. He kept every newspaper article and magazine. In fact, he made me go find an old dusty box he's been keeping in his closet for all of these years." Lance stopped and wiped a tear from his eye. "It was shocking, Jules."

I knew from Lance's raw emotion and because he was calling me Jules that he had completely shed his exterior façade. I was talking to the real Lance.

"You won't believe it. I'll show it to you. It's a huge box of literally everything that's ever been written about me."

"That's wonderful."

"And heartbreaking." He brushed his cheek. "I wish I would have set my ego aside earlier. We could have had many years."

"But it's better than losing him and never having a moment like that."

"Definitely." He nodded. "We talked about my mom and her wishes. We talked about Leo. That's when my father dropped a bomb. He thinks that my brother is trying to kill him."

Chapter Four

"What?" I shouted.

"Quiet," he hissed. "You never know what listening ears might be around."

"What do you mean?" I looked around the bakeshop. A line of customers had gathered in front of the espresso bar where Andy was demonstrating a pour-over technique. Bethany stood nearby snapping pictures on her phone.

"I mean I'm being followed." Lance's voice was barely audible.

"You are?" I glanced around again.

"Don't be so obvious." Lance intentionally faked a yawn, stretching his long arms over his head. "Play it cool. No sudden moves. Actually, you should laugh. Pretend like I said something funny."

I didn't feel like laughing, but complied and tried to fake a chuckle.

"That was atrocious, darling. To think I've been begging you to take the stage." He made a tsking sound under his breath.

"Why do you think your brother is trying to kill your father? Especially if your father is already in hospice."

Lance's eyes darkened. "Money."

"I don't understand." How many times had I said that in the course of our conversation? I was having a hard time wrapping my brain around the fact that Lance had grown up in Medford, let alone was a member of the Brown family.

"Wait, so you think that Leo is following you?"

"Probably. More likely, he's hired someone to follow me. I can guarantee that he'll show up here soon. Now that I'm back in the picture he won't let me out of sight." He folded his napkin and looked nonchalant. "Don't move, but when you have a chance in a minute or two, take a look at the table up by the espresso machine. There's a guy in a black leather biker jacket with black leather pants and a ghastly goatee. I saw him this morning in Lithia Park. Then again on the bricks, and now here. That can't be a coincidence. I'm sure Leo hired him to tail me."

"Why?" I kept my gaze on Lance.

Lance frowned. "I don't know. My father is convinced that someone has been tampering with his morphine drip. The only people with access to his room are the hired nursing staff, hospice workers, and Leo. It stands to reason that Leo is the most likely culprit."

"You said for money." I shot a quick glance toward the coffee counter. Sure enough, a man dressed entirely in black with a thick dark goatee and matching hair was nursing a coffee and staring straight at us. When he caught my eye, he grabbed a newspaper and buried his face behind it.

"That's my best guess. It must have something to do with my father's will or maybe Leo's trust. Our parents established separate trusts for each of us. I don't know the specifics of Leo's trust, but if it's anything like mine he probably receives a very generous monthly stipend along with his salary."

"Does your father's death change the trust?"

"No." Lance shook his head. "Not unless Leo's trust is set up differently. My mother's goal was to have the money from the trust fund us for our lifetime. It was intentionally set up to pay out slowly versus giving us a huge lump sum. She was astute. We might have been young when she died, but she knew our personalities were already set."

"So, what's his motivation for wanting to kill your father? On his deathbed?"

Lance pretended to stretch, but I could tell he was trying to check on the mysterious guy in the biker jacket. I wanted to see if the man was still watching us, but I fought the urge to look. "I can only guess, but it has to be money. Everything is about money, isn't it? Leo's been putting on a good show, feigning concern and having Sarah, his personal assistant, sit at our father's bedside around the clock. But I know better." He sighed. "If you had asked me even a month ago if I thought my brother was a killer, I would have said no. Leo's not the sharpest tool in the shed, but I never pictured him as a cold-blooded killer. Greed—Shakespeare had it right. 'Quarrels unjust against the good and loyal, Destroying them for wealth.' You know, 'The Scottish Play.' "

Unlike the Professor, Lance wasn't usually prone to quoting Shakespeare.

"If Leo doesn't think he's getting enough from the trust then our father's death will ensure a large payout from the company."

"That's terrible." I'd never had siblings, but couldn't imagine arguing over money if I had. Nor could I fathom even considering the thought of harming my parents.

"That's my family." Lance tried to put on a brave face, but I could see through his façade.

"How can I help?"

He sighed. "Yes, well, just getting this off my chest is helpful. Thank you for listening."

"Of course. I'm always here for you, Lance."

"The feeling is mutual, darling." He patted his heart. "On to the Brown family crisis. I've hired a private investigator to do her own digging. I have to find out exactly what's in the will, and what Leo stands to gain."

"A private investigator?"

"Yes, yes. I've been assured that she's the best money can buy. The Professor is doing some sleuthing for me as well."

"He is?" Suddenly I realized the connection. The Professor had been making several trips to Medford lately. I had assumed it was because he was trying to work on finding a replacement. When he had proposed to Mom, he decided that it was time for him to scale back. He intended to stay on as a consultant and pass his detective badge on to Thomas and someone new—most likely Detective Kerry, who had been filling in recently. Now I wondered if one of the other reasons that he'd been spending so much time in Medford was due to Lance.

"Close your mouth, Juliet. It's not becoming to sit there gaping." He winked.

"Thanks," I said with thick sarcasm. "If you've hired a private investigator and the Professor is helping you, what do you need from me?"

"Other than delicious coffee, pastry, and to stare at those starry blue eyes?"

This was more like the Lance I knew.

"From you, darling, I need a few extra invites to the wedding of the century."

"You want invites to the wedding?"

"Yes. I know it sounds odd, but it was Megan the PI's idea. She wants to come as my date. She's worried about leaving me alone, knowing that someone is tailing me. Once she hatched the idea to tag along to the wedding, she decided it might be a good idea to invite my dastardly brother and his goons. She seems convinced that we'll learn something revealing if we can get them out in the wild so to speak."

"You think someone would follow you to the wedding?" I was sure that my face must have revealed my confusion.

"What better place than at a wedding? From what I hear it's going to be the party to end all parties."

"Right." I sat up. "Will Leo even come? He doesn't know anyone in Ashland."

"Oh, he'll come. He'll bring his entourage. He doesn't go anywhere without his lawyer and personal assistant, and trust me, he doesn't want me out of his sight right now."

Perhaps that was in the Brown family DNA. Lance

was known for being flanked by young actors and theater groupies whenever he was seen around town.

"Rumor has it that you've been doing some devious
planning of your own. Color me impressed. When you
mentioned that you were going to throw a surprise wedding, I didn't realize that *everyone* would be in on the
gig. The entire town is absolutely ready to burst."

"How did you hear that?" I felt my jaw open again.

"Please, it's me. I have eyes and ears everywhere." He
sounded exasperated. "Don't worry, the Professor is
none the wiser. He and I met for a slice of pie yesterday
and he's positively beside himself trying to come up
with a fall date and the perfect locale. He has no idea
what you have up your sleeve."

"You think?"

"That. Or he has a fabulous game face." His eyes
twinkled devilishly. "In any event, it's the perfect excuse
to invite Leo. I'll tell him I want him to get to see me in
my element, and what could be better than a Midsummer Night's Dream wedding? Inviting him to a wedding
would be too obvious. This, however, is simply a town
celebration. A grand reopening of my new winery. He'll
never know, and hopefully Megan will get what she
needs to lock him up."

"Okay, if you think it will help." It still wasn't clear
to me why Megan, the PI, wanted to observe Lance's
brother out of his typical routine. I would have to ask
the Professor. Maybe it was a police tactic.

"You're the best." Lance checked the expensive silver watch on his wrist. "Oh dear, is that the time? Must
run. Ta-ta." He stood, blew me air kisses, and then
pranced to the front door.

I checked to see if the biker guy was watching. He must have left because Sterling was wiping down the table.

Was Lance right? Was he being followed? I thought about the woman I'd seen wearing similar black biker gear. I had wondered if she was following me. Oh no. Could Lance be rubbing off on me? Was I paranoid too?

It was possible that Lance was overdramatizing things about his family. The theater was his business after all. But my gut told me to believe him. I was going to have to keep my eyes open and be sure to pay extra attention to anyone out of the ordinary. If the biker guy returned to the bakeshop I was going to confront him, regardless of what Lance said.

A new thought pushed through as I picked up our coffee cups and plates. Lance might be in danger. If his brother was trying to kill their father, what would stop him from trying to kill Lance too? If their father was dead and Lance was out of the picture Leo would inherit everything. As in millions. If that wasn't motive for murder, what was?

Chapter Five

Mom breezed in not long after Lance left. She balanced a box of creamy embossed invitations with red wax seals. "Your invitations arrived," she said, tucking her gingerbread-colored hair behind one of her ears. It was cut in a stylish bob that accented her apple-shaped cheeks and warm, walnut eyes. She wore a pair of red clogs and a light cardigan.

I reached for one of the elegant invites.

"You know, I'm not sure why you were stressing about ordering official invites," Mom said, placing the box on the pastry counter. "Everyone in town already has next weekend on their calendars. I think at this rate the grand reopening of Uva is going to be the biggest party Ashland has ever seen."

"I know, but Lance insisted," I lied, setting the invite on the top of the pile. We had already handed out secret invites to friends, family, neighbors, and business owners, but these were decoy invites that I had made just to throw Mom and the Professor off the trail. "It's probably silly, but relaunching the winery is a big deal and

Lance thought it would be best to send a formal invitation. You know how he is."

"True." She surveyed the bakeshop. "How's everything coming along? I feel like I'm completely out of the loop up here. I've been in the basement so much lately. Roger has been keeping us busy with these final decisions, and then Doug and I have been touring every venue around trying to firm up a plan for this fall." The lines around her eyes crinkled. "There's so much activity up here. It looks like every square inch of counter space has pastries on it. Have we had a boon in orders, or is that for the relaunch party?"

I tried to block her view. "It's not as much as it looks. The Green Goblin is hosting a brunch and we had two last-minute custom cake orders."

She started to move toward the kitchen. "I should be helping. It looks like you're slammed. Why didn't you say anything? I feel terrible leaving you in the lurch."

"Remember, you're supposed to be scaling back," I reminded her. "We have it under control. You just focus on the basement and the wedding plans. I've got everything else covered."

Mom stood on her tiptoes to steal another look at the kitchen. "As long as you're sure."

"I'm sure." I steered her away from the kitchen. "Are you hungry for lunch? Sterling made some delicious Italian subs. I can snag us a couple and fill you in."

She gave me a suspicious look. Was she onto us? Mom was Ashland's resident baker/therapist. She had an incredible listening ear and a knack for getting people to open up. I wondered if she had managed to butter up an unsuspecting local with her understanding smile and get them to dish on what was really going on at Torte.

"Hey, Mrs. C.," Andy called, rescuing me. "You've gotta come try my cold-brew special."

With a parting grimace, she headed in his direction. Whew. Saved by espresso.

I watched her hug Andy and greet a group of regulars. She was a fixture at Torte. I didn't know how I was going to fill her shoes when and if she ever decided to retire permanently. Before I made it to the kitchen, the bell on the front door jingled and Thomas walked in. He wore his standard blue police uniform with blue shorts and hiking boots. "Hey, Jules. Do you have a sec?" He motioned toward Mom, who was happily chatting with our customers.

"Sure." I handed him an invite. "Outside?"

"Yep." He held the door open for me.

"Are you on park duty today?" I asked, pointing to his shorts and hiking boots. Ashland's small and friendly police force were tasked with a wide range of duties, including patrolling Lithia Park.

Thomas laughed. "You know me, I wear shorts any chance I can get." He paused and held up a finger. Then he turned to a group of women who were loaded with shopping bags and about to step off the curb next to us. "Crosswalk, ladies! Use the crosswalk, please."

I smiled to myself. This was life in Ashland, where the police had to caution tourists to use the crosswalks and spent a good chunk of their day giving directions and restaurant recommendations.

The ladies blushed and offered an apology. They hurried to the crosswalk where they squealed with delight when they spotted Lance. He was quickly enveloped in the group of theater lovers.

"Poor Lance," I said to Thomas.

"Nah, he loves it." Thomas pointed to Lance who had whipped a pen from his pocket and began signing autographs.

"Fair enough." I chuckled. "What's up?"

"Just checking in on operation wedding 111." Thomas peered inside Torte's front door. He had given our efforts to keep the upcoming nuptials under wraps the code name 111. When I asked him why, he had grinned and said, "It's kind of like an emergency. A *love* emergency." If memory served, I think I gave him a playful punch.

Thomas glanced around to make sure no one was listening. "My mom said to tell you that the flowers for the bouquets will be in by Friday. She said if you have time you should stop by. She's putting garlands of greenery and flowers together to go with the Midsummer Night's Dream theme." We had decided to have the ceremony take place underneath a giant oak tree above the vineyard. We would string strands of golden twinkle lights from the tree and then intertwine them along the rows of grapevines so that the entire hillside was aglow.

"Great." Thomas's parents owned A Rose by Any Other Name and had offered to make the bridal bouquets, boutonnieres, and reception flowers as their gift to Mom and the Professor. That had been a consistent theme among many of the shop owners in the plaza. From the decoy invitations to the musicians, and even the wedding spread, everyone in town had come forward and insisted on giving us huge discounts or donating product for the festivities. My friend Chef Garrison, at Ashland Springs Hotel, was going to oversee catering. He was bringing a team of his servers for prep and cleanup at a majorly reduced rate so that our staff could enjoy the wedding. I had been humbled by the town's response, although not surprised given how much both of them had contributed to the community over the years.

"How's it going with your mom? Do you think she has any idea?" Thomas asked.

I reached over and tapped one of the window boxes. "Knock on wood, no. But she just noticed how many pastries we have piled up in the kitchen. I've got to keep her out of there. What about the Professor? Are you keeping him busy?"

"You have no idea, Jules. I looped Detective Kerry in on the secret. She's actually been really helpful. She's been making the Professor go over every single manual and police procedural with us. He never would have believed it if it were me asking, but with Detective Kerry asking he hasn't even raised an eyebrow."

"Brilliant."

His cheeks warmed with color, giving his youthful face an even more earnest look. "I do what I can." He winked. "I've also convinced him that we need an app."

"An app?"

"Yep. An Ashland mobile app. One of the department's goals is two-way communication. Kerry and I were talking about it and it's a great way to keep citizens informed. We'll send text alerts with emergency updates. People can submit anonymous tips, even send in photos from local events. What do you think?"

"Great idea."

Thomas beamed with pride. "Thanks. Designing it is going to be fun and hopefully another distraction for the Professor. Anything else you need help with? I heard Carlos is coming in soon."

I stiffened. When I had returned home to Ashland, Thomas and I had rekindled our friendship. He'd been a great shoulder to cry on, but given that we had dated during high school there had been a constant, underlying tension between us whenever Carlos was around or even when his name was mentioned. "Yeah, he and Ramiro are both coming." I kept my tone upbeat. "I really had to stretch the truth with Mom. I told her this was the only week that Ramiro could come. Otherwise, I'm sure that she would have been suspicious."

"Cool. Let me know if they want a police escort from the airport. Maybe Carlos and I can be a tag team for the Professor. They seemed to get along well when Carlos was here last time, and I could use another distraction besides reviewing moving violations."

If Thomas was upset about Carlos's upcoming visit he gave no indication. I felt my body relax. "You bet. Good plan. I'm sure Carlos would love to help entertain Mom and the Professor."

A homeless man, wearing tattered clothes, wobbled toward us. He was barefoot and obviously under the influence of something. Thomas gave me a fist bump. "Operation wedding 111 continues." Then he made his way toward the man. "Hey, hey, Mr. Frank, how you doin' today?" He put his arm around the homeless man's shoulder and led him away from the plaza.

Ashland was lucky to have Thomas on the beat. His approach, whether dealing with a street person or a tourist, was always kind and heartfelt. He loved technology so creating a mobile app would be a fantastic project for him and for Ashland. I smiled and returned inside.

"Hey, can I steal a couple of those beauties from you?" I asked Sterling, who was slicing thick four-inch stacks of his loaded Italian subs in the kitchen.

"That depends on who they're for." Sterling motioned to the window. Richard Lord and Lance were standing across the street in front of the Lithia bubblers. The group of tourists had released Lance from their clutches, but it didn't look as if he had found relief in his conversation with Richard. "Richard's not coming in for lunch, is he?"

"Good Lord, I hope not."

Bethany chuckled. "Good Lord, that's funny." Rows and rows of cooling chocolate chip cookie cups lined the island. She and Steph had filled each cup with melted dark chocolate. Once the chocolate had cooled we could pour vanilla milk into the shots. I couldn't wait to give the final product a try.

I hadn't even realized the irony. I smiled at her and then returned my attention to Lance and Richard. Spit spewed from Richard's lips as he tapped Lance's collarbone.

"What's that all about?" Sterling asked.

"Good question. I have a couple guesses. Maybe something about Uva. Or perhaps Richard is mad that his new gastronomic menu is bombing and he's decided to blame Lance."

"Why would he do that?" Bethany asked. She removed her apron, which was spattered with red food dye. Her gray T-shirt had a silhouette of a coffee mug with the saying I LIKE YOU A LATTE printed across the chest.

I shrugged. "Why Richard Lord does anything is always a question."

She dabbed her apron with soap and water.

"What happened to you?" I pointed to her hands. They looked as if she had submerged them in the dye.

"Don't ask."

Stephanie picked up a gallon jug of red food coloring. "Things got a little crazy here with the last batch of buttercream. I was whipping the frosting and asked Bethany to add in the food coloring. The cap came off and dye went everywhere."

Bethany held up her stained hands. "Yeah, it looked like a murder scene. I should have taken a picture before cleaning it up. Hashtag #KitchenFail!"

"Do you need help?" Spills and accidents were common in a commercial kitchen. I'd had my fair share of disasters when it came to food dyes.

Bethany finished scrubbing her apron and walked to toss it in the laundry bin. "No, I think I've got it. Should be fun to have lobster hands for a while. How long does this stuff last?"

I cringed. "Uh, maybe a day or two."

"Awesome." Bethany stared at her stained hands. "Maybe I'll have to find a new dress to match my fingers for the wedding." She gasped and threw her hand over her mouth. "Sorry. I forgot that your mom is here."

"Don't sweat it. She's up front. There's no way she can hear us."

Sterling offered me two plates with his sandwich and sides of balsamic apple coleslaw. "Lunch?"

"Thanks. Call if you need me. I'll be in the dining room with Mom." I left them to continue the cleanup.

Mom sat at a window booth. I slid in across from her. "Compliments of Sterling," I said, handing her a plate. "Sorry it took me a minute. Thomas stopped by to say hi."

"No problem. I was catching up with some friends anyway. This looks incredible." She glanced in the direction of the kitchen. "He's really coming into his own, isn't he?"

I nodded. "Yeah. I don't have to give him much direction, and he's constantly testing and experimenting with new ingredients. It's so much fun to watch him develop."

She frowned.

"What?"

"I hope we don't lose him. Or any of the team for that matter." She glanced at the coffee bar where Andy was pouring shots and dancing to the beat of the music playing overhead.

"Have you heard something?"

Mom shook her head. "No. It's just that as Sterling gains more confidence and experience he'll be able to parlay that into a traditional chef position. I wouldn't put it past someone like Richard to try and poach our staff."

That was one of the cons of the baking business. It wasn't uncommon to mentor young pastry chefs only to have them leave to launch their own bakeshops or go to work for bigger operations. The same went for restaurants. I couldn't begin to count the number of sous chefs Carlos had trained who went on to open their own restaurants. Carlos's philosophy was that it was a cycle. Each of us had once been on the other side of mentorship. He believed that as seasoned chefs it was our duty to give back and teach the next generation. So much so that he made a point of visiting each grand opening of the chefs who had come up the ranks with him.

If Sterling landed a job at one of Ashland's premier restaurants I would be thrilled for him and equally devastated. If he went to work for Richard, I would die. But I knew he would never consider a job offer from Richard Lord, even if it was twice what we could pay him. I also knew we were going to have to focus on staffing soon, not only because of the expansion but because eventually Stephanie and Andy were going to graduate from college. Neither of them had talked specifics, but it was likely that their future with Torte was limited.

"True," I said to Mom. "But let's focus on that later. Right now, let's talk about happier things—like the party at Uva and the wedding. The last I heard you were thinking fall? Is that still the plan?"

She nibbled on her sandwich and salad. "Yes, I've resigned myself to a fall wedding, not that it's anything to scoff about. Fall here is one of the most majestic and beautiful seasons. The good news is that every venue we've looked at has availability. We're hoping to nail down a date by the end of the weekend. I'd like to get invites out in the next few weeks."

"I think fall will be beautiful."

Her face perked up. "Don't you think? The colorful trees, the fall produce. You'll have to start dreaming up something with apples."

"Count on it. Have you seen Lance?" I asked, glad to have a reason to change the subject.

"Briefly. We said hello in passing, but that's it. How is he?"

"Better." I filled her in on my earlier conversation.

"Hmm." She considered my words after I finished. "Doug had mentioned something about checking on a few things for Lance, but I had no idea that he was a member of the Brown family. What pressure."

"Exactly. And Lance wants to invite his brother to the Uva launch, even though he might be plotting to kill their father."

Mom's face clouded. "I suppose I could make a joke about that going hand in hand with Shakespeare, but that seems in poor taste. Do you think there's legitimacy to Lance's story or could it just be Lance being Lance?"

"My thoughts exactly. I think it's highly possible that Lance is exaggerating, but then again we're talking about millions and millions of dollars and people do crazy things when it comes to that kind of money."

She took a bite of the tangy coleslaw. "Sadly, that's quite right."

I finished my sandwich. "In other news, Carlos and Ramiro arrive in two days."

"How are you feeling?"

I bit my bottom lip. "Honestly? Nervous. I don't think I've ever been this nervous to meet someone before."

"You mean Ramiro?"

I nodded.

"Honey, he's going to adore you. You have nothing to worry about."

"Yeah, I hope so."

She squeezed my arm. "I know so."

Before we could continue, the sound of someone clearing their throat made us both turn our heads. The Professor stood next to the booth holding a bouquet of pale pink peonies. "Flowers, for my lady." He gave a half bow.

"Doug. What are you doing here?" Mom's cheeks warmed with color.

I was happy to see him, but wished there was a way I could keep them both out of Torte until the wedding. The longer either of them were here, the more likely they would start to question our marathon baking.

He placed the flowers in her arms. "May I?" He pointed to the empty space on the bench next to her.

"As if you need to ask." She scooted closer to the window to make room for him.

"What are you two lovely ladies up to on this brilliant afternoon?" The Professor stared at the box of invitations.

I reached for one of the invites. "These are for our grand reopening party at Uva."

The Professor pushed a pair of thin glasses onto the bridge of his nose and read the invitation. "Yes, wonderful." He placed his arm around Mom's shoulder. "I must admit, I do wish that we might have found a way to pull off a midsummer wedding."

Leaning into his shoulder, she smiled at me. "Don't worry, Doug. I was just telling Juliet that I think the stars have other plans for us. Don't you think fall will be a gorgeous time to host a celebration?"

"Yes." The Professor removed his glasses. "I hear the words of George Eliot: 'Delicious autumn! My very soul is wedded to it, and if I were a bird I would fly about the earth seeking the successive autumns.'" He covered Mom's hand with his. "I cannot imagine anyone else with whom I would want to fly off in search of new autumns."

Maybe Thomas was right. The Professor's heartfelt poem didn't make him sound like he had a clue what we were really planning.

Tears welled in Mom's eyes. "I agree, Doug."

They shared a sweet kiss. My heart swelled, and then momentarily sunk. I hoped that they would both like the surprise, and that I hadn't overstepped my bounds. I was about to excuse myself, when I remembered my conversation with Lance. "Before I go, can I ask you something?"

The Professor stared at the chalkboard on the far wall where we posted a rotating weekly quote, along with coffee and pastry specials. He read this week's quote aloud, "'Love asks me no questions, and gives me endless support.' One of my favorites from the Bard. How fitting. And, yes, please ask me anything."

"It's about Lance. He told me that you've been helping him do some background checking into his family."

"That's correct." His face was passive.

I decided that there was no point in tiptoeing around the subject. "He told me that he thinks his brother is trying to kill his father."

The Professor rubbed his beard. "Indeed?"

"Yes." I explained Lance's theory on Leo wanting access to the Brown family fortune and how Lance had hired a PI.

"I see. It sounds as if I might be overdue for another conversation with Lance."

The Professor had a way of playing his cards close to his chest. "I would advise you to steer clear of our dear friend's family feud," he continued. "I've learned that nothing good comes of immersing ourselves in someone else's family dynamics. And in this particular situation I fear that there is something most concerning in the midst."

"Right." I nodded and stood. "You two lovebirds enjoy yourselves." I returned to the kitchen, undeterred by the Professor's warning. Lance was in trouble and I had to help.

Chapter Six

The next week passed in a frenzy of wedding details. Mom delivered the remaining fake invites to the downtown business community and to no one's surprise the guest list tripled overnight. I kept her out of Torte's kitchen with dozens of menial checklists for the renovation project. Roger had been a godsend. When I told him that I was having a hard time keeping Mom away, he agreed to occupy her with paint samples and trips to the tile store.

With two days to go before the big bash, Torte was bursting at the seams. Trays of hand-pressed tarts lined the walk-in fridge. Boxes of decorating supplies, stacks of cakes, and tubs of frosting took over every free square inch in the kitchen. I'd been running back and forth between the winery and Torte, which left my feet aching and had me never quite grounded in one place or the other. Chef Garrison's team had been a dream. They had helped prep dozens of appetizers and gone beyond the call of duty, assisting us in stringing up garlands and arranging tables in Uva's barn, which would serve as the dance floor and dessert buffet.

The entire vineyard had been completely transformed for the wedding. Thousands of twinkle lights and paper lanterns had been stretched from the trees and wrapped among the vines. A wooden arch entwined with garlands of greenery had been erected on the top of the hillside looking over acres and acres of lush grapevines. I couldn't envision a more beautiful spot for Mom and the Professor to share their vows.

In addition to the outdoor spaces we would utilize the deck attached to the tasting room to serve dinner. Guests would wind their way through tables loaded with appetizers, meats, and salads. The layout would hopefully make serving and restocking the dinner buffet relatively easy because Chef Garrison's staff would be working in the kitchen directly off the deck.

Picnic tables and chairs had been arranged throughout the grassy hilltop, and a wooden dance floor had been installed in the barn, which was my favorite space. Jose, Uva's previous owner, had renovated an old dilapidated barn on the property, salvaging huge timber beams and a stone fireplace. An iron chandelier with tapered candles hung above the dance floor. The warm interior smelled of chestnut and oak. It was the perfect spot to house our desserts. I couldn't wait to see my tiered wedding cake displayed in front of a low-burning fire, to watch Mom and the Professor take the first turn on the dance floor as husband and wife, and to toast them with a celebratory round of champagne.

Everything was coming together as planned. Fingers crossed, it looked like we were ahead of schedule. The only thing remaining would be the flowers and food, which were perishable and would be delivered the morning of the wedding.

As if dividing my time between the winery and bakeshop wasn't enough to frazzle my nerves, the fact that Carlos and Ramiro were arriving in less than an hour had me running on high. I was acutely aware of my pulse rate as I directed the team on the last remaining tasks and left for the airport. Carlos and Ramiro had flown out of Spain with layovers in New York and Portland. I could only imagine how exhausted they were going to be when they landed in Medford. I had already prepared a simple dinner—a Greek pasta salad with artichoke hearts, marinated chicken, cherry tomatoes, red onions, black olives, goat cheese, and fresh basil that I tossed with a lemon vinaigrette. I would serve it with homemade parmesan-and-olive bread, salad, and Carlos's favorite chocolate cake. If Ramiro was up for it, I thought I could give him the quick tour of Ashland. Lance offered to give them an exclusive behind-the-scenes tour of OSF and front-row tickets to whatever shows they wanted to see. I had Mom and the Professor on call. I wasn't sure if Carlos and Ramiro would want company or just want to go to bed and try to stave off jet lag. Either way, dinner and a crisp bottle of white wine was chilling in the fridge. I told Mom I would call her once I got to the airport and let her know if she and the Professor should come by or not.

I took the long route from Uva, past miles of sepia-toned hills and dotted with green vineyards. As I followed Ashland's back roads, there were signs posted warning of aggressive deer and wildfire danger. My stomach swirled as I left the two-lane highway and steered Mom's car onto I-5 north to Medford. It was a short drive and one I could almost do with my eyes closed, but today it felt as if time was sluggish. The car moved like molasses. Anticipation pulsed through my veins. I couldn't believe that I was finally going to meet Carlos's son. What would he be like? I hadn't spent much time around teenagers. What if he hated me?

Stop it, Jules, I scolded myself. If Ramiro was anything like Carlos I was sure that I would love him instantly. I just wanted to get the initial meeting over with.

The Medford airport was small with one main terminal that housed a gift shop, restaurant, and information booth. I found a parking space and opted to go inside to meet them.

Airports see more love than maybe any other place on the planet. I watched as a couple embraced and kissed each other in a passionate good-bye. A family waiting next to me reunited with a bunch of bright balloons, happy tears, and enthusiastic hugs. Would that be us? Or would my first meeting with my stepson be awkward and stilted?

I held my breath and tried to force my heart rate to return to normal. Suddenly, I spotted Carlos, walking arm in arm with a young teen who could almost have passed as his twin. Ramiro was taller than I expected. He had the same olive skin and dark hair as Carlos and a slight swagger to his walk. I sucked in a breath. This was it.

"Julieta!" Carlos broke into a jaunt. When he made it to me he embraced me in a lingering hug. He smelled of sandalwood and musk. His familiar touch made my stomach queasy. "*Mi querida,* you look wonderful."

Ramiro lagged behind. He stuffed his hands in his pockets and stared at his sandals.

"You must be Ramiro," I said, breaking away from Carlos. "I've heard so much about you."

"Sí, me too." He greeted me with a kiss on each cheek.

"You look so much like your dad." I couldn't take my eyes off him. The teen girls who hung around Torte after school were going to swoon at the sight of Ramiro. Like Carlos, he had the same chiseled features, dark hair, olive skin, and impish grin. His brown eyes held a hint of playfulness about them.

Carlos tussled Ramiro's hair. "Sí, sí, he is handsome, no?"

"Yes," I agreed.

Ramiro pushed Carlos away. I could tell that we were embarrassing him, so I changed the subject. "How was the flight?"

"Long." Carlos twisted from side to side.

"Yeah. That's an understatement." I looked to Ramiro. "What would you like to do? I have dinner waiting for you at my apartment. I can show you around town, or you can just crash."

"Crash?" Ramiro scrunched his face, making him look younger than fourteen.

"Oh, sorry. Sleep." I grinned. Ramiro had grown up with his mother in Spain. His English was remarkable, but I had to remember that American slang probably didn't get translated into his textbooks.

"Ah. Crash. I was thinking about the plane and trying to understand your meaning. You mean sleep." Tiny flecks of gold sparkled in his eyes when he laughed.

"I'm fine. I would like to see Ashland. Papa, is that okay with you?"

Carlos wrapped one arm around Ramiro and the other around me. "Sí, let's go explore."

I wondered if people walking past us would think of us as family. I'm sure I must have looked like the odd woman out, sandwiched between two Spanish men with my fair skin and light hair. Regardless of whether I looked the part Carlos was my family, and now Ramiro was too. My nerves calmed as we waited for their bags. The anticipation that had been bubbling inside dissipated. Ramiro and I had much to learn about each other, but at least the initial meeting was over, and given his playful spirit I had a feeling that we were going to get along just fine.

"The hills look like Spain," Ramiro commented in the backseat as we drove into Ashland. His observation made sense. Ashland boasts a Mediterranean climate with long days of summer sun. At two thousand feet above sea level, our fair city is nestled in the Siskiyou Mountain Range, allowing for cool evenings and bringing abundant wildlife—free-range turkeys, herds of deer, cougars, coyotes, and even black bears—into neighborhoods and backyards. Native Ashlanders simply waved hello to deer running loose on front lawns on their way to the market or theater. Tourists, on the other hand, often stopped to pose for pictures and videos with our four-legged residents.

"We should take him to Uva," Carlos said. I was acutely aware that Ramiro was in the backseat, as I steered off the freeway onto the back road leading into town. We hadn't had a chance to speak about the winery, and I didn't want to burden Ramiro with what might be a long, drawn-out conversation.

"You want to go there first?" I met his eyes. A shot of adrenaline pulsed through my body. Regardless of how many times I had tried to ignore and abandon my feelings for Carlos, there was an undeniable pull and chemistry between us.

"Sí." Carlos glanced behind him. "I have told Ramiro all about the winery. The beautiful slope, the rocky soil, and our plans."

"Our plans?" I raised a brow. Carlos hadn't mentioned anything about the future or even why he had decided to buy a stake in the vineyard.

His bronzed hand touched my knee. I clutched the steering wheel to try and control my emotions. "We have plenty of time to talk about the future, *mi querida*."

Ramiro smiled at me in the rearview mirror. I wondered what Carlos had told him about us. Had he explained our separation or glossed over the fact that we were worlds apart?

In front of me the road switched from pavement to dirt, offering a welcome distraction from what was next for Carlos and me. We wound up the bumpy road, past rows and rows of grapevines to the crest of the hill. Uva sat, like a mighty fortress, at the top. "Here we are," I said, pulling into an empty space in front of the building.

"Wow, it's huge." Ramiro jumped out of the car.

Carlos beamed with pride. "Sí, it is one of the oldest vineyards in the region, with well-established grapes."

I watched him point out how the grapes had been intentionally planted on the rocky terrain so that they would have to fight for survival. Carlos was an expert when it came to wine. As part of his training as a chef he had taken a variety of classes and workshops from world-class sommeliers and toured vineyards on practically every continent. The thing that made his style unique was his ability to put people at ease when it came to wine. He was knowledgeable without being pretentious. When he hosted tastings on the *Amour of the Seas* he was known for whipping up whimsical pairings. Like a buttery chardonnay with salty potato chips, or a deep red blend with decadent chocolate cupcakes.

"It is wonderful, no?" Carlos pointed to the paper lanterns hanging from the trees and the colorful burlap banners strung along the deck. "You have already done so much."

"Just for the wedding," I replied. As if on cue, a yellow Hummer rumbled up the dirt road, kicking gravel and dust in its wake. "Oh no," I muttered under my breath.

"What is it?" Carlos looked at me with concern.

"Richard Lord."

"Ah, sí. I must meet with him."

"Not today. You and Ramiro just got here."

Carlos waved dust from his face. "It is okay, do not worry, Julieta."

Richard slammed the brakes, sending out another cloud of dirt. I stepped away. Ramiro pointed down the hill where a few vineyard workers were kicking a soccer ball. "Is it okay if I go explore?"

"Go for it." I looked to Carlos for confirmation.

"Sí." He nodded. Ramiro sprinted down the hill. As much as he resembled his dad, he was still a kid at heart. I appreciated that he wasn't trying to act older. "He is a good kid, yes?" Carlos noted as we both watched Ramiro run through the vines.

"He's amazing." I squeezed Carlos's hand.

Richard Lord lumbered out of the Hummer. True to his typical fashion he wore a pair of tight white golf shorts that did little to enhance his bulky frame. He paired the shorts with a ridiculous green Hawaiian shirt with neon-yellow pineapples. He looked like a Sasquatch ready to board a cruise. "The rumors are true, huh?" His heavy gait left footprints in the dirt as he stormed toward us. "I heard that you were in town and figured Juliet would bring you out here to try and dig her claws in."

"What does that even mean, Richard?"

Carlos clutched my hand in an attempt to try and appease me. Then he dropped it and walked over to Richard. "It is good to see you again." He held out his hand.

Richard made a point of grasping Carlos's hand and then clapping him on the back. It sounded like it must have stung, but Carlos's face remained passive. "Two of my business partners in the flesh. What do you say we pop open a bottle of pinot and have a little chat on the deck?" His tone indicated that it wasn't a request.

We followed Richard up the short steps that led to the deck. He paused when he reached the top and puffed for air. If walking up five steps left Richard out of breath he was in worse shape than I had thought. "Hey, what's that crew doing down there?" His booming voice echoed as he pointed out the workers kicking the soccer ball.

"Playing football," Carlos said, with a wink to me. "It is wonderful. It makes the grapes happy and happy grapes mean wonderful wine."

Richard hiked his golf shorts over his belly. "I'm going to have words with them about that. There's no time for play. They're on the clock. They should be working."

Carlos shrugged.

"Where's the help around here?" Richard yelled.

"We're closed," I reminded him. Uva's tasting room was open each weekend and three days a week, in addition to hosting special events. When our good friend Jose owned the winery he and his wife shared duties in the tasting room. Otherwise, they hired seasonal workers to help with the harvest, crush, and vine maintenance. Hiring someone to oversee the tasting room was one of my top priorities. I didn't have time to manage that on top of everything else. As long as we hired someone with experience they could coordinate volunteers. Many local wineries used trained volunteers to pour in their tasting rooms. It was a win-win. The volunteers received payment in the form of wine, and the tasting rooms didn't have to take on the expense of extra staff.

"What would you like to drink?" I asked. "I'll get us a bottle inside."

"You better make it two." Richard sneered.

"Anything you like is fine," Carlos replied, taking a seat next to Richard at one of the hand-carved wooden tables with a sweeping view of the vineyard.

I unlocked the sliding glass doors that led inside. Jose and his family had lived and worked in the house. He had converted an old barn adjacent to the house into a tasting room. The main floor of the home consisted of a large chef-style kitchen, a family room, office, and small bathroom. Upstairs there were three bedrooms and an additional bathroom. I'd been mulling over ideas for the house since I had learned that Carlos and I were part owners. My latest brainstorm was to rent it out for private parties and weddings. We could update one of the bedrooms upstairs into a bridal suite. Mom didn't know it yet, but she was going to be my test bride. In my conversations with other winery owners, I had learned that many of them supplemented their income by renting out the property. The possibilities were endless, from opening the space up for family reunions to renting as an Airbnb.

The kitchen as it stood looked very bare without Jose's family's dishes and plates. The last time Carlos was here we had dined outside under the stars. Jose and his wife had treated us to an authentic Mexican feast. I remembered the kitchen feeling alive with energy and laughter. Today it felt sterile.

At least it has wineglasses, I thought as I removed three glasses from the cupboard near a wall of wine bottles. Jose had left stemware, barware, and the equipment needed to make wine, all of which came with the sale. I scanned the wine racks and decided on a 2012 bottle of pinot noir. That year's crops were record-producing. The summer had been warm and dry. Vintners throughout the Pacific Northwest had deemed it the best year for wine in decades. Many went on to win awards for that year's near-perfect bounty.

I returned to the deck with the bottle of pinot and handed Carlos and Richard glasses.

"What did you pick?" Richard snatched the bottle from my hand. He had to hold it a foot from his face to read the label. "Twenty twelve. That was a good year." He sounded disappointed that I knew my wines.

Richard struggled to uncork the wine. He tugged so hard that he snapped the corkscrew in half. "Great."

"May I try?" Carlos offered.

"It's ruined." Richard set the broken corkscrew on the table.

"That is okay. I do not need a corkscrew. Watch." Carlos picked up the bottle of wine. He stood and removed one of his leather shoes.

"What's he doing?" Richard asked.

"No idea." I shrugged.

Carlos placed the bottle of wine inside his shoe and then walked over to the stone wall at the far end of the deck. He held the top of the bottle and began banging the shoe against the wall. Slowly the cork emerged, like a tortoise from its shell. After a few heavy hits, he removed the bottle from his shoe and twisted the cork the rest of the way with one hand. "Voilà!"

"How did you do that?" Richard's face puffed out.

"A trick I learned from a French chef many years ago. It is good to know, sí?" He poured the raspberry-colored wine into our glasses. "You never know when you might need to open a bottle."

It didn't surprise me that Carlos could remove a cork without a bottle opener. And I had to admit that watching Richard's reaction made it even sweeter.

Carlos put his shoe back on and sat down. "A toast to new ventures."

We clicked our glasses together.

"About that." Richard took a huge swig of his wine. "What is your intention with the property? I'm in a position to buy out your shares immediately."

"Buy out?" Carlos looked confused.

"Yes, as in adios. See ya later. I'm willing to pay fair market value for your share in the winery." Richard held his wineglass to the light and swirled it so fast I thought it might slosh on me. I scooted my chair away. "I explained this to Jose when he sold me my shares. I'm in a position to diversify my investments. I'm not sure if Juliet told you that we're offering free wine tastings every afternoon at the Merry Windsor to our guests. It's been a huge hit."

What Richard failed to mention was that he wasn't serving Uva wines for his free tastings. My friend Chef Garrison had told me that the Merry Windsor was "treating" their guests to cheap boxed wines and stale crackers and cheese. It was a classic Richard Lord move, which I'm sure was brought on by the fact that Chef Garrison had started hosting happy hour tastings for guests at Ashland Springs with some of the Rogue Valley's best wines and elegant bites. Richard was notorious for copying anyone he considered to be competition. Although I did wonder why he kept mentioning wanting to diversify his investments. What was he scheming now?

"But we don't want to sell," Carlos said, sounding surprised.

"Look, you don't know Southern Oregon like I do. People aren't going to take to foreigners, especially around these parts. I'll cut you a deal to get your investment back. No harm done."

"No." Carlos swirled his wine. I could tell from the vein pulsing in his forehead that he was fuming, but he kept his composure. "We are not interested in selling. Are we, Julieta?"

"Nope." That wasn't entirely true. Adding the winery to my already full plate had been one of the reasons I hadn't been sleeping well, but I refused to bow to Richard Lord's whims. Not to mention that spending time at Uva in preparation for Mom's wedding had deepened my attachment to the vineyard.

Richard polished off the wine in his glass. He stared at us with his bulbous eyes while he poured himself a refill. "Have it your way, but you realize you have to get my sign-off on everything we do around here."

Carlos shook his head. "No, this is not true."

"I think it is, actually," I said, taking a sip of the wine. Hints of berries came through in the crisp, clean pinot.

"No, it is not," Carlos insisted.

"But Carlos, we're equal partners. The three of us and Lance."

Carlos ran his finger along the rim of the wineglass. "Did you read the paperwork I sent you?"

"Yeah." I had skimmed the contracts. "Most of it."

He chuckled.

Richard's face had gone as red as the wine. "What are you talking about?"

"The contracts. When Jose and I made our deal, he was worried about the winery being torn down and turned into a housing development. He sold three portions of shares in order to ensure that wouldn't happen."

"Right, but that makes us equal," I said.

"No. You see, Jose was to keep a small percentage— five percent—for himself. But he decided against it and offered that to me. Those shares belong to you solely, Julieta. We are the majority shareholders in Uva."

The look of dismay on Richard's face made me almost feel sorry for him. Almost.

Chapter Seven

Richard almost spit his wine all over us. He pushed to his feet. "What? You have more shares than me? How? How is that possible?"

Carlos topped off his glass of wine. "It is how Jose wanted things."

"This is unacceptable. I'm going to consult my lawyer."

"Sí, it is a good idea. I hope that we can work together. I would like to hear your thoughts on the vineyard."

Richard fumed. "I have to go." He pointed a fat finger at my face. "You'll be hearing from my people, Juliet. I know this was your scheme. You and your mother are always up to something."

"No, Julieta had nothing to do with this," Carlos said, standing as if to protect my honor.

"Like I said, you'll be hearing from my lawyers." He tugged at his Hawaiian shirt and stomped down the stairs.

I doubted that Richard had "lawyers." Maybe he had *a* lawyer. And I would bet that his lawyer was also my lawyer. It was hardly as if Ashland was teeming with law firms.

"He did not take that well." Carlos sat down.

"That's Richard. I tried to warn you. Why didn't you say anything about my five percent?"

"This is why I sent you the contracts. You did not look at them?" He sounded hurt.

"Sorry. I've had so much going on with the wedding and renovations that I didn't take the time to fully review them."

"It is okay. Do not worry." Carlos raised the bottle of wine. "Would you like more?"

I shook my head. "No, I'm fine. But like Richard, I don't understand. Why did Jose sell you his shares?"

Carlos and Jose had hit it off immediately when they first met. They shared a common language and a love for organic food and wine. Jose had struggled with the decision to sell Uva. Ultimately, he decided that the financial burden wasn't worth the stress to his family. However, he did not want to see the vineyard that he had spent years building up being torn into plots for subdivisions—a common trend in the farmland surrounding Ashland as of late. "He had planned to keep a piece for himself, but when his wife decided that they would move home to Mexico he did not want to have to worry about the taxes and banking. He asked if I could afford a bit more. He did not want to give this option to Richard because he knew that Richard does not care so much about the vineyard."

That was true. I knew that if Richard had complete control of Uva he would develop the property immediately.

"Was it legal?" I asked.

"The sale?" Carlos tilted his wineglass. "Sí. Of course. It is good. It should not be a problem."

I hoped he was right. There was something about his tone that made me nervous, made me think that he wasn't telling me everything. I wasn't sure how the business had been set up. Did every stakeholder have to sign off on selling more shares? Or could it be that because Carlos was already a shareholder he had first right of refusal to buy Richard out? The last thing I needed was a court battle with Richard Lord.

Ramiro arrived, dripping with sweat and smiling broadly. "They are very good soccer players." He plopped down next to Carlos.

"Would you like something to drink?"

Carlos offered him his wine. *"Vino?"*

I knew the drinking age was lower in Spain but I wondered if kids Ramiro's age drank.

Ramiro laughed. "No, do you have some water?"

"Of course. Let me get you some." I went to the kitchen to get him a glass of ice water. If Carlos and I really did own the majority shares we could potentially do some amazing things here, I thought as I piled ice into a glass. Then again, was Carlos even considering staying?

I returned with water and the three of us chatted under the warm late-afternoon sun about Spain and Ramiro's friends and soccer team. The vineyard smelled of warm grapes and baking pine needles. Conversation flowed with ease. Ramiro was bright and engaging. He spoke with his hands (like his father) while he regaled us with tales of surfing off the coast of Spain where he was almost stung by a stingray and once came within a few feet of a shark.

Chef Garrison pulled up about an hour later in a white van with the Ashland Spring's logo painted on the side. "Jules, hey! I wasn't expecting to see you today," he said, jumping out of the driver's seat. He was accompanied by three staff members, one of whom looked familiar. I stared at the guy as they unloaded trays of supplies from the back of the van. He was in his early to mid-thirties, with jet-black hair, a bunch of tattoos, and a goatee. Where did I know him from?

Suddenly, it dawned on me—Torte. This was the guy I'd seen hanging around Torte the other morning. The guy that Lance thought was following him. What was he doing here?

I excused myself from the table after introducing Carlos and Ramiro, and followed Chef Garrison inside. "Can I talk to you in private for a minute?" I asked.

Chef Garrison set a gallon of olive oil on the kitchen counter. "Sure." He looked at me with concern. "Is something wrong?"

I pointed to the office. "No, I just want to go over something with you," I lied, and led him to the office and shut the door behind us. Carlos wasn't a fan of my meddling. I didn't want him or anyone else to hear our conversation. "Sorry, I know I'm acting weird, but I want to ask you about one of your staff members," I said to the chef.

"Shoot." Chef Garrison glanced in the direction of the kitchen.

"It's the guy with the goatee," I said. "I saw him

hanging around Torte a few days ago. Has he worked for you long?"

"Adam? Uh, no. He came from a temp agency, but he's been great. A good, solid worker. I hired him as dishwasher but he's done some serving for private events too. Why? Did something happen at Torte?"

"No. I'm sure it's nothing. It was just weird to see him here. He was acting a bit strange at the bakeshop. Almost like he was watching us work. I'm sure I sound paranoid." I didn't want to betray Lance's confidence.

Chef Garrison leaned his head back and nodded. "No. You're not paranoid. That's on me. I told the staff who are working this event to stop by Torte and buy a pastry and take a look around. I know this is a special event for the entire town and I thought it would be helpful if they had a taste of what the vibe of the wedding is going to be like, and where better to get that than Torte."

"Good thinking." I smiled, feeling more at ease. Maybe Lance was being paranoid. It was much more likely that Adam had come to Torte on his boss's request rather than to tail Lance. I thanked Chef Garrison and went back outside to join Carlos and Ramiro.

We didn't stay much longer. Ramiro's spurt of energy was followed by a crash. His head kept drooping. Twice I caught him blinking rapidly to keep his eyes open.

"Should we go?" I suggested.

Carlos took one look at Ramiro and nodded. "Sí, I think we both may need a catnap soon."

"Would you like me to invite Mom and the Professor over for dinner, or are you ready to call it a night?"

Ramiro rubbed the corner of his eye. "Could we stop for an espresso?"

"Absolutely!" I flashed him a grin. "I don't know what your dad has told you, but I never turn down the chance for a coffee."

He helped pick up our glasses. If they were in the mood for coffee we could pop into Torte. I knew that the team was dying to see Carlos again, especially Sterling. They had grown surprisingly tight when Carlos had visited last winter.

The drive to Torte only took a few minutes. I pointed out nearby wineries and hop farms. "Oh, before I forget," I said, pulling into an angled parking space at the end of the plaza. "The wedding is a surprise. The story is that you're both here for the Uva grand opening party. And, I might need to recruit you to help distract the Professor."

"This is so romantic, Julieta," Carlos said with a thickness in his voice.

"I see, so you mean they will surprised at the party." Ramiro exited the car. A group of young girls walking arm in arm stopped in mid-stride and gaped at him. I was used to women ogling Carlos. It was no surprise that Ramiro got the same treatment. It was also impossible not to be drawn in by their Mediterranean looks and radiant charm.

"Exactly." I waved to the girls, who realized I'd seen them staring at Ramiro. They giggled and ran off toward Lithia Park. "This is Torte." I motioned to the bakeshop and couldn't help but smile. Bethany had outdone herself with the front window display. It was a scene from a Parisian picnic with a red and white checkered blanket, bottles of blackberry sparkling sodas and lemonade with pink and yellow striped straws, a basket bursting with bundles of our French baguettes, a collection of summer pastries like butterfly and ladybug cupcakes, and sugar cookies cut out like flowers. Customers sat at outdoor tables with blue and red umbrellas sipping lattes and noshing on buttery croissants.

"It is *precioso*." Ramiro's toothy grin made his face light up.

"Come inside. Everyone is excited to meet you, and I promise that Andy, our barista, makes the best espresso on the West Coast."

"Sí, that is good."

Inside, the bakeshop was relatively quiet. There was a group at one of the window booths. I did a double take because at first glance I could have sworn that one of the men in the group was Lance. He had the same lean, lanky frame and catlike features. It wasn't Lance, though. His features were harder and his outfit—a flannel shirt and jeans—completely wrong.

"Boss, you brought the fam." Andy's voice made me tear my eyes away from the booth.

"Right." We moved toward the espresso bar. "You remember Carlos, and this is his son, Ramiro."

Andy squeezed his hand into a fist. He bumped it twice on his chest and then flashed a peace sign. "Welcome to America, bro."

Ramiro laughed. He mimicked Andy's fist-bump greeting. "Thanks, bro."

"Can I get you something? A hot chocolate?" Andy opened a canister of beans. "These beauties were delivered about an hour ago straight from the roaster."

"The smell is so good." Ramiro stepped closer to get a better whiff. "Can I have an espresso?"

Andy's mouth dropped open. "Mad props, kid. I like it. Start 'em young on straight shots of this nectar of the gods." He gave Ramiro another fist bump. "One espresso coming up."

"Carlos." Sterling joined us at the counter. He and Carlos exchanged a hug. "So good to have you here."

"Yes, it is good to be here again. Julieta tells me you have been improving very much. I cannot wait to cook with you."

Sterling almost blushed.

"This is my son, Ramiro." Carlos introduced them.

I noticed Steph and Bethany had stopped cleaning up in the kitchen. Bethany's face betrayed her. She gazed at Carlos with a starstruck, faraway stare. I couldn't blame her. Carlos was devilishly handsome and had the same effect on pretty much every woman who crossed his path. "Come up." I motioned to them.

Bethany pinched her cheeks and smoothed her wavy hair down. She checked her apron for stains. Steph tossed a dish towel in the sink.

"Here's the rest of the team." I finished the introductions, watching as Bethany blushed. I wondered if Andy would take notice. Bethany had had a little crush on Andy, but thus far he was completely oblivious. Steph, on the other hand, was immune to Carlos's wiles. She stayed just long enough to be polite before returning to the kitchen.

Carlos and Sterling took off together, striking up a conversation about cuts of meat and the best way to slice salami. Andy had a captive audience in Ramiro. He talked him through each step of the espresso-making process. Bethany gave Carlos one final glance before recovering her composure and joining in on the coffee discussion. She hadn't been around the last time Carlos was in town, so this was her first introduction. I wasn't the least bit worried. I knew that her real feelings lay with Andy and that she was way too young for Carlos to even turn an eye.

I scanned the bakeshop. Aside from the booth with the gentleman who bore a striking resemblance to Lance, there were only two tables in use. Could the man be Leo, Lance's brother? There was one way to find out. I left Ramiro in Andy's capable hands. Then I picked up a carafe of coffee and began circulating through the tables.

"Anyone need a refill?" I asked, holding up a carafe when I stopped at their booth.

The man who looked like Lance handed me his cup. "As long as that's not decaf. There's a special place in hell for people who drink decaf."

"Wow, that's a strong sentiment." I laughed, refilling his cup.

"Wasn't kidding." His voice sounded like Lance's, except with an edge.

The woman sitting across from him turned cherry red. "You're not going to like this, Leo, but I was about to ask her if she had any decaf."

Leo! It was Lance's brother. I wondered if I should say anything.

"Sarah, no employee of mine is drinking decaf. Man up and have another cup."

Sarah winced. She showed us her hands, which were quivering. "I can't. I already have the shakes. Too much coffee and too many late nights crunching numbers and watching over your dad." Her fingernails were painted bright red to match her plaid shirt, which she had accessorized with funky plastic bangles and a chunky black and red plastic necklace.

"You always have the shakes," he scoffed. "Good thing you know your stuff, otherwise I'd have to kick you to the curb."

I wondered if this was how they interacted with one another. Was Leo kidding? Or was he really a jerk?"

The man sitting next to Sarah chimed in. "Who cares what coffee she drinks, Leo?" He appeared more poised. I would guess that he was in his late fifties. He wore a dress shirt, a purple bow tie, and slacks and had a stack of file folders in front of him.

"You know why I care? Because of all those damn tree huggers. They're the ones who drink decaf. Not my guys out in the field. Can you imagine Jim or Rusty coming in here and ordering a decaf? It's not American."

I couldn't believe the difference in attitude between Lance and his brother.

"If you want I can have our barista brew a fresh pot of decaf." I addressed Sarah. "We have a number of customers who prefer our coffee without caffeine for a variety of reasons." I found myself wanting to defend her.

Leo sighed. "Whatever. Like I said, the girl knows her stuff. She's a master at balancing my books and I think she knows more about my company than I do."

"Decaf would be nice." Sarah shot me a look of thanks. I got the sense she was embarrassed by Leo's strange attempt at praise.

"I'll be right back." I topped off Leo's and the other

man's cups. "Hey, Andy, can you brew a half-pot of de-caf?" I asked, setting the empty coffee carafe on the bar.

"You bet." He nudged Ramiro in the waist. "You want to grind the beans for me?"

"Sí."

"This kid knows his coffee." Andy was not easily impressed. I knew that was high praise coming from him. "He told me he and his friends starting drinking cappuccinos in fifth grade. I think I need to move to Spain."

"What? And leave this?" I swept my arm along the counter. "What would Ashland do without you?"

"If Ramiro sticks around they won't need me. I'll be out of a job." Andy winked.

Once the decaf had brewed I returned to the booth.

Sarah offered her cup and a smile of relief. "Thanks again. I would have been up all night with the jitters."

Leo made a grunting sound under his breath.

She ignored him. "Do you own this shop?"

"I do. I'm Jules, pastry chef and decaf coffee pur-veyor."

"Jules, as in Juliet?" Leo said.

"Yes, that's right."

He stared at me with interest. "I think you know my brother."

"Who's that?" I decided it might be better if I didn't let on that Lance had mentioned anything about his brother.

"Lance. He's the director of tights or something at the playhouse."

Sarah laughed uncomfortably. The other man shuffled paperwork in one of the file folders and ignored Leo's dig.

"Lance is amazing. He's the best artistic director that OSF has ever had." I could hear my voice getting higher. Lance hadn't exaggerated. Leo was obnoxious.

"I'm Jarvis." The man wearing the light blue dress shirt extended his hand. "Jarvis O. Sandberg, attorney."

I half expected him to hand me a business card.

"Oh, and I'm Sarah. Decaf lover." Sarah introduced herself. "I manage the Brown Family trust, and try my best to keep these two on task." She chuckled awkwardly. Neither Jarvis nor Leo laughed.

"Nice to meet you all. What brings you to Torte?"

Jarvis tapped the stack of crisp files. "Work."

"We get that a lot." I shifted the coffee carafe from one hand to the other. "SOU students call this their 'office.'"

"I have an office in Medford," Jarvis replied.

"We're here on business, is what he means," Leo said. "Waiting for that fruitcake brother of mine to show up."

I had to resist dumping the rest of the decaf on his lap. How could he be so rude about Lance? And to someone he barely knew?

"Lance is meeting you here?" I asked, through clenched teeth.

"Yep. Said we had to come meet him at an artisan coffeehouse. We have these in Medford too, you know. It's called Grandma J's Café where you can get an entire stack of hotcakes, eggs, hash browns, and all the coffee you can drink for the same price as one of your fancy lattes."

No wonder Lance had left his family behind.

"I can smell the patchouli from here. Artisan Chunky Monkey, what is that? My God. Call it coffee. I'll take coffee from a can any day over what they serve in this hippie town."

It wasn't very often that someone came into my shop and offended me so blatantly. Nothing in Torte smelled of patchouli. We prided ourselves on serving top-notch baked goods that were infused with love. Sure, Ashland had a free-spirited community but that was one small piece of my beloved town. Ashlanders are diverse and worldly. Our small city attracts professors, playwrights, actors, and adventure seekers—people from varying corners of the globe.

In that moment, I had made up my mind that Lance was right. Leo had to be plotting to kill their father. I wanted to kill *him*.

Instead, I shifted the conversation. "I'm sorry to hear about your father. Lance mentioned that he isn't doing well."

Leo looked down at his coffee cup and didn't answer.

Sarah tried to console him by reaching out for his hand. "Thank you. It's been a hard time for everyone at the Brown Family Group. I'm afraid the senior Mr. Brown doesn't have much time left."

Leo threw her hand off. "What do you know? The old man keeps on ticking. Nothing has stopped him yet. He'll probably keep going for another twenty years."

Jarvis cleared his throat. "This coffee is delicious." He smoothed the stack of files.

I got the sense he was uncomfortable with the topic of Mr. Brown's failing health.

"It's fantastic," Sarah agreed. "Do you roast your own

beans? I'll have to buy some for the office. Working with a bunch of lumberjacks means that our coffee usually comes from a can."

I was about to tell her that we sourced our beans from a local roaster, but Leo jumped in.

"My brother says you're having some kind of tutti-frutti party he wants us to come to. Says it's a new potential investment for the Brown Group." Leo sounded disinterested.

Is that how Lance had pitched it? As a potential investment deal? In what, Uva?

I kept my face neutral. "Yes, we're having a launch party for the vineyard. You're all welcome to come. It's a community event. We're hosting a Midsummer Night's Eve party in honor of reopening the winery."

"That sounds like fun," Sarah said, fiddling with the cheap plastic bracelets around her wrist.

Leo gnawed on his fingernail. "I'm not wearing a costume. I already told my brother that there was no way he was going to get me in tights."

"Costumes are optional." I forced a smile. "I should get back to work, but maybe I'll see you again this weekend."

I left them bickering about costumes. Lance's brother was loathsome. I didn't want him anywhere near the wedding. But I had made a promise to a friend. I just couldn't help but wonder if Lance had another reason for inviting Leo. He wasn't really thinking of selling his portion of Uva, was he? There was no way that I could work with Richard Lord *and* Leo. No way.

Chapter Eight

I skipped inviting Mom and the Professor to dinner. Ramiro and Carlos scarfed down dinner and were asleep minutes later. My apartment wasn't exactly spacious, but I set Ramiro up on an air mattress on the living room floor. Carlos took the couch. He insisted, despite my attempts to give them my bed.

Even if my sleep hadn't been impacted by the stress of everything going on, trying to sleep knowing that Carlos was only a few feet away was nearly impossible. I tossed and turned all night before finally giving up sometime around four. Odds were good that Ramiro and Carlos would sleep for hours, so I tiptoed into the bathroom and got dressed. The kitchen was stocked with coffee, eggs, fruit, and bread and pastries that I'd brought home from Torte last night. They would be fine once they woke. I left a note, telling them to come find me at the bakeshop later and to help themselves to anything in the kitchen.

Hopefully they could have a leisurely morning. My morning was not going to be quite as calm. There were still about a thousand things to do before the wedding. Carlos had offered his services. Having his skilled hands in the kitchen would be a tremendous relief. Ramiro also agreed to help with anything we needed. Obviously, he wasn't a formally trained chef like his father, but we would take any extra help we could get, even if it meant asking him to fold napkins or sprinkle sugar on cookie cutouts.

I headed down the stairs from my apartment. Elevation, the outdoor store, was at ground level. Their front window had huge banners offering twenty percent off kayaks. Ashland wasn't just known as a destination for theater lovers. Given our proximity to dozens of lakes and rivers, adventure-seekers used Ashland as base camp for summer explorations. It wasn't unusual to see groups of men and women dressed in rafting gear with sunglasses, waterproof hats, and Bull Frog sunscreen meandering between couples in evening wear headed for the Elizabethan theater.

Continuing along the sidewalk I passed Puck's Pub and A Rose by Any Other Name. Torte sat in a peaceful slumber at the end of the plaza. Aside from chirping crickets and the sound of the Lithia bubblers a quiet calm permeated downtown. I paused and breathed it in.

The morning stillness was shattered by my phone buzzing. I was startled.

Who was calling me this early? I unlocked the front door and tugged my phone from my bag. Lance's face flashed on the screen.

"Lance? What's going on?" There was no reason for Lance to be calling me now.

"He's dead, Juliet. Dead."

"Who?" My thoughts went immediately to Leo. I had taken such an instant dislike to him that part of me wouldn't have been sad to hear that he was dead. I felt along the front wall and flipped on the lights.

"My father." Lance's voice cracked. "He's dead."

"Oh, Lance. I'm so sorry. What can I do? I'm at Torte. Do you want to come down for a coffee? It's just me. Or I can bring you something, or come to your place. Anything. Anything you need, I'm here."

"No. I had to get out of that house." Lance paused. "I'm driving aimlessly around Medford trying to figure out what to do next. I know Leo killed him, Juliet. Or put one of his henchmen up to it. You have to help me prove it."

"Okay, okay. Lance, try to breathe. Should I come get you? You probably shouldn't be driving. I'm sure you're in shock."

"I'm fine. The man was in his eighties. He lived a good life. He knew this was coming." There was brief silence on the phone. "The only thing I'm in shock about is that my brother went through with it. I was there, Juliet. I was with him last night. He was awake and alert. We talked. He ate some pudding. I went to bed and woke up a few hours later to the sound of alarms blaring in his room. Leo claims that he died peacefully in his sleep, but I saw his machines—all of those tubes and his breathing machine. They were *unplugged*, Juliet."

I didn't know what to say.

"Someone pulled the plug, and I'm sure it was my brother."

"Lance, are you sure?" My skin felt clammy.

"Positive, but I made a terrible mistake."

Construction equipment beeped in the background. "What kind of a mistake?"

"I left the room. I thought I might be sick. Seeing my father's lifeless body was . . ." He didn't finish.

"I know," I said with sympathy.

He coughed twice. "In any event, I stepped out of the room for a moment and when I returned everything was plugged back in. How will we ever prove that Leo killed my father?"

"Can we?" I hated to sound unhelpful. "We'll have to talk to the Professor. I have no idea what to do."

"What about fingerprints on the cord or plug-in? There has to be some evidence, somewhere." Lance's voice hit a shrill pitch.

"Look, why don't you drive home, or come here. We'll find the Professor and talk to him together." I hoped that my tone sounded calming.

"Okay. Okay. I'll call him. Sorry to dump this on you. I've been a terrible friend lately. I'll make it up to you somehow."

"Lance, don't be ridiculous. That's what friends do. Really, I'm here for anything you need. Anytime. You can call me at two o'clock in the morning. I'll be here."

He let out a sorrowful sigh. "That's why I love you, darling. I'll check in later."

We hung up. I stared at the still kitchen. Suddenly, my stresses and worries seemed minor. Lance had lost his father. Unfortunately, I knew all too well that there was no escaping grief. The pain of losing my father had left me forever altered. After he died, I remember seeing a therapist who walked me through the stages of grief. While the exercise had been helpful in understanding that my erratic emotions were normal, the idea of grief being linear and something that could be mastered was misleading. Grief was part of me. It had made me stronger, but I carried my father's loss and his memory with me. I wished that I could fix things for Lance, but I knew that the only thing I could do would be to stand with him in the days and weeks and months ahead. To offer a listening ear or temporary distraction while he learned to find a way to make space for his grief.

I headed for the kitchen. I needed to clear my head and the best way to do that was to bake. After tying on an apron, I washed my hands and began proofing bread yeast. Had Lance called the Professor? I should have asked him to let me know. Before I got my hands sticky with bread dough I shot him a text. What was standard procedure for a death like this? Would an autopsy or any sort of formal investigation be performed since Lance's father had been sick? I thought about my brief conversation with Leo, Sarah, and Jarvis. They seemed like an unlikely trio. My first impression had been that Sarah appeared to be in charge. Leo didn't strike me as mastermind or genius. Could he have planned to kill his father? What kind of person would unplug their parent from life support?

I shuddered at the thought. I couldn't imagine anyone killing their parent, but after meeting Leo yesterday I had to admit that it wasn't out of the realm of possibility. Then again, Lance had a tendency toward hysterics. There was an equal chance that his father had died from natural causes and that no one had tampered with his life support.

One important question that I hadn't asked was whether there was anyone else in the room. Hopefully,

Lance would come by soon and we could sit down and talk more.

With the yeast rising I combined flour, a touch of sugar, and salt in the mixer. Once the yeast had bubbled up, I added that to the dry ingredients and let the kneading attachment in our industrial mixer do the heavy lifting. When the dough was stretchy I would finish it by hand and pat it into greased loaf pans.

I wanted to get through our morning orders quickly so I could focus most of the day on the final wedding prep. With extra hands around, we could divide our efforts between Torte's kitchen and Uva's. Chef Garrison and his team would be finishing the remainder of the prep work on-site. Once we had beautiful rows of pastries stacked in the front case and a pot of soup simmering on the stove, we could send a crew to Uva with the premade desserts to assist Chef Garrison. Carlos could oversee those efforts and I could pop back and forth throughout the day.

Since none of my staff were likely to get a breather in the next couple of days I wanted to make a hearty, simple lunch just for them—a Greek chicken sheet-pan lunch. Sheet-pan meals were like modern-day casseroles. The ingredients could be combined, placed on a sheet pan, and baked together. I went to the walk-in and removed organic chicken breasts. Then I gathered green beans, lemons, garlic, onions, Kalamata olives, and fire-roasted tomatoes. I diced onions and garlic. The strong scent made my eyes begin to water. Next, I sliced the chicken into thin two-inch strips, rinsed the green beans, and tossed everything together with olive oil. I seasoned it with salt, pepper, and fresh oregano and basil. I squeezed in the juice of half a lemon, and sliced the rest of them into wedges. After greasing a sheet pan I spread the ingredients on to the tray and returned to the walk-in where it could marinate for hours. At lunchtime, we could pop it into the oven, bake for twenty to thirty minutes, and have a delicious savory meal.

With my Greek chicken marinating, I switched gears and returned my focus to finishing the morning bread. I wanted to get it done and delivered as quickly as possible because I still needed time to work on the wedding cake. Hiding it from Mom had been a team effort. We had pieces of the cake stashed all around the bakery. On multiple occasions we had had to scurry to hide sugar flowers or lie about a last-minute custom order that wasn't listed on the whiteboard.

The cake was going to be five layers, designed like a fairy garden. The bottom tier would resemble the forest floor, the next would feature delicate, blooming spring flowers, each painted by hand, the third layer would have two trees made of modeling chocolate. The tree branches would stretch toward one another, a symbol of Mom and the Professor's love. They would be decorated with sugar flowers and butterflies. The final two tiers would be completely covered in handmade sugar flowers in pink, purple, peach, and green. I'd been working on the sugar art whenever I had a spare minute. Thus far, I had amassed a few dozen sugar flowers, but we were going to need many more. I was going to have to recruit Steph or Bethany to help later.

Each layer of the cake would consist of a different flavor—strawberry shortcake vanilla cake with cream cheese frosting and fresh strawberries; lemon butter with lemon curd and French buttercream; a traditional milk chocolate with chocolate ganache; almond with marzipan and raspberries; and a spice cake with cardamom and orange buttercream. There should be something to please every palate. In addition to the tiered wedding cake, we had baked extra sheet cakes to cut and slice. The dessert table would include tarts, pies, petit fours, chocolates, and custards. I didn't think there was any chance we would be short on sweets. Our mantra at Torte was that you could never have too much of a good thing. Better to be overprepared and send the bride and groom home with boxes of goodies than to run out of dessert.

I couldn't stop thinking about Lance as I slid puffy loaves of bread into the oven. To have spent so many years disconnected from his father and then to have him die right after reuniting must be heartbreaking. It made me think about Mom. Returning home to work by her side was one of the best decisions I had ever made.

I dusted powdered sugar on a loaf of sweet bread. The front doorbell jingled. Stephanie arrived and greeted me with some kind of a grunt.

"Morning," I offered.

She washed her hands, tied on an apron, and stared at the coffee bar. "Andy's not here yet?"

"Nope. You're stuck with me."

"Can I make coffee?"

"Knock yourself out." I watched her trudge to the espresso counter. "Actually, you might want to make a large pot. We're going to have extra hands in here soon."

Her purple braids swung with her curt nod. She was a woman of few words at her best. Without coffee, she was practically mute.

I returned to my bread. By the time the rest of the team showed up the bread orders were complete. Loaves of sourdough, sweet raisin, cinnamon swirl, marble rye, and whole wheat were stacked in neat rows on the island, awaiting delivery.

"It's great to have Carlos back," Sterling commented, reaching for an apron.

"He's not back," I replied with a bit too much force.

Sterling kindly ignored my tone. "Ramiro looks just like him. It's crazy."

"I know. I'd seen pictures of him, but the resemblance is even more striking in person."

"He seems like a good kid." Sterling pushed up the sleeves on his hoodie. His tattoos were expanding. In addition to a hummingbird on his forearm, which I knew he had inked in a tribute to his mom, there was an infinity loop, a half-moon, and a short poem.

"Yes. I'm just glad to have our first meeting over. I haven't been that nervous in years."

"Tell me about it." Sterling's intensely blue eyes flashed. "We've all been counting down the days till Carlos's arrival. Hopefully, you'll be able to chill now."

"Have I not been chill?"

Sterling's eyes lightened. "Nah, I'm messing with you."

I thought about hitting him with a wooden spoon, but instead I called the whole team into the kitchen. "Thanks for putting in such an amazing effort lately, everyone. I know it's been a bit of a whirlwind around here and for the next couple days that's probably going to ramp up. I want to send Sterling and either Steph or Bethany to Uva today to do the prep work for the wedding with Carlos."

Bethany raised her hand, which was still tomato red from her food-dye incident. "Pick me. Pick me!" Then she blushed and turned to Stephanie. "I mean unless you want to go." I noticed that she had more makeup on than normal and had tied her wavy curls up with two gold barrettes.

Steph shrugged.

"Okay, Bethany, you and Sterling will go with Carlos. Andy, you'll be at the espresso bar; Steph, you can do pastries. I'll do the morning deliveries and then divide my time between here and the winery. We've hired extra staff for the weekend, too." A wave of dizziness hit me as I listed off everything we had left to do. "I made a sheet-pan Greek chicken lunch, so whenever you get hungry, stick it in the oven at three twenty-five for twenty to thirty minutes. Oh, and there's one more thing that I think you should all know. Lance's dad died. He may be in later today. If I'm not here, please send him out to the winery."

"That's too bad," Andy said. "I didn't know Lance had a dad."

Bethany chuckled. "Everyone has a dad, duh."

"I mean I get that obviously he had to have had a dad at some point. I guess I didn't know he kept in touch with family." Andy stuck his tongue out at Bethany, causing her neck to warm with bright pink splotches. "I've never heard him say anything about his family."

"Me neither," I concurred with Andy. "I only recently learned that he has family nearby. On that note, his brother and some of his colleagues may be in later today as well. Lance has asked to extend an invitation to them. If they come asking for me, I want to talk to them.

Otherwise, I'm going to be focused on the painstaking task of cutting out dozens of paper-thin sugar flowers today and am going to hole myself up back here."

"You got it, boss," Andy replied with a salute. "No distractions, unless it's Lance and his *brother*." He made an exaggerated face while emphasizing "brother."

I decided it was best to keep my staff in the dark about Lance's family dynamics. There was no point in worrying them, especially because I didn't know if there was a reason to worry yet. Even if Lance was right, the task of proving that someone had disconnected Mr. Brown from his life-support machines seemed impossible.

"Perfect. Thanks again, guys. I don't know what I would do without the four of you." My throat tightened. "I know we're going to have to hire more help, but you are literally my dream team."

Sterling flicked a pizza cutter, making the stainless steel wheel spin. "Jules, we've got your back. Torte is the best place in Ashland. And your mom is like a mom to all of us. We want her wedding to be amazing too."

I blinked back a tear. "I know, and that's why I can't thank you enough."

"You can thank me in free food anytime," Andy teased. "My mouth is already watering over the thought of a Greek chicken lunch. Is it lunchtime yet?"

"Free food is always on the table," I bantered back. "In fact, I'm planning to order a bunch of pizzas for anyone who wants to come help decorate and make sugar flowers tonight."

Andy snapped, "You had me at free pizza."

Steph tugged on one of her braids. "School's out for summer, so I'm free."

"Me too," Bethany added, stealing a quick glance at Andy.

Sterling looked around at his coworkers. "I was already going to say yes, but now if I don't I'm going to sound like a tool."

I laughed. "Great. You'll get paid your regular salaries."

"Plus pizza. Don't forget about the pizza," Andy said.

"Absolutely, plus pizza, and we'll be at the winery so wine and soft drinks are on me."

Everyone returned to their stations. I breezed through the morning deliveries, eager to get back to work on the wedding cake. As I crossed Main Street past the Lithia bubblers I spotted the woman in the black leather jacket whom I had seen Clarissa meeting with the other morning. She was sitting on a park bench in deep conversation with none other than Adam, Chef Garrison's employee, whom I'd seen hanging around Torte. Weird.

I half expected to see a bunch of motorcycles parked in the plaza because Adam was dressed in black leather chaps and a biker jacket. The woman reached behind her and pulled out a rolled-up piece of paper. She handed it to Adam. His face darted from side to side. Was he checking to make sure no one was watching them?

He stuffed the paper into his jacket, stood, glanced around again, and then headed north on Main Street toward Ashland Springs. At the same time, the woman looked up and met my eyes. She froze.

What was her deal?

Her face betrayed her. She looked like a deer caught in headlights.

A city truck rumbled past the bubbling fountains. The

woman used the distraction to push to her feet and quickly walk away.

As soon as the truck passed by, I made a beeline for her. She took off in the opposite direction toward the Merry Windsor. Fortunately, I have long legs and used to run track in high school. I caught up with her in five quick strides. "Hey, do I know you?" I asked, when she gave up and stopped in front of Richard Lord's hotel. From the outside the hotel resembled an English manor house with its stone foundation, slate tile roof, brick chimneys, and half-timbered black and white framing. It was no wonder that when tourists saw pictures of the romantic inn online and noted that each room in the hotel was themed after a Shakespearean character, they booked a stay at the Merry Windsor. Little did they know that it was no more than a cheap façade. The inside of the hotel was rundown with old, water-stained carpets and the smell of mildew. Richard's themed rooms consisted of faded drapes and bedding, gaudy brass doorknobs and lighting, and a few pencil-drawn sketches of Helen or Romeo in costume. Many times, I had overheard tourists complain about the hotel not meeting their expectations.

She leaned against a white arbor on the side of the hotel. "I don't think so. The name's Megan."

"I saw you hanging around the bakeshop a few days ago." I pointed to Torte.

Her deep-set eyes gave away nothing. She flipped the collar up on her leather jacket. "Nope. I don't know what you're talking about."

"I'm Jules. I own Torte, the pastry shop across the street." I pointed to Torte's bright awnings. "I'm sure that I saw you meeting with Clarissa from the arts council last week." It wasn't like me to be quite this pushy, but it couldn't be an accident that I had seen her and Adam on the same day at Torte and now together this morning.

Something flickered in her eyes. "Right. I had a meeting at your pastry place. Good stuff."

"What brings you to Ashland?" I asked.

"Work." She reached into her jacket pocket and removed a business card. "I'm doing some work for Lance. I think you might know him."

I read her card: "Megan Antonini, Private Detective." This was the PI Lance had hired?

"You're Jules. He told me about you." Her fierce stare was unsettling. "You're hosting the wedding, right? He told me you were cool with us crashing the party. Thanks for that."

I wasn't sure if I should trust her. Her attitude had shifted so quickly. "What are you doing on the plaza this morning?"

She glanced around us. Two guests had emerged from the hotel with paper cups of coffee. "Surveillance."

"On the Merry Windsor?"

"No. For Lance. You heard, right? His dad died this morning, and there are some extenuating circumstances that I'm not at liberty to discuss."

If she knew about Lance's dad I was more inclined to believe her. "Yeah. He called me earlier."

"Then you know we're at mission critical right now. It's imperative that I follow up with every lead as soon as possible, since this case might be hard to prove."

No one in Ashland spoke like Megan. What did

"mission critical" even mean? And why was she in Ashland if Lance's dad died—or had been killed—in Medford?

"I know it's kind of unconventional to do a sting at a wedding. Lance told me about your secret plans. I appreciate you being game to letting us crash the party. I'm hoping to bag a killer this weekend."

That sounded like the last possible thing I wanted to have happen at Mom's wedding. I sighed. What had I gotten us into? Then in the same breath, I thought about Lance. I had to help him.

Megan continued. "Look, I don't want to be seen talking to you. It could give us away, but if you see or think of anything between today and the wedding, you call me. Got it?"

I nodded.

In a flash, Megan ducked behind the Merry Windsor and disappeared. I stuck her card in my jeans pocket. She reminded me of an actor playing a spy. Something about her demeanor didn't add up.

"Julieta!" Carlos's voice rang across the plaza. He and Ramiro were en route to Torte. I crossed the street and caught up with them. Even in casual attire, a polo shirt and crisp white shorts with navy stripes, Carlos looked as if he had stepped out of the pages of a *GQ* ad.

"How did you guys sleep?"

"Ah, wonderful. Sí, it was a great sleep for me." Carlos kissed my cheeks. I drank in the scent of his aftershave with hints of woodsy smoke.

"Did you eat?"

Ramiro grinned. "Sí." He wore a pair of board shorts

and a yellow T-shirt with the cutout of a surf board and a "hang loose" sign. "I like your blueberry muffins."

"He ate the entire plate that you left for us. I did not even get one bite." Carlos patted Ramiro's hard stomach. "I don't know where you put it. Feel this stomach. His abs are like steel."

I didn't imagine that Ramiro wanted me to touch his abs. "I'll take your word for it," I said to Carlos.

Ramiro shot me a look of relief.

"Glad you liked the muffins. What's next for you guys? Should I put you to work or do you want the grand tour first?" I waved toward the plaza where a group of through hikers was practicing qigong. Nearby two "travelers," as locals referred to Ashland's rotating population of young street people, sat braiding each other's hair, with a mangy dog curled up on their backpack. They had crafted a sign out of cardboard that read: THERE'S MUCH ADO, BUT WE GOT NOTHING. I had to give them credit for the playful Shakespearean pun. However, I didn't drop any money into the hat propped next to their sign. Ashland's vagabond population had been an ongoing debate at city council meetings and at OSF. Most of the travelers were harmless, but panhandling had become a problem on the plaza. Some days it was impossible not to be accosted with requests for spare change on every corner. Travelers would beg tourists for their boxes of leftovers or, as one sign in front of Torte had read: I WON'T LIE, IT'S FOR WEED. The Professor and Thomas had been trying to crack down on the issue, while still maintaining a professional relationship with the travelers.

"Good sign," Ramiro said as we passed by. One of the travelers flashed him a peace sign.

"Put us to work. We have plenty of time after the wedding to see Ashland, but I think there is not much time for cooking now, no?" Carlos said, putting an arm around Ramiro's shoulder. One of the things that I appreciated most about Spanish men was their ability to show physical affection. Carlos never flinched when it came to holding my hand or kissing me on a crowded sidewalk. He expressed his love for Ramiro with the same abandon.

"If you're sure, I would love the help. But you didn't fly thousands of miles just to cook. There's so much I want to show you. I was thinking we could take a day trip to Crater Lake, cross into California. I want to show you Mount Ashland and the old western town of Jacksonville."

Carlos nodded. "Yes, but there is time for this later. The wedding is in two days and we are here to be of service. We have almost a week together after the wedding. We want to help."

Ramiro agreed. "It's true. I'm happy to be in the kitchen with Papa."

As much as I wanted to take off and show them my beloved Southern Oregon, I was relieved that they were still up for the task of wedding prep. I told them my plan for the day and that I had invited the team for a work party at Uva later.

"I've been wanting to try American pizza," Ramiro said. "They say it is nothing like the pizza we have in Europe."

"Is pizza popular in Spain?" I asked.

He ran his fingers through his thick dark hair. "No. Not so popular. More like a flatbread. My family and I go to Italy in the summer and that is where the best pizza is found."

I felt a tiny twinge of jealousy. Ramiro already had a family. He had grown up with his mother and uncles, aunts and cousins. I was just his father's wife. What was my role in his world? Carlos and I had talked a few times about the idea of having children. It never made sense when we were living on the ship. That vagabond lifestyle was no way to raise a child. For the first time, I found myself longing for a family of my own.

"Well, I don't know how authentically American the pizza here in Ashland is, but you will have to give it a try and let me know how it compares." I plastered on a smile. "Should we head inside?"

They followed me into Torte and were welcomed by my staff. After they left to start prep work at Uva I went downstairs to touch base with Roger.

He and Clarissa were locked in what appeared to be a lover's spat. They stood in front of the wood-fired pizza oven, talking in hushed, angry tones.

"I've had enough," Clarissa seethed, thrusting her index finger into Roger's chest.

I tried to tiptoe away quietly, but Roger spotted me. He moved away from the pizza oven. "Jules, we were just talking about you."

Clarissa spun her head in my direction. Her icy glare made a chill run down my spine. I had obviously interrupted something. "Roger, we'll continue this discussion later." She twisted an expensive diamond watch on her petite wrist. "I'm late."

"Hopefully I'll see you at Uva's launch party," I said as she brushed past me.

Roger answered for her. "We'll be there. Wouldn't miss it for the world."

Clarissa didn't answer. Her stilettos echoed on the floor as she made her exit.

"Sorry, I didn't mean to pop in unannounced," I said to Roger.

His eyes followed his wife out the door. "This is your property. You can come and go as you please." He dropped the subject and moved to show me the painter's progress. The basement property was coming to life with its creamy walls and rustic brick fireplace.

"Everything is on track. We are slotted to move the kitchen equipment this weekend. You're still planning to close for the wedding?"

"Yep." The basement smelled of drying paint. "As long the timing works for you guys, it's great for us. You can get everything moved and put in place here by Monday?"

"Not a problem. I have a group of heavy lifters scheduled to be here tomorrow morning. And you'll be glad to know that I sent your mother on a wild-goose chase in search of handles and pulls with my contractor right before Clarissa arrived. She should be busy looking at dozens of cabinet pulls for at least an hour or two."

"Thanks."

Roger brushed dust from his pants. "I have to say that she didn't appear very pleased with me when I told her that I needed a decision by close of day and that the hardware store had boxes of silver, ceramic, plastic, and glass pulls for her to look through."

I grinned. "We're evil."

We walked through the new kitchen layout one final time. Mom and I had opted for white quartz countertops. They would be durable and a bright workspace for detailed designs like painting fondant and molding modeling chocolate. I had faith in Roger. He had kept me informed throughout the entire process. Plus, we had been through this before. When we upgraded our kitchen equipment a few months ago, we had closed the bakeshop for a long weekend to paint and install the ovens. Fingers crossed, everything would go according to plan.

"Unless you have any other questions, I think we should be set," Roger said.

"I do have one question, but it's not related to construction."

"What's that?" He ran his finger along the smooth countertop.

"I noticed Clarissa meeting with a woman I met this morning, Megan. Are you familiar with her?"

Roger shook his head. "No, but Clarissa is president of the Ashland Arts Council. She's always meeting with business owners and donors for her galas and fundraising drives."

Part of me wanted to bring up the fact that Megan was a PI, but I decided against it. I didn't want to get involved in a potential marital dispute. I also wanted to find a time to speak to Clarissa alone. Could she have crossed paths with the Brown family through her work at the arts council? It was too much of a coincidence that she happened to be meeting with the same PI whom Lance had hired. Was there a chance that any of these coincidences tied into Lance's father's death? There had to be some connection, and I intended to find out what it was.

Chapter Nine

Later in the evening, the mood at Uva was alive and electric. Carlos blasted Latin samba music. Walking into the kitchen was sensory overload. The scent of rosemary flank steak made my stomach rumble with hunger. Sterling stood at the gas stove searing the thin-sliced steaks. Ramiro was filling fluted cups of filo dough with a savory herb-infused couscous with cherry tomatoes and sweet corn. Carlos danced over to me. "Julieta, the food it sings to life. This will be the most beautiful wedding anyone has ever seen. Except for our wedding." His apron was spotted with sauce. His eyes were bright. Carlos belonged in the kitchen.

I had fallen for him almost immediately when I met him on the ship. It wasn't only due to his sultry eyes or his classic features. Carlos loved food. He saw it as his mission in life to create dishes that inspired. Watching him dote over a simmering stew or caress a fillet of fish with butter and lemon made my knees go weak. It was hard to resist his charms most days, but in the kitchen, it was nearly impossible. He managed to maintain control of his staff while infusing life and fun into his food.

Sometimes if my shift ended early on the ship, I would leave the pastry kitchen and stand in the doorway of the galley and watch Carlos work. He was like a conductor, orchestrating a grand arrangement as he danced between the line cooks and waitstaff, singing in Spanish and adding a final sprinkling of chopped herbs to each plate.

"You guys have made great progress." I nodded to the platters of stuffed olives, mini-quiches, and vegetable skewers. The distraction of having Carlos in the kitchen was welcome. I felt like I was about to reach my maximum level of stress. Every time I had a few minutes of head space my thoughts went to Lance. How was he holding up? The day that my father died would be forever etched in my memory. I remember a wave of wooziness assaulting my body when he took his final breath, Mom dropping to her knees, and the sound of his heart flatlining on the machine. To think that Lance's brother could murder their father was unimaginable.

Carlos's silky voice brought me back to the moment. "Sí, it has been wonderful to work with Sterling again. You were right, *mi querida,* he is becoming a true chef."

Sterling gave Carlos a half bow. "I'm learning from the master."

"They call him the maestro in my village in Spain," Ramiro said, sharing a look with his dad.

"Maestro. That's good." Sterling added a spear of rosemary to the grilling flank steak.

"No, no. This is no good. I am not a maestro. Cooking is not about being an expert. It is about getting your hands dirty. You must try and fail many times. This is something only the best chefs understand."

Chef Garrison, who had been reviewing the wine list with his staff, removed his white coat and joined us. "Carlos, it's been a pleasure to cook with you today," he said, shaking Carlos's hand. "Jules, I think we're set. I should get back to the restaurant. I've tasked Adam with finishing the wine list. He should be done soon. Unless you need anything else, I'll see you tomorrow."

"Thanks so much, we couldn't have done this without you." I gave him a hug.

"Happy to be part of it." He waved to the rest of the team and left.

I went over to Adam. Even though he was wearing an Ashland Springs uniform I could still picture him in his black leather biking gear from earlier. He was stacking rows of Uva wines on the far counter. "Hey, how's it going?" I asked.

He flinched and moved to block my view of the wine. "Fine."

"Do you need any help?" I wasn't sure if it was because of Lance's assertion that he had been followed, but there was something about Adam that made me uncomfortable.

"Nope."

"I'm happy to pull one of my staff over if you need an extra set of hands," I pressed.

"Chef told me to inventory these. Then I'm outta here."

Why had Chef Garrison asked him to inventory our wine? I had made it clear that his waitstaff could open as many bottles as was necessary to keep the wine flowing tomorrow night.

Adam turned back to the wine and started counting bottles. I half expected him to stuff a bottle into his pocket. There was something strange about him. I considered telling him that I'd seen him with Megan earlier, but Bethany appeared from the front of the house. She was carrying a tray of sugar cookies cut in the shape of wedding cakes. The cookies were precariously stacked.

I hurried over to help her.

"Thanks, Jules." She sighed with relief when I caught the side of the tray. We placed it on the empty square of space on the countertop. The cookies would be frosted with royal icing and adorned with flowers to match the sugar flowers on the actual cake.

"That was a close one." She took half of the stack off and made a few smaller piles of unfrosted cookies. "I'm excited to try the piping technique you showed us earlier." I had taught them how to flood the cookies with royal icing. The process is very simple. Just like it sounds we created a thin royal icing and flooded the top and side of the cookie with it to coat the entire surface with icing. Once the icing hardened we then piped an intricate lace design onto each cookie by hand. "Andy and Steph are on their way."

"Sounds like I should order pizzas, then." I pulled out my cell. "Any requests?"

Sterling glanced at Ramiro. "Make sure you get something really American for him. You know, like Canadian bacon and pineapple."

Ramiro stuck out his tongue. "Pineapple on a pizza?"

"It's a thing." Sterling shrugged. "It's not my favorite but people love it. You have to try it."

"I'll get a small," I said to Ramiro, whose scowl made

it clear that he was not sure about the idea of pineapple on pizza.

Steph and Andy showed up after I hung up with the pizza place.

"Put us to work, boss." Andy had flipped his SOU cap backward. "You know I can't bake to save my life, but I'll do whatever you need."

Andy knew how to brew a killer cup of joe but baking wasn't his forte. "That's okay, I was hoping to put you in charge of setting up the chairs outside."

"You just want me for my muscles." Andy flexed. "I see how it is."

"Hey, if you got them, I'll put them to work." I walked him outside to show him where to arrange the chairs. Then I set up a workspace closest to the front of the house to finish my sugar flowers. I drank in the smells and sounds of the happy kitchen as I rolled and pressed dainty sugar flowers. Customers often ask why wedding cakes are so expensive, but if anyone watched how much work went into the process of designing a custom cake they wouldn't question the expense. Every wedding cake that we created at Torte was unique. Our goal was to tell a story about the bride and groom through the flavor and details on the cake. Some brides opted for more traditional cakes like a classic three-tier cake frosted with French buttercream hand-piped with an elegant star tip, while others preferred to express their creativity in cake. Some of my favorite nontraditional designs included sculpted cakes and geometric shapes like squares and triangles. The sky was the limit when it came to wedding cakes. If a bride could dream it, we would bake it.

I had forgotten how much fun it was to have Carlos

running a kitchen. His laughter was contagious. Hearing my team crack up every few minutes at one of his jokes brought a smile to my face.

I thought about Mom. She and the Professor had been banned from Uva. I didn't want either of them anywhere near the winery until tomorrow night. She had promised me that they were going to have a simple dinner and take an evening stroll through Lithia Park. Would Lance's father's death change their plans? I wished I had had a chance to talk to the Professor. Lance had mentioned that he been helping dig into the family's estate, but had Lance had a chance to loop him in? It was such crummy timing with the wedding tomorrow.

The pizza arrived about an hour later. We took a welcome break. I noticed that Adam had left. I must have missed his exit. Carlos poured glasses of wine for those of us of drinking age, and I cracked open root beers, ginger ales, and cherry sodas for the rest. Ramiro scrunched his nose at the sight of the Hawaiian pizza. "People think this is good, yes?"

Stephanie rolled her eyes. "No. It's gross. It's like an eighties trend. It's totally dead now. Foodies wouldn't touch that stuff."

She should know, I thought. Stephanie kept abreast of the latest food trends. She was also a secret Pastry Channel junkie. If I didn't think it would send her into a sour mood, I would have teased her about it.

Ramiro held out the slice of pizza like it was alive. "You think I should try it?"

Andy reached for a slice. "Dude, it's awesome. Don't listen to Steph. She's a food snob. She likes her pizza with truffles and arugula." He made a "hang loose" sign and pointed to Ramiro's shirt. "You're a surfer. That means you must be a pretty chill dude. Trust me, this is beach pizza."

"Yeah, because any good chef would tell you that I'm eating real food, not canned pineapple," Stephanie said, taking a slice with chunks of fresh mozzarella and basil.

"Right, if you want to spend like ten thousand dollars on one slice of pie." Andy tore into his piece with his teeth.

I knew their banter wasn't anything serious. The two of them bickered like siblings. However, I also knew that they would protect each other at a minute's notice.

"Try it," Andy said through a mouthful of pizza.

Ramiro took a tiny bite of the pizza.

"You didn't even get any of the good stuff." Andy frowned.

Sterling sipped a root beer. "This feels like some kind of hazing ritual. You don't have to eat that if you don't want to, man."

Ramiro squinted. He braced himself and took a big bite. Everyone watched with bated breath. He opened his eyes after a second and grinned. "I like it. It is very good. Surprising. But good." He took another bite.

Carlos clapped him on the back. "Sí, this is why as chefs we must always be open to trying new things. Our taste buds they will surprise us. It is like training for your mouth. If you only taste the same flavors again and again you will not have to make your taste buds work. You must force your palate to work. It is like a muscle. Without working it out, it will become flabby."

"I never would have thought of Hawaiian pizza as

stretching a palate," I said, taking a slice of salami and black olive.

"Sí, but it is the same as any of you coming to Spain and trying one of our signature dishes." Carlos was talking to everyone now. He thrived in moments like this. "It is our job as chefs to lead the way. We must show people the way to food. It is the only understanding we share. It is the only way we will find peace on this planet. We must come to the table together and break bread and drink wine. This is how we will solve the world's problems."

Andy raised his bottle of ginger ale. "Cheers to that."

We clinked our glasses together. "Cheers."

Ramiro polished off two slices of the Canadian bacon and pineapple pizza along with a slice from each of the other four pizzas I had ordered. Carlos was right. The kid could eat. "I will have to tell my friends about this American pizza," he said, wiping his hands on a napkin.

Bethany nibbled on a piece of crust with her stained fingers. "Which one was your favorite?"

"That one." Ramiro pointed to one lonely slice of Hawaiian. We all laughed.

"If you stay much longer, we're going to turn you into an American, bro." Andy chomped down a fourth slice. As long as I had known Andy I had never once seen him turn down food of any kind. Mom and I liked to tease him about his ability to put away food without ever gaining an ounce of weight. I appreciated that my staff had embraced and included Ramiro. It was evident in his wide grin that he was loving being an honorary member of my American "crew."

Carlos and Ramiro shared a brief look. Ramiro started to say something, but Carlos interrupted him. "I would like to do a walk-through of how we will be serving the feast tomorrow night."

I wasn't sure why he was intent on changing the subject, but he was right, we needed to make sure that everyone knew what they were responsible for and where they were going to be stationed. We cleaned up the pizza boxes. Carlos took the lead in setting up the rotation for dinner and appetizer service.

Our work party lasted well into the early morning hours. It was close to one in the morning by the time Carlos, Ramiro, and I flipped off the lights, locked Uva's kitchen, and headed for my apartment. While Ramiro showered, Carlos and I shared a cup of tea on the couch. He draped his arm around my shoulder.

"What are you thinking, Julieta? You are lost in your thoughts, no?"

"Sorry. I was just reviewing everything for the wedding in my head. I didn't forget something, did I?" I didn't want to bother him with the news of Lance's dad. There was no point.

He massaged my neck. "No. It is perfection. Everything will be wonderful."

I hoped that he was right. I needed a moment of quiet to absorb the mix of emotions pulsing through my body. Tomorrow, my mom was getting married. My family was changing and expanding. Change was good, but lately it felt like everything was in flux. I wanted to be in a place to fully appreciate the moment when Mom and the Professor exchanged their vows, and the only way to accomplish that was to force myself to sleep.

Chapter Ten

I woke the next morning to the sound of scrub jays squawking outside my window. Mom often would save a loaf of sourdough and take it to the park to feed the jays. I wondered if they knew that today was her big day and had come out for an early serenade. Nervous jitters rumbled through my empty stomach. I crawled out of bed and pulled on a pair of old sweatpants and T-shirt. I twisted my hair into a ponytail and squished my toes into flip-flops.

Carlos snored lightly on the couch. Ramiro was sacked out on the air mattress. They had agreed to help Thomas distract the Professor and get him to Uva on time.

I gathered my things and left without causing them to so much as blink. Mom didn't know it yet, but she and I were spending the morning at her house. I had packed a hearty breakfast last night, along with makeup, my dress, and a change of clothes for after the reception. Most importantly, I had tucked a gold-embossed creamy invitation into my bag. After weeks of secrecy, this morning I would hand Mom the invitation to her wedding. When we first hatched the plan of a surprise wedding I had imagined keeping Mom and the Professor in the dark until it was time to walk down the aisle. But then reality set in. How would I get her into her wedding dress or keep her away from the wedding cake? Not to mention that every bride should be pampered on her wedding day. I wanted Mom to languish in love while we painted our toes and curled our hair. Just like she had done for me when I was getting ready for high school dances.

Mom and the Professor were flying to Greece on a red-eye after the reception. The Professor had already put a deposit down on the trip, and thanks to Thomas's sleuthing we had been able to have the Professor's travel agent book the trip earlier. I had snuck over and packed her suitcase with flowing sundresses and swimsuits. Thomas had done the same for the Professor. We had also arranged for a car to pick them up at Uva and take them directly to the Medford airport. This was my last day to spend with her before she became "Mrs. the Professor" as Andy had affectionately deemed to be her new married name. I wanted everything to be perfect for her, and wanted to soak in our last few hours together.

The street lamps along Main Street shimmered, along with the rising sun, on the path to Mom's house. I drove past sleepy shops and turned onto Mountain Avenue with its towering sequoia and aspen trees. The steep road that led to my childhood home was familiar. Thomas used to race his bike down the hill, much to the discontent of Mom, who was convinced that he would break an arm or leg. He never did, but he did boast that his bike clocked thirty miles an hour. I remember telling him that it was probably best to keep that stat to himself. I smiled at the memory and pulled into the driveway.

My throat tightened as I knocked on the solid wood door. This was really happening. She was getting married today. "Mom, are you awake?" I stepped inside, and was immediately flooded with the familiar smells of my childhood—the lemon-scented wood floor cleaner and a fragrant bundle of fresh herbs sitting in a vase in the entryway.

"Juliet, is that you?" she called from upstairs.

"Yep. I brought breakfast." I placed my dress on the banister and went into the kitchen. Mom hadn't changed anything since my dad died. The house had been built in the 1920s and they had decorated it with mission-style furniture. Windows with the original pressed glass looked out onto the forested hillside. The kitchen had oak floors that gleamed in the morning light. A collection of framed photos rested on a desk near the window. I paused and picked up a picture of me and my parents. It had been taken at my elementary school carnival. I had won the cakewalk and was holding one of my dad's custom black cherry tortes.

I fought back tears.

"Juliet, what are you doing here so early?" Mom came into the kitchen. She was wearing a thin, creamy bathrobe and matching slippers. The minute she saw me holding the picture, she pulled me into a hug. "Oh, honey, I know. I miss him too."

"Sorry. I feel like all I've done the past few weeks is cry." I sniffed.

Mom released me and handed me a tissue. "It's okay. There's a lot going on."

"I know, but I'm a mess." I brushed salty tears from my cheek. "It's Carlos, and the expansion, Uva, everything."

Her eyes misted. "Do you remember your dad talking about the days of water?"

"The days of water?" I shook my head.

She twisted her old wedding ring that she now wore on a chain around her neck. "He used to say that our best days were the days of water. Days when life-affirming tears rolled down our cheeks just as yours are now. Happy tears, sad tears, it doesn't matter. It's the act of feeling deeply that makes us human. Your father knew that and embraced it every day of his life. That's what I want for you, more than anything."

Her tender words made my eyes well again. "Thanks, Mom." I dabbed my face with the tissue.

Tiny wrinkles creased her cheeks when she smiled. "I'll tell you what you need."

"What's that?" I felt more centered. Instead of fighting the tears, allowing them to flow had released something.

"How about a pot of coffee. Strong coffee."

"That I can do." I moved to the other side of the kitchen and set to work brewing coffee and arranging the fresh fruit, cheese, and box of pastries I had brought for brunch.

"What's all this?" Mom asked, tucking her hair behind her ears.

I held up a finger. "It's a surprise."

"A surprise? I love surprises." Mom clasped her hands together.

"I hope you like this one," I said, handing her the invitation.

She ran her fingers over the paper and used her pinkie to free the wax seal on the back of the envelope. "What is this?"

"Just read it."

I bit the inside of my cheek while I watched her read the invitation. What if she hated the idea? What if a surprise wedding had been a terrible mistake?

Her mouth hung open. She dropped the invitation on the counter.

"Is it bad? Do you hate it?" I winced and waited for her reply.

"Hate it? I love it!" She danced over and hugged me. "A surprise wedding, today? It's summer solstice. Midsummer's Eve. How did you pull it off? Does Doug know?" Her words strung together as she spoke. "Wait! The launch party. Of course! Why didn't I put two and two together? You've been planning this all along? Who else is in on it? Everyone?"

"Everyone." I laughed. "Well, not the Professor. We wanted to surprise both of you."

She punched me playfully in the shoulder. "But everyone else? The team at Torte?"

I gave her a sheepish grin. "More like everyone in Ashland."

"Juliet, how did you do it? What about the flowers, and food . . ." She stopped in midstream. "That's why Carlos and Ramiro are here?"

"Yep." I reached for two coffee cups. "It's been a community undertaking. Everyone wanted to be in on the surprise. You and the Professor just get to show up tonight and revel in the experience. Oh, and you need to pack because you fly out to Greece tonight. I put some things together for you, but I'm sure you'll want to take a look and add anything I might have missed."

"What?" Her eyes were wide. "I can't believe it. It sounds wonderful. Beautiful. Thank you."

"I'm so glad that you're happy about it; all of a sudden I was starting to panic. What if you hated the idea?"

She patted my hand. "I could never hate anything you do."

I offered her a buttery croissant. "You know what they say, butter makes everything beautiful."

"I've never heard that." She took the plate.

"Good, then maybe I just coined a new mantra for the bakeshop." I picked at a lemon poppy seed scone. "Now, where to start on our day of beauty?"

"You tell me, you're the expert. I'm still feeling like this is a dream." She held out her wrist. "Do you think that feeling will go away if you pinch me?"

I chuckled. "No, but maybe a cup or two of my wedding-day brew will ground you in reality." I poured us each a mug of coffee. "Although, aren't brides supposed to float through their wedding day anyway?"

Mom took the coffee. "True."

We reminisced over pastry and fruit. I savored my coffee and the moment.

"Oh my gosh, in the excitement I forgot to ask whether you heard about Lance's dad? He called me yesterday to say that his father had died, but I was so busy I never had a chance to talk to him. Did he call the Professor?"

She popped a deep purple blackberry in her mouth.

"Yes, Doug mentioned it last night. He's worried about Lance."

"Me too. It's always hard to peel back the theater façade and get to the real Lance."

"True." She cradled the mug of coffee in her hands. "Doug is personally invested in the case, because it's Lance. He said this is the first time in all of his years of knowing Lance that he doesn't think that Lance is intentionally dramatizing the facts. I hope he's able to enjoy the day. He's convinced that Mr. Brown was killed, but last night he barely touched our dinner. He has no idea how they can prove it, and since the murder took place in Medford, his hands are tied. Doug has a number of friends on the case who are sharing as much information as they can, but ultimately it's not his case."

I hadn't even thought about that.

"Hopefully the wedding will be a good distraction. Doug doesn't do well when he's tied up in bureaucratic procedure." She looked pensive.

I felt bad for bringing up the subject. As much as I wanted her opinion on whether the Professor had any theories or an idea of how to prove that Lance's dad had been killed, this was her wedding day. Neither Mom nor the Professor needed to worry about anything other than savoring their love.

"Shall we go get started on our beauty transformations?" I asked, trying to wink. "Carlos, Ramiro, and Thomas have big plans for the Professor today. I'm sure they'll keep him happily entertained."

She took a final sip of her coffee. "Let's do it."

We spent the next few hours laughing on her bed like we used to in my teenage years. I remember many late nights plopped on her queen bed with its white down comforter, telling her about my dreams and aspirations. Things had shifted between us. Now she was the one taking off for new and grand adventures.

The day passed like a magical dream straight from the pages of a Shakespearean play. By late afternoon it was time to pack our things and Mom's wedding dress and head to Uva. The grounds were abuzz with activity when we pulled into the parking lot and I quickly ushered Mom upstairs to the bedroom where she could change. I didn't want her to see the romantic scene we had created until she was walking down the aisle. I touched up her makeup and lay her dress out on the bed.

Once we finished primping, the moment came for her to put on her dress. We had found it at a dress shop in Jacksonville not long after the Professor popped the question. The minute she had tried the dress on, we both knew it was *the one*. She removed it from the closet and I helped her get it over her head without ruining her makeup or loose curls. The dress was made of off-white silk. It was cut with an empire waist and fell below her ankles. She was a vision straight from the pages of one of Shakespeare's plays. The ethereal dress brought out the olive undertones to her skin. Her wavy locks framed her heart-shaped cheeks, which glowed with excitement. At Uva, we would add the final touch—a floral headpiece with ribbons of flowers and greenery that would cascade down her back.

"Mom, you look incredible." I placed my hand over my heart.

She bit her bottom lip. "You think so?"

"I know so." I turned her toward the mirror on the door that led to the master bathroom. "Look."

Her breath caught as she took in her reflection. We stared at each other in the mirror. "Mom, you're beautiful."

She waved her hand in front of her face. "Don't start. Don't look at me like that. Otherwise, I'm going to tear up and ruin your makeup job."

I kissed her cheek. "I promise. I won't cry. At least not until the actual wedding."

Mom smoothed the front of her dress. "Now what about you? Are you going to change now?"

I glanced at my own reflection. I looked pretty funny in my baggy sweats and T-shirt with long curls and enough makeup to grace the stage. "I'll change later. I still need to check on everything at the winery, and depending on how far the staff has gotten I might need to jump in and help."

"I can help too," Mom offered.

"No way. This is your wedding day. I'm going to go get you a light snack and a glass of something bubbly. You can sit outside on the deck and watch everyone else run around."

She scowled. "Juliet, you know that I'm not good at sitting still."

"Too bad. You have exactly thirty minutes until the guests start to arrive, and you are going to enjoy it."

I left to check in with the team in the kitchen and get her a glass of champagne. The kitchen was a blur of activity. Chef Garrison's crew from Ashland Springs had arrived and were wiping down plates and glasses, stacking dinnerware, and carrying warming trays onto the deck. I spotted Adam among the staff. He was wearing the standard uniform—black slacks, black work shoes, and crisp white button-down shirt—but his neck tattoos and dark goatee made him look more like a criminal trying to dress up to go before the review board.

Stop it, Juliet. Like Mom had said earlier, even the Professor doubted that Lance's story hadn't been embellished. My imagination was getting the best of me. The odds that Adam had been tailing Lance were slim.

Carlos's booming voice made me turn my attention to the stove where he conducted the crew. "No, that must go out last," he said to a waiter about to uncover a platter of bread. "Do not uncover that until the very last minute. We want it to be fresh and springy. We do not want it to sit even for an extra minute and get hard and stale."

The waiter took his hand off the plastic wrap.

"How's it going down here?" I asked.

The way Carlos looked at me made my cheeks burn. "Julieta, you are lovely."

I motioned to my T-shirt. "I'm in my sweats."

He ran his fingers through my curls. "I like your hair like this. It is soft and romantic." He let his hand slide along my neck. Then he paused and stared at the ceiling. "The lights they make your hair look like gold."

"Thanks." I gulped. "Is everything okay with food prep?" I changed the subject.

He held on to my hair for a second longer. Then gave his head a slight shake as if forcing himself back into the moment. It was a feeling I knew all too well. "Sí, we are ready. Chef Garrison has the dinner service prepared. Ramiro and I will go change and then after the ceremony the staff will have trays of appetizers and chilled wine ready for the guests." He nodded to the far end of the kitchen where round trays were lined with crystal stemware and bottles of Uva's white blend were resting in buckets of ice.

"How is Helen?" Carlos wiped his hands on his crisp, white apron.

"Good. She's a bit nervous. But she looks amazing. What about the Professor? How was he today?"

Carlos's eyes twinkled. "He is wonderful. I had Ramiro deliver his invitation, and he was very touched."

I could picture the Professor's response.

"Thomas suggested we go golfing. Ramiro drove the cart. He was a speed demon, zooming down the rolling hills. We were a good foursome. The Professor is quite skilled at golf and Ramiro thinks that Thomas is the 'coolest.' He wants to become a police officer now."

"That's funny." I stole a glance at a platter of gorgeous hand pies. "Do you think he was okay with the surprise?"

"Yes, yes. He put on a good show, but I think that he had an idea of what was happening."

"Really?" I made way for a waiter carrying a tray of crystal vases filled with sand. These would be used to display grilled kebabs.

Carlos nodded. "Do not say anything to Thomas. He is very excited about surprising his boss, but the Professor and I shared a look. This is not a man who can be easily fooled. I am sure he knew about the secret, but I also know he will happily play along."

That was true. The Professor was one of the most brilliant men I had ever met, and he had spent a lifetime solving crime. It was silly that we had thought that we could fool him. I agreed with Carlos though. Why say anything? The guests would be arriving soon, and the Professor was such a good sport I was sure that he eagerly stepped into the role of surprised groom.

I glanced outside. "What about the setup? Does anything else need to be done?"

Carlos shook his head. "I think it is good, but you can see for yourself."

I hesitated. "I was going to bring Mom a glass of wine or champagne and a little snack."

"I will do this. You go to see what you think." He practically pushed me out the sliding doors.

The deck had been completely transformed. Twinkle lights had been strung in vertical rows from end to end. Garlands of sweet, fragrant jasmine and evergreen boughs hung between the lights. Long tables had been covered in white linens. Tapered white candles and more greenery had been interspersed between stacks of plates and silver serving trays. The railing had been wrapped in white roses and peonies. I breathed in the succulent scent of the flowers and descended onto the grassy area.

Here more garlands with bountiful white roses and sprigs of jasmine stretched from the top of the rose-colored altar out into a group of oak trees. Rows of chairs covered with white linen had been arranged facing the altar. Glowing paper lanterns hung from the trees, and torches lit the path down into the grape fields where more twinkle lights danced in a happy welcome. To the right of the altar the grass housed circular tables. The barn doors had been opened revealing a wooden dance floor and even more golden lights.

It was more stunning than I could have imagined. Mom and the Professor were going to love it. I returned inside and checked in with Steph who had been tasked with placing the sugar flowers on the wedding cake. We would take it out to the barn after the ceremony.

She was wearing a dress. A black dress, but nonetheless a dress. Mom and the Professor weren't sticklers for formality. I knew that they wouldn't care that Stephanie had broken tradition and worn black to a wedding. In fact, I wondered if that etiquette even held true anymore.

"Is this what you wanted?" she asked. The black dress hit just above her knee. She had tied a purple ribbon in the same shade as her hair around her waist, and wore a thick black ribbon around her head. Her cheeks were dusted with purple glitter.

"You look great," I said.

She scowled. "I heard you kind of have to wear a dress to a wedding."

"No. Mom wants you here. She doesn't care what you wear."

Stephanie shrugged. "It's fine."

"The cake is looking equally great," I said, very pleased with how it had come together. It could grace the cover of any bridal magazine. Each tier retained its own unique style and yet the cake as a whole looked cohesive. If I didn't know that each delicate, wispy flower had been made by hand, I would have thought they were real. "Do you need anything else before I go change?"

"Nah, we're good." She tugged at her dress. "Have you met that guy, Adam? He's one of the waiters."

"Yeah. Why?" My eyes scanned the kitchen, but I didn't see him.

"He's super uptight about the wine. Won't let anyone touch it. Bethany grabbed a bottle to take some pictures for Instagram with the cake and he freaked out on her."

"Really?"

Steph twisted the ribbon around her waist. I could tell that wearing a dress was out of her comfort zone. "Yeah. He's weird."

"Okay. I'll talk to Chef Garrison about it, but this is Mom's wedding. If you want to take a bottle of wine for pictures or anything, you have my permission."

"Cool."

I returned to the bedroom upstairs. Maybe it wasn't just my imagination. The fact that Stephanie thought Adam was acting strangely made me reconsider my initial reaction to him. When I had a chance later I was going to have to check in with Chef Garrison. But for the moment, I had a wedding to focus on.

Mom and Carlos sat on two Adirondack chairs on the small balcony. They were laughing easily.

"What are you two up to?" I asked, stepping outside.

"Carlos suggested that we turn this into *Romeo and Juliet*. Since we have a balcony after all." Mom turned to me. Her face was bright. "Have you seen the view from up here?"

I shook my head. Then took in the aerial view. The vineyards and grounds looked as if they were aglow. Everything I had seen from ground level looked even more spectacular from this vantage point.

"Carlos also suggested that Doug and I take some

photos from up here. Don't you think they'll look beautiful?"

"For sure." My eyes traveled down the long windy road that cut through the vineyard. I could see headlights in the distance. "Guests are starting to arrive."

Mom raised her glass of white wine. She took a sip. "That's my cue."

Carlos left to change. I put on my dress. A dreamy sky-blue knee-length dress with strappy sleeves and a flared skirt. It had a hint of an Elizabethan style. Delicate white flowers had been embroidered along the waist and neckline. The color brought out the blue in my eyes and blended nicely with my fair skin tone.

"Honey, you look divine," Mom noted as we looped arms and took the stairs one at a time. We hid out in the office where a box contained both of our bouquets and headpieces. I placed Mom's floral crown on her head. The contrast between the greenery and dainty white flowers was striking. A Rose by Any Other Name had made a floral tiara for me too. I felt like I was living in a fairy tale as I secured it to my head with bobby pins. Then I handed Mom her bouquet. "Are you ready for this?"

She beamed with delight. "I am. I really am, honey."

A knock sounded on the door. It was Carlos. He had changed into a black suit with a pale blue tie. My throat tightened at the sight of his slicked-back hair and dashing eyes. "It is time, Helen." He poked his head inside.

She gave me a final grin, then squeezed my hand. I went first. Carlos steadied me with a firm grasp on my wrist. "Julieta, you are a vision," he whispered in my ear as we rounded the front of the winery and made our way toward the music.

A medieval minstrel band complete with flutes, a harp, a trumpet, and guitar, played the "Wedding March." I didn't trust myself to speak. As we approached the archway, Carlos dropped my arm and faded into the background. I was aware of the crowd of friends and family, but my eyes focused on the Professor who stood underneath the arch of flowers. His face held such happiness that I thought my heart might explode.

I marched slowly, knowing that Mom was behind me. Once I arrived at the archway, the Professor kissed both of my cheeks. The guests stood as the minister cued the band to play "Here Comes the Bride."

Mom floated above the ground. Her smile was wide. Her eyes were dewy. I barely heard the minister speak as they exchanged their vows. It wasn't until the Professor cleared his throat to recite a custom poem that he had written for Mom that my tears really began to flow.

"Dearest Helen," he began. His eyes were locked on Mom's. I noticed that she clutched his hands to help steady him. Time stood still. It could have been the fifteen hundreds. The Professor in his king's costume with a regal tapestry coat, jacquard shirt, and tights, and Mom in her equally resplendent wedding gown.

"By moonlight, by sunlight, in stillness, in brightness, you are my shield and I shall forever be your shadow. I'll follow you through summer's glare, through winter's darkness. You, the beacon of my heart, my everything, my everywhere. I will dry your tears, hold you in moments of sorrow. I will sing to you from mountains and serenade you from the sea. We will dance boldly into an unknown future, wrapped in each other's embrace. Let the rain fall, let the west wind blow, let the snow swirl and the earth shudder. Our love will stand strong. I will stand with you, by you, for you. You, my beloved." His voice cracked. "My wife."

Mom stood on her tiptoes to kiss his cheek. The Professor dabbed his eyes. And then the minister announced that they were husband and wife.

Suddenly, they were kissing and everyone was on their feet and applauding.

I followed behind them as they danced down the aisle toward the oak trees. Mom was married, and I couldn't be happier. If only I could have held on to that moment. Little did I know that the joyous occasion was about to take a nasty turn.

Chapter Eleven

As promised, waiters flanked the aisle holding trays of chilled wine and puff pastry with goat cheese, tomatoes, and basil, mini-quiches, shrimp puffs, skewers of grilled chicken and veggies, Italian meatballs, and antipasto.

The Professor kissed my hand as I made my way through the greeting line. "Well played, dear Juliet. I don't believe that I've ever seen your mother's eyes shine so bright. A perfect surprise, I must say."

I studied his kind face. "You were *both* surprised, right?"

"But of course. Why would you think otherwise?" He tipped his velvet cap decorated with jewels. I caught a hint of sarcasm in his tone. "Thank you for arranging such a wonderful day. I very much enjoyed spending the afternoon with Carlos, Ramiro, and Thomas."

"Word has it that you beat them all at golf."

The creases in the Professor's cheeks widened with his smile. "A gentleman never shares his golf score." There was a brief lull in the line, as the waitstaff brought out trays of red and white wine. "Juliet, I assume you've been in contact with Lance?"

I nodded.

The Professor lowered his voice. "I'm afraid I haven't been able to accomplish much in the way of information about his father's murder."

"You think it was murder?" I fluffed the skirt of my dress.

"Most definitely." He scanned the crowd. "I do fear that there's not much that can be done. Even if I had a suspect, I can't make an arrest, and as you well know your mother and I will be leaving tonight. Do keep an eye on Lance. I know that your friendship means the world to him."

"Of course. Is there anything else I can do?"

He waved to a guest wearing an elaborate gown. "Alas, no. I had a private conversation with Thomas this afternoon and have shared everything. I also put in a call to a friend in Medford who has promised to keep him and Detective Kerry in the loop."

The line began to move. The Professor kissed my cheek. "Again, many thanks, my dear."

I continued on, wishing that the Professor didn't have to think about murder on his wedding night.

Soon the reception was in full swing. Music wafted from the barn, where a five-piece band serenaded the happy couple. People mingled and nibbled on appetizers. They wandered the grounds. Once dinner service had been set out on the deck they queued up and loaded plates with flank steak, garlic, herbed whipped potatoes, a strawberry field salad with toasted almonds and balsamic vinaigrette, and Torte's bread assortment with hand-churned butter.

I didn't have a moment to myself. Everyone wanted

to congratulate me on Mom's wedding. I kept checking in with the kitchen staff, and made sure the dessert bar and cake would be ready to go once guests had finished dinner. Confident that Chef Garrison had everything under control, I went to double-check how many tables had been set up in the barn for our dessert spread.

The band played low as people noshed at high bar tables that had been placed around the dance floor. The dessert tables flanked the stage. They had been covered with greenery and cascading bouquets. As I made my way through familiar faces, I did a double take when I spotted a couple slow dancing. It was Thomas and Detective Kerry. They looked quite cozy and completely oblivious that anyone was watching them. I had never seen Detective Kerry in anything other than a pencil skirt or tailored slacks and a professional blouse, but tonight she wore an ankle-length red silk dress with a plunging neckline. Her hair fell loose to her shoulders, giving her a soft appearance. I had always thought that she was pretty, albeit serious. Tonight, she looked stunning. Thomas didn't notice when I walked by them on my way to the dessert tables.

I stopped short of the tables, though, because Adam and Megan, Lance's fake date, were standing behind the speakers. Megan wore a skintight black leather dress and combat boots.

"Get out!" She socked Adam in the shoulder. He didn't flinch. "I'm serious. You need to go. Now! You can't be here."

Adam puffed out his chest. Was he going to hit her?

Without thinking I raced over and jumped between

them. "Hey, break it up." I held out my hands to keep him away from her.

"It's fine," Megan said to me. Then she shot Adam a scathing look and stomped away.

"Aren't you supposed to be serving?" I asked Adam, who was staring at Megan. A shiver ran down my spine. The way he was watching her made me nervous. She didn't appear to be a woman who couldn't hold her own, but his beady eyes and intense gaze were unsettling.

"Yeah." He gave me a half nod and followed after Megan.

I did not trust the guy. Every interaction that I had had with him made me more confident that Lance had been right. He was up to no good. I checked the dessert tables and returned outside.

Wine flowed freely and the sound of laughter filled the starry night. On more than one occasion Carlos and I locked eyes. I found myself wistful and wishing for a moment alone. Blame it on the dewy feeling of love that was thick in the sultry night air.

"Jules!"

I turned to see Sterling and the rest of the Torte crew gathered at a picnic table. They waved for me to come join them. "Well? What do you guys think? A success?" I asked, taking a seat on the edge of the table.

"Double thumbs-up, boss." Andy held up a glass of fruit punch in a toast. He looked grown-up in slacks, a forest-green dress shirt, and navy and white striped tie.

"Wow, everyone looks incredible." It was true. Sterling had opted for black with a dark suit jacket and silver tie. He and Steph sat on one side of the picnic bench with their knees touching. Bethany wore a glittery headband in her curls and a cute eggplant pixie dress.

"Oh my!" Lance's voice sounded behind me. "The gang's all here."

"Lance." I turned and embraced him. "How are you?"

He shook his head, and addressed the team. "You won't mind if I steal away your fair leader for a moment?"

"Take her," Andy said with a wink. "If she sticks around here any longer she'll put us to work."

Lance linked his arm through mine. "Don't you sweat the thought for a minute, you handsome young devil. Should any of you ever consider a change in careers, contact Uncle Lance."

"Hear that, boss?" Andy called as Lance and I walked away. "We're going to be stars."

"Pastry stars," I bantered back.

"Darling, you look absolutely ravishing." Lance planted a kiss on each of my cheeks.

"You too." I kissed his cheek. He had outdone himself as always. His costume must have come from OSF. It was made from rich maroon velvet, embroidered with gold thread, and complete with a doublet, breeches, cape, and pleated white ruff collar.

We paused at an empty high bar table. "How are you? I've been thinking about you nonstop. You never came by Torte yesterday."

Lance plucked a single white rose from the bouquet in the center of the table. "I didn't want to trouble you. I know how much stress you've been under."

"Your dad died." I put my hand on his forearm.

He massaged the petals on the rose. "True."

"Did you speak with the Professor?"

"Yes. Although I got the distinct impression that he thought I was mistaken about my father's breathing machine. He said something to the effect that 'grief and shock are clouding my vision.' I assure you that my vision wasn't clouded. Someone unplugged my father's life-support machines." He ripped a petal from the rose.

"I don't think so. I just talked to him, and he's sure it was murder."

"Really?"

"Yes. On that note, who else was there when your father died? Leo, right? Was anyone else there? A nurse? Doctor?"

"No." Lance pressed a petal between his fingers. "Just Jarvis and Sarah."

"Didn't you say that your dad died in the middle of the night?"

He tossed the petal on the grass and fiddled with his collar. "Yes."

"That means that Jarvis or Sarah could have pulled the plug."

"Perhaps." He stared toward the vineyard. I turned to see what he was looking at. Megan was talking to Leo, Sarah, and Jarvis.

"I finally met her," I said, nodding toward Megan. "She wasn't what I expected."

"She's a diamond in the rough." Lance kept his gaze focused on his brother.

"Has it been helpful her being here? Has she uncovered anything new?" I could tell that Lance wasn't listening.

"Huh?" He realized that I was talking. "Yes, yes, she's been most helpful. But I don't want to be left out of this conversation. I'll see you soon. Ta-ta." He tucked the rose into his breast pocket and strolled down the hill.

I watched his long strides. His gait appeared relaxed, but I knew that he was consumed with his father's death. I just wished there was something else I could do to help.

"Not so fast, Juliet." Richard Lord's voice boomed to my left.

Could I make a break for it? I glanced toward the deck where the waitstaff were setting up the buffet. No chance. Not in my strappy sandals and dress.

"Hi, Richard." I sighed and turned around. "Are you enjoying the wedding?"

"Enjoying this? It's a spectacle if you ask me. Everyone knows your mother can't afford anything this lavish. Nor can Doug. What does he make on a police salary?" Richard reminded me of a fat British lord. I had to credit him for coming in costume, but thought that someone might want to suggest that he not accentuate his girth by wearing a purple cape that made him look like a giant blueberry.

"I'm not sure how my mom's or the Professor's finances are any of your concern."

Richard flipped his cape, making it billow out behind him. "Your finances are of my concern. Stretched too thin, aren't you? Like I told that slippery snake husband of yours, I'm willing to cut you a deal and buy you out tonight. You won't see another offer as good, so if I were you I would take it."

"No, thanks." I plastered on a fake smile. "Thank you so much for your concern though. I know it must be heartfelt. What I'm curious about is why the rush to buy us out? Let me guess. Do you have an investor waiting in the wings? Buildable property around Ashland is at a premium, isn't it?" I paused and pointed to the grapevines. Lit up with twinkling lights they stretched as far as my eye could see. "Uva's acreage would be very desirable for the right buyer, wouldn't it?"

Richard became visibly flustered. He tossed his cape from side to side. "You don't know what you're talking about, young lady. And trust me, you don't want to make an enemy of me. I can make things very difficult for you and Torte." With that he huffed away.

I had obviously hit the mark. Richard didn't care about Uva. He wanted our shares so that he could turn around and double—or triple—his profit by selling to a developer. No way. I didn't care if I had to forgo sleep for the next year, my brief conversation with Richard had solidified my determination to do whatever it took to make the winery a success.

Don't let him ruin your night, Jules, I told myself as I made my way to the deck. Dinner service went without a single hiccup. Guests raved about the herb-encrusted steaks and rustic mashed potatoes. I couldn't wipe the grin from my face. Mom and the Professor looked equally happy as they circulated among the tables, stopping to chat and thank each and every guest. I wondered if they were going to have a chance to taste the feast.

I decided to pop into the kitchen and ask the staff to box up plates for them. They would be the envy of the plane later with savory leftovers to tide them over until they landed in Greece. On my way inside I bumped into Clarissa. She wore a striking evening gown and a piercing glare. She was surrounded by Leo and his "goons" as Lance called them—Sarah and Jarvis.

"You all made it," I said with a smile. I looked around for Roger, but didn't see him.

"If you're looking for my husband, he's off getting more wine—as always." She scowled. Then she turned to Sarah and rolled her eyes. Roger didn't strike me as a big drinker, but then again, I only knew him in the context of our expansion.

"I didn't know that you all knew each other."

Sarah steadied her wineglass. She looked younger than I remembered from our first meeting at Torte. Maybe it was her outfit. Her dress looked more like something I would imagine a high school student wearing to the prom. It was hot pink with silver rhinestones. "Clarissa has asked Leo to be a new sponsor for the arts council," Sarah offered.

"Oh." I wasn't sure what else to say. Given Leo's apparent disdain for Lance's profession I was surprised to hear that he would fund any kind of art program.

As if reading my mind, Leo snarled, "What, you don't think the Brown Group is good enough for the art council or something?"

"Me?" I pointed to my chest. I couldn't tell if he was talking to me or Clarissa. He swayed slightly. Sarah reached to steady him and spilled her wine down the front of her dress.

"Oh no!" Her wineglass landed on the grass without breaking.

Jarvis reached into his suit jacket and removed a pristine white handkerchief. He bent over and picked up the glass with the handkerchief.

Quirky, I thought. "We have some club soda and

water in the kitchen," I said to Sarah. "If you want to come inside, I can help you with the stain."

"Thanks." She gave me a look of relief.

Leo yanked Jarvis's arm. "Come on, I want to go find my brother."

Clarissa snapped her fingers at me. "While you're inside, please bring me a glass of wine. The waitstaff has been dismal. I haven't seen a waiter in an hour, or my husband."

I ignored her dig and led Sarah inside.

"Uh-oh. Party casualty," Chef Garrison said, when he spotted Sarah's stained dress.

"There's always one. I'm going to find some club soda. It should do the trick." I took Sarah to the opposite side of the kitchen and found a towel and the soda water. "Are you good? Do you need anything else?"

"No, this is great. Thanks. You're a lifesaver."

Since it was just the two of us, I used the opportunity to see if she would spill anything about Leo. "How do you like working for the Brown Group?"

She poured soda onto the towel and started dabbing her dress. "It's fine. I don't love having to deal with snooty types like Clarissa."

"I'm surprised that Leo's thinking of sponsoring the arts council. It doesn't seem like . . ." I trailed off, trying to find the right words so as not to offend her. She did work for the guy after all.

"His cup of tea?" Sarah offered. "The truth is Leo wants to work with Clarissa's husband, Roger. I guess he's a highly sought after architect and he turned Leo down on a new building project. Clarissa told Leo that if he supports the council, she'll make sure her husband takes the project."

"Ah." I nodded.

Sarah continued to sponge her dress. The wine stain had turned the hot pink an even more garish color. "It's a lot of deals like that, but I have free rein. Leo isn't book smart. He likes being in the field, so it's a good job for me. The entire Brown family has been good to me."

"I was so sorry to hear about Leo's father," I said, wondering how she would respond.

She dipped the burgundy-stained towel into a pitcher of water. "It was a sad day for the Brown Family Group. Mr. Brown will be sorely missed, but in many ways it was a relief. He was in a lot of pain at the end. He was barely cognizant. He couldn't talk. He couldn't eat. It's probably better that he went quickly."

"Right." I gave her a solemn nod. Hadn't Lance said that his father had been alert and eating pudding right before he died?

"This is a lost cause." Sarah stared at her dress. "Is there a bathroom I can use? I might take it off and give it a good scrub."

"Sure." I pointed her to the bathroom and went to get a glass of wine for Clarissa. The kitchen was a display of organized chaos. Food trays had been devoured and piled in the sink. The staff was getting ready to set up the dessert bar. Servers steadied loaded trays on their arms and the wedding cake had been placed on a cart and was about to be wheeled outside. It was a good thing I had thought of packing up dinner for Mom and the Professor because the very last of the dinner trays was being sent out. Relieved that things were running so smoothly, I poured a few glasses of white wine, placed them and the bottle on a tray, and returned to the party.

Clarissa was waiting where I had left her, but she had been joined by Lance and Megan, the PI.

"How are you enjoying the reception?" I asked the group, holding the tray with both hands.

Clarissa stared at her perfectly manicured nails. "I thought the steak was overdone and the potatoes lacked flavor. Don't say anything to your sweet mother, but I would not recommend the caterer she used."

Great. I thought about mentioning the fact that I was the caterer, but instead ignored her snide comment. Part of me wondered if she knew that Torte had catered the event and was intentionally trying to slight me.

Lance coughed and then cleared his throat. "Let me take that from you, darling." He took the tray from my hands, picked up a glass of wine, and passed the tray around. "Honestly, you've outdone yourself, Juliet. This is an absolute show stunner."

"Show stunner?" I said, as Megan offered me the last glass of wine on the tray. I declined. "No, thanks. Go ahead, help yourself."

She took the glass and handed me the empty tray. They looked like an odd pair. Lance in his Shakespearean costume and Megan in her biker bar dress.

Lance drummed his fingers on his chin. "How much have I had to drink tonight, ladies? Show stunner. Hmm. Maybe I've coined a new phrase. Or perhaps I'm slightly tipsy." He pretended to stumble.

Megan sipped her wine.

"I believe you know Clarissa and Megan, right, Juliet?" Lance asked me in the way of an introduction.

I nodded. "Yes, we've had the pleasure."

A group of teenagers trying to get a conga line started danced past us. Ramiro was in the middle of the line, grinning and cheering.

"Do tell, darling. Could that be the offspring of your dark and debonair—or maybe devilish—husband?"

"Yep, that's Ramiro," I said to Lance, watching Ramiro dash off with the teens.

"Just as delicious as his father, isn't he?"

Lance started to say more, but was cut off by the sight of Megan clutching her throat and gasping for air. She dropped her wineglass, which rolled away from her feet.

"Are you okay?" I tossed the empty tray on the grass.

Her face turned beet red. She waved her hand in front of her face. "Something in the drink," she managed to cough out.

I stared at Lance. He sprinted off to find help.

Clarissa stared at us.

"Go get the Professor. See if there's a doctor here," I commanded.

She stood there frozen.

"Go get help!" I yelled.

Megan continued to cough. I helped her over to the base of the deck and had her sit on the bottom of the stairs. "We need water," I called to one of the servers, before realizing it was Adam. He raced away.

"Did you choke on something?" I asked.

She clutched her throat and shook her head. "No, the drink. The drink."

"Are you allergic?" I racked my brain to think about the ingredients that went into making white wine. Usually if people had a reaction to anything in wine it was the sulfites. Could Megan have had an extreme reaction to the sulfites?

Adam came back with a glass of water. His hands shook so violently that water spilled from the glass.

I placed the cold cup to Megan's lips. "Do you think you can try to take a sip?"

She nodded, still struggling for breath.

After getting a couple of sips of water down, her wheezing sounded slightly less intense. I could hear an ambulance siren in the distance. Lance was running toward us with one of Ashland's pediatricians.

Megan dug her nails into her wrist. Her voice was raspy. "Something in my drink."

I tried to make sense of what she was saying. "Are you choking? You swallowed something?"

She shook her head and heaved her shoulders. "No."

Her eyes bulged. She dug her nails into her neck, drawing blood. "Poison."

"What?" I started to stand. She grabbed my arm. "For you," she managed to whisper.

The pediatrician pushed me aside. My heart pounded. Megan thought that her wine had been poisoned and it was intended for me!

Chapter Twelve

The happy vibe at the reception took on a somber tone as the ambulance sped off with Megan. The paramedics seemed to think that she would be okay, but it was too soon to know. Clarissa and Adam had both disappeared.

Lance promised that he would meet her at the hospital. I wanted to go with him. What had Megan meant about her wine being intended for me? Had she simply had a reaction to something she had eaten?

Mom and the Professor came over to confer.

"What happened?" Mom's brow crinkled.

"I don't know. We were talking—Megan, Clarissa, Lance, and I—and all of sudden she started clutching her throat and coughing." I shivered at the memory. There was no chance that I was mentioning Megan's parting warning.

The Professor's face hardened. "Perhaps it would be best if we delayed our trip, Helen?"

Mom nodded. "I know. I was thinking the same thing."

"No way. You two are going. The paramedics said

that they think she's going to be fine. They took her to the hospital as a precaution. There's nothing you can do. Lance and I will go check in on her later, I promise." I pointed to the barn where the band had resumed and guests had begun to dance. "Go enjoy the rest of the night. Your flight leaves in four hours. You should dance and cut the cake. Think of the incident as a little blip on the radar and nothing more."

Mom forced a smile. "I don't know, what do you think, Doug?"

The Professor sighed. "Juliet makes a fair point. One of my favorite sayings is, 'Sadness is but a wall between two gardens.' Perhaps we should plant our garden on the dance floor?"

"Is that Shakespeare?" Mom asked. "I don't recognize it."

"No. That piece of wisdom comes from Kahlil Gibran."

"It's lovely," I said.

Mom frowned. "Speaking of not recognizing something. Who's Megan? I don't think that I know her."

The Professor's eyes felt like they were burning into my forehead. Obviously, he knew who Megan really was.

"Lance's date," I replied, trying to keep my face as passive as possible.

"What? Lance's date? The woman in the black leather dress?" Mom's face scrunched up in disbelief. "Her and Lance? There must be more to that story."

The Professor cleared his throat. "My dearest Helen, I see them waving to us. I believe our guests are eager for cake, and everyone is familiar with the Bard's most famous sentiment when it comes to cake."

"Let them eat cake," Mom and I said in unison.

We laughed, which broke the pall hanging over us. "Your cake is calling." I nudged them toward the barn. The Professor shot me a look of thanks. It was unnecessary. This was their wedding night. Nothing but joy should surround them.

The mood lightened when Mom and the Professor cut into the cake. Guests oohed and aahed when we wheeled the elegant tiered cake onto the center of the dance floor. They linked hands and sliced into the bottom layer. I helped plate slices dense with buttercream and fresh strawberries. There's an art and a system to cake cutting. One of the services that we offer our bridal customers at Torte is cake cutting. Hiring a professional baker to cut and serve the wedding cake ensures that each slice will be uniform and that the cake will feed everyone in attendance.

In culinary school, we studied cake-cutting charts and watched endless demonstrations. There are a variety of methods that bakers use, from the "Circular Method" to disassembling the cake to cut the bottom layer first. I prefer this option because it allows me to cut and serve a cake for two hundred people in less than fifteen minutes. Plus, if there's any cake leftover, it will be the top smaller layers that can easily be stored in the freezer.

Guests love watching the bride and groom slice into silky layers of buttercream, but the mechanics of dissecting a cake into individual pieces takes away the romance of the occasion. I cheered with everyone as Mom and the Professor fed each other carefully and polished off their dainty bites with a kiss. Once they had been swept into the crowd, I waved Bethany over to help.

She wiggled her fingers that were now a warm shade of pink. "Show me how it's done."

I began by cutting a two-inch strip down the side of the bottom tier. I used a cake cutting comb and a knife to gently lay the strip on its side. This is the part of the process that makes most novices nervous because they worry that the cake will fall apart. It won't. Once the strip was on its side I simply used a ruler to cut even one-inch slices.

"That looks easy enough," Bethany said, picking up a pastry knife. "Should I start on the next tier?"

"Go for it. Just go easy when you slice the first strip. If you cut too quickly you'll smash the layers together and the filling will squish out."

"Wish me luck." She snapped a picture of the growing row of plated cake.

Guests lined up while Bethany and I carefully sliced piece after piece. Mom's mantra has always been, "Never underestimate the power of pastry." That certainly rang true as guests noshed on our strawberry-shortcake cake and lemon cream. Mom and the Professor took a turn on the dance floor. Tears returned as I watched the Professor whisper in her ear.

A deep voice interrupted my thoughts. "They are very much in love, no?" Carlos massaged the small of my back. "Julieta, shall we join them?"

As much as I knew I should decline, I let my heart lead. Carlos wrapped one hand over mine and pulled me onto the dance floor. He was a good dancer. He moved to the music, his body swaying to the beat as he swirled me around. I'd forgotten how good it felt to be in his arms.

The dance floor was packed with familiar faces. Sterling cradled the back of Steph's neck as they moved to the middle of the wooden floor. Bethany danced with someone I didn't recognize, and Andy chatted with the band.

We danced past Mom and the Professor who grinned. "We should have taken lessons from them, Doug." Mom nudged the Professor.

"It is necessary in Spain," Carlos said, leaning me into a dip. "Dance is like food. It is the language of love. You are doing beautifully."

Mom chuckled, but got pulled into a conversation with another guest.

The music slowed. Carlos pressed his cheek to mine. He smelled of sautéed onions, garlic, and musky aftershave. We weren't exactly dancing any longer. More like falling into each other. I couldn't let myself get lost in the moment.

When the song ended, I untangled myself from his arms. "I have to go find Lance," I lied, leaving him standing in the middle of the dance floor.

I could feel the flush on my face, as I left the barn and headed for the grapevines. It was true that I did want to find Lance, eventually. But first I needed some space. Having Carlos here was dangerous. I was falling for him again—hard. I couldn't let that happen. Getting over him had been one of the most challenging things I had ever done. I wasn't sure I would survive it a second time.

I was angry at myself for letting him back in. I had

worked so hard at building an exterior and keeping my heart in check, but every day I was with him I found myself spinning in a dizzy swirl of emotions.

"Pull it together, Jules," I told myself as I plucked a leaf from a grapevine.

"I thought I might find you here." Lance's voice made me jump.

"Lance, what are you doing?"

He ripped a leaf from the vine. "Same as you, darling. Escaping."

"Why do we always end up like this?"

"Because we're made from the same cloth. Hopeless romantics, creatives, closet introverts, just to name a few."

I wrapped the leaf around my pinkie. "What do you think happened to Megan?" I wasn't ready to process Carlos yet, even with Lance.

"Why do you think I've been meandering through these grapevines for the past half hour?" Lance asked.

"Did you hear what she said?"

He shook his head.

"She told me that there was something in her drink. She thinks it was poisoned."

Lance clutched the leaf to his chest. "Seriously?"

"Yeah, and she said that the wine was meant for me." I sighed and breathed in the scent of the grapes.

"My God." Lance dabbed his brow. "Why? Who would want to poison Ashland's pastry queen?"

I shrugged. "I don't know. She was in bad shape. Maybe I misunderstood her."

Lance glared at me. "Hardly. When have you ever misunderstood any situation?"

"Thanks for the vote of confidence, but I promise I've had plenty of mishaps." The stars flickered above us. I rubbed my arms to keep warm.

"I find that hard to believe."

"Let's assume that I heard her correctly. Why would someone want to poison her drink, or mine?"

"Your guess is as good as mine. She told me that she had some new information for me, but you know what it's like for me when I'm mingling with the public. I haven't had a single minute to myself since we arrived. Hence my traipsing through dusty vines and risking ruining my Italian leather shoes." Lance tugged up his pantaloons to prove his point.

"It has to be connected to your father's case, don't you think?" I asked.

Lance nodded. "It must be, but what's the connection to you? Who poured the drinks?"

"I did."

He cackled. "Now that would be quite Shakespearean. The daughter knocks herself off at her mother's wedding. Classic move. Absolutely classic."

"Lance, this is no time to joke around."

"Coping strategy." He yanked another leaf from a grapevine.

"Okay, fine. I poured the wine in the kitchen and brought it outside."

"Did anyone touch it before you poured it?"

I thought back through my steps. "No. I poured it myself and placed the glasses on a tray. I brought it outside for Clarissa, but then you were there talking to her with Megan. In fact, I handed the tray to you first."

"That's right." Lance dropped the leaf and clapped

his hands together. "Now we may be on to something. Let's think this through. Why so many glasses? Weren't there exactly four glasses on the tray?"

Were there? I retraced every move. "You're right. I poured four glasses. Not for any specific reason. There just happened to be four glasses on the counter. I figured if I was bringing Clarissa a glass I could offer the three remaining glasses to other guests."

"This is good. This is really good. Then what?"

"Then I came outside. The three of you were talking. You took the tray."

Lance rubbed his temple. "I did. Then what did I do?"

"You were joking about being tipsy."

"Ha-ha! As if. I'm as sober as a rock right now." He twisted the ruff collar around his neck. "I've got to take this thing off. It's itching. I have newfound respect for my actors who have to wear these things." He scratched his neck. "But seriously. No drop of liquor has touched these lips tonight. I have to be on my A game with Leo."

"Did you hand the tray to Clarissa?"

"Yes." He snapped twice. "That's it. When I gave it to her it had three glasses."

"Wait. Did you take a glass for yourself first?"

"Definitely. I wanted a prop. I do much better talking to my public with something in my hands."

I rolled my eyes. "So, Clarissa took a glass, then she gave the tray to Megan. I remember Megan offering me a drink, and I know for sure there was only one glass of wine left on the tray."

"Where did the fourth glass go?"

"No idea. Megan took the last glass when I declined."

Lance's lips formed a tight seal. "You realize what this means, don't you?"

"What?"

"Either someone tried to kill Megan. Or someone tried to kill you."

"But who? And why? We were right there. I know Clarissa doesn't like me. I have no idea why, but I can't imagine the president of Ashland's art council trying to kill me. How could she have done it? She was holding a tray of three glasses."

"That's it. Maybe that's why one is missing. It could have fallen when she dropped the poison in."

"We would have seen her. Or heard her, don't you think?"

"True." Lance nodded. "And that would have been taking a risk. How could she guarantee which one of you would take the drink?"

My stomach churned at the thought.

"The more likely scenario is that Megan tampered with the drink."

"What? She's in the hospital, Lance."

"I know. Think about it. It's brilliant. No one would suspect her. Maybe it was a warning."

"For what?"

"How should I know."

"You hired her. Do you think she's the type to tuck a vial of poison into her evening bag?"

"No, but she is a PI. She's probably got quick fingers."

"Fine, but again, why would she want to warn me?"

Lance frowned. "I haven't put that piece together yet. However, I have been worried that she's a double agent."

"A double agent?"

"I've been subtly dropping details about my family estate to see if they get back to Leo. I think she might be working for him too."

"Really?" I breathed in the earthy scent of the grapevines.

"Really."

We were quiet for a moment. The lively sounds of the band and happy guests dancing under a canopy of shimmering little lights seemed a world away.

"There is another possibility, you know," Lance finally said.

"What's that?"

"Someone else could have poisoned the drink. There are hundreds of people here. What if someone snuck past us? We were talking for a while. It's dark. Perhaps our culprit splashed in a couple drops of the poison and scurried away."

"That's a stretch."

"But not out of the realm of possibility." Lance paused and craned his neck toward the reception. "It looks like the happy couple is about to make their grand exit. What do you say we see them off and then take a detour to the hospital? I do believe that a tête-à-tête with Megan is in order."

We linked arms and weaved through the grapevines. This was it. Time to say bon voyage to Mom. I was happy for her, but wished that I didn't have to worry that someone may have just tried to kill me.

Chapter Thirteen

Tears flowed as I stood with Carlos, Ramiro, and Lance and waved good-bye to Mom and the Professor. The crew from Torte gathered round. Mom stopped to kiss each of them on the cheek. Sparklers lit up the night sky. The scent of smoke hit my nose. Mom and the Professor ran through a sea of tiny white flames into a waiting vintage carriage. Andy, Bethany, Sterling, and Steph waved sparklers in both hands, creating a wave of color in the air. Lance squeezed my right hand. Carlos held my left hand. Ramiro twirled a gold sparkler, making the shape of a heart appear. This was my family. I had to remind myself of that fact. I had created a family in Ashland. My heart felt full.

The rest of the reception was a blur. Clarissa and Roger must have left, because I never saw them after the wine incident. Nor did I see Leo, Jarvis, or Sarah.

Hiring Chef Garrison and his crew from Ashland Springs was the best decision we had made. I didn't have to worry about cleanup or storing whatever leftovers remained. If Megan hadn't choked on her wine, I might have stayed late into the evening and danced with Carlos, but the Universe had other plans for me.

Carlos and Ramiro had started helping the crew tear down some of the peripheral tables that weren't in use. Most guests had begun to trickle away, but there were still a handful of lingering couples taking a turn around the dance floor or savoring a plate of desserts.

Lance tapped my shoulder as I carried a tray of used dishes toward the kitchen. "Don't you have people for that?"

I adjusted the stack of plates. "For dishes? Yes."

"Good. Then put those down and let's jet."

"Jet?"

He took the pile from my hands, and waved over a waiter whose tower of dishes looked as if it were about to crash and shatter into a thousand pieces. Then he proceeded to load the poor guy up with my stack of dishes. "We have work to do. Let's go."

I shot the waiter an apologetic smile as Lance yanked me away from the deck. "Where are we going?"

"To the hospital, of course. Megan was my ride so I need you to drive."

I dug my heels into the grass. "Hold on. You want to go to the hospital? Now?"

"When else?" Lance sounded exasperated. "The clock is ticking. We're wasting precious time."

"But I have work to do. I can't just leave." I motioned to the crew of waitstaff circulating around us.

"That's why you hired people. You must learn how to delegate, Juliet. Take my advice. You're going to burn out and end up spread too thin. As in too thin like butter."

He snapped and waved his finger in a zigzag in front of me.

While his words held truth, I didn't see how they were relevant to snooping around Megan's hospital room. "What about Carlos? And Ramiro? I can't just leave them," I protested.

"Details. Details. You can come back for them. This won't take long. We'll scoot over to the hospital and have you back in less than an hour. No one will be the wiser."

I hesitated. Lance grinned. He knew that he had won.

"Fine. But we should make it quick. I need to help with cleanup."

"Deal." Lance shook my hand, and linked his fingers through mine. No one seemed to take notice as we headed down the hill to my car.

"I would say the wedding was a success." Lance bowed to a couple getting into the car next to us. The woman's dress got caught in the door. Lance tapped on the window and pointed to the packed gravel road. "Your dress, honey," he mouthed. The woman opened the door and Lance helped her tuck her dress around her feet.

"Do you think everyone had fun?" I asked once he had rescued the damsel in distress and returned to the car.

"You mean minus an attempted murder."

"Minus that." I sighed. "Did you talk to Leo again?"

"Jarvis wouldn't let me near him," Lance said, twisting his collar. "The suit is like my brother's shadow. Anytime I tried to talk to Leo, Jarvis was right next to him. I don't trust the guy. I'm telling you, he's like a henchman with surprisingly decent taste in menswear.

Did you see his feather bow tie? It's a custom design. Probably cost him upward of two hundred and fifty dollars. The question is, what kind of cash is my brother paying him if he can afford a tie like that?"

Leave it to Lance to critique Jarvis's style.

"He's a lawyer, isn't he?" I kept my eyes focused on the bumpy road. There were no streetlights in the country.

"Yes, but how many Medford lawyers do you know who wear designer bow ties?" He paused. "What am I saying? How many Medford lawyers do you know who wear bow ties at all?"

"What about Sarah? Did you talk to her?"

"Not much. She kept running back and forth to the kitchen. I think she was obsessed with trying to get out the stain on her dress. Very Macbeth of her. I shouted, 'Out, damned spot, out, I say!' to her. She didn't get it. Not a surprise, and her garish dress is definitely Medford. I wanted to tell her that the stain actually made it look better."

"Lance." I punched his shoulder.

"What? I'm simply saying what you know you're thinking. Who wears cheap, pink satin with fake rhinestones to a wedding? My brother must not be paying her enough."

We came to the main road, complete with streetlight and cement. Lance was unusually quiet on the remainder of the drive to the hospital. "Are you thinking about your dad?" I asked as we drove past a horse sanctuary.

He stared out the window. "Among other things, yes. Why am I so stubborn, Juliet?"

"You're not stubborn."

"Please." Lance let out an exasperated sigh. "I could have reached out to my father years ago, but I didn't. I chose to simmer in bitterness and hold my own pity party. I wasted so much time. Now he's gone and the possibility that we're going to be able to prove that someone killed him is looking pretty bleak. I'm going to have to live with that guilt for the rest of my life. I could have done something to stop it, and I didn't."

"No. What could you have done?"

He gnawed on his fingernail. "I could have camped out next to his bedside around the clock. I could have insisted on police protection."

"Lance, don't beat yourself up. And don't lose hope. Maybe that's why Megan was poisoned. She might have proof that your father was murdered. We could be close to learning the truth."

This seemed to calm him down. "The important thing is that you *did* reach out to him. Like I said before, what a gift to be able to have that kind of closure. Not everyone gets that lucky," I continued.

He didn't respond. We turned onto the main road leading back to town. "What about you? Carlos is as dashing as always and, judging from the way he was looking at you tonight, I would say he has set his sights on a permanent residence here in Ashland."

"Do you think?"

Lance scoffed. "Juliet, you are one of the wisest and densest women I have ever met."

"Thanks."

"No one could accuse you of having an ego, but seriously, darling, men drool at your feet and you take no notice. How is that possible?"

"Carlos wasn't drooling at my feet."

"I beg to differ."

Thankfully, we arrived at the hospital and he dropped the subject. I wasn't sure if they would let us see Megan. Lance pranced his way to the nurses' station, ripped off his starched collar, and buried his face in his hands. "You must let me speak to Megan, she was my paramour. The love of my life. What if she doesn't recover? This could be my one and only chance to say good-bye."

Were those real tears he had squeezed out of his eyes?

The nurse must have bought his act. "You'll have to speak to the officer on patrol. I'm not sure if the police are letting visitors in," she said. "Room 224. Down the hall on the right."

To my surprise, Thomas was standing guard outside Megan's room. "Thomas, what are you doing here?" I asked.

Thomas perked up when he saw us. He was still wearing the chocolate-brown suit that he'd worn to the wedding. A boutonniere with a single white rose and three sprigs of rosemary was pinned to his breast pocket. He looked like an older version of my homecoming date. His eyes still hold the same spark of interest and inquisitiveness. "Uh, I was about to ask you guys the same question."

Lance scratched his exposed neck. The collar had left a red rash in a perfect three-inch circle. "Do tell. It appears that you're guarding the door."

Thomas was well versed in Lance speak. He winked at me. "More like watching."

"Why?" I asked.

"I had a chat with the Professor." His boyish face

shifted. "While golfing we had a long discussion about your dad's case."

Lance folded his hands together and waited for Thomas to say more.

"Look, you guys know that our hands are tied with Medford taking the lead, but the Professor has done some legwork and I'm going to follow up on his leads. He pulled me aside before he and your mom left and suggested I head over this way and check things out. I wanted to make sure that I was the one to come. You know how the Professor is. I could see him calling off the honeymoon or something." Thomas tried to sound casual, but I noticed his posture was rigid and he hadn't budged even an inch from Megan's door. "Did they get off okay?"

"The happy couple?" Lance interjected with a flick of his wrist. "Yes, yes. They're blissfully on their way to the Greek isles and completely unaware of the drama unfolding here."

"I wouldn't say that," I said to Lance. "If the Professor sent Thomas here he must have suspected that something wasn't right about Megan's reaction to the wine."

Thomas nodded. He lowered his voice. "I just spoke to the resident on call and he confirmed that she was poisoned. We've sent the glass to the lab in Medford to run toxicology tests."

"Really?" A new wave of nausea assaulted my body. I had hoped that Lance and I were blowing things out of proportion.

"Jules, are you okay?" Thomas reached out to steady me.

"I'm fine. It's hospitals. They give me the jitters."

That wasn't a lie. I had spent way too much time in the hospital when my dad was sick. The smell of industrial bleach and the fluorescent lighting stirred up unwelcome memories.

Thomas gave my arm a squeeze before letting me go.

Lance pursed his lips. "You have to let us in. We have to speak with Megan. It's most urgent."

Thomas rolled his eyes. "Lance, you know I can't do that."

"Not even if it could mean life or death for our dear Juliet?" Lance raised one groomed eyebrow.

"What?" Thomas frowned and looked to me.

Lance continued. "That drink might have been meant for Juliet. Megan is the only person who knows the truth."

Thomas shook his head. "Wait, what? The drink was meant for you?"

I shrugged. "I don't know. That's what Megan said to me as she was being taken away in the ambulance. She probably wasn't coherent. Or, I could have heard her wrong."

"Why would anyone want to poison you?" Thomas's face dropped. He focused on Lance. "You really think that Megan suspected the drink was intended for Jules?"

"Our dear Juliet is trying her usual tactic of making light of a ghastly situation. We both are acutely aware of the fact that Juliet has rarely misunderstood *anything*. She happens to be one of the most astute people I know." Lance laced his fingers together. "Why she was the intended victim, I don't know. Nor do I understand the connection to my father's death, but I'm certain that Juliet didn't mistake Megan's words. Agree?"

Thomas hesitated for a second. He glanced down the empty hospital corridor. I wondered if he was looking for Detective Kerry. If she caught Thomas sneaking us in to see Megan, I was sure she would try to get his badge taken away. I didn't want to get him in trouble, but knowing that the doctor had confirmed that Megan's drink had contained poison changed everything. "Okay, but just a couple minutes, and I'm coming with you."

He unlocked the door and ushered us inside. Megan lay in the hospital bed. Her face had lost most of its color. "Sorry to bother you, but these witnesses have come forward with some new information," Thomas said. "I need to ask you a few more questions."

Megan tried to sit up. She winced, then pressed the remote control to move the bed to a more upright position. Was she really in pain, or was it an act? Lance's theory that she was the person who slipped something in my drink was far-fetched, but then again stranger things had happened, especially here in Ashland.

Thomas removed an iPad Mini from his jacket. His iPad was like an extra appendage. Had he brought it to the wedding? What about his gun? I wondered if it was strapped to his ankle, carefully hidden beneath his dress slacks. "Ms. Capshaw claims that you said something about the wine being intended for her?"

Megan nodded with force but didn't speak. She clutched her hand to her throat. She looked like a different woman. Gone was the tough leather exterior. Her eyes held an unnerving desperation.

"The doctor told us that her vocal cords were damaged by the poison. They're sending a speech pathologist and ENT down from Medford tomorrow, but in the meantime, they don't want her to speak," Thomas explained. "Anything you want to ask will need to be a yes or no question, or I can have her type her answer on the iPad."

Megan's response was immediate. She motioned rapidly for Thomas to hand her the iPad and began typing. Lance fiddled with his ruffled collar, rolling it into a tight ball and then watching it spring out again, while we waited to see what Megan had written. After what felt like an hour, she handed the iPad back to Thomas and stared at me.

Thomas read what she had written. "You're sure?" he asked her without filling Lance or me in.

Megan nodded and made a slicing motion across her neck.

Thomas let out a long sigh. The sound of footsteps echoed in the hallway. He shot his head in the direction of the door. "Let's go." He forced us out the door.

"What's going on?" I asked.

Thomas shook his head and moved his eyes in the direction of the nurses' station. Detective Kerry was marching down the hall straight for us. The sound of her heels echoed through the corridor. Her silky red dress billowed behind her. "Hold on a sec. Let me do the talking."

Detective Kerry approached us with a curt nod. "Were you talking to the victim without me?"

Thomas twisted his boutonniere. "Kerry, I got some new info from Lance and Jules." Was it my imagination or did he blush slightly when talking to her?

She scowled. "I hope you didn't let civilians in there."

"Us? Civilians?" Lance chimed in. "Don't be ridiculous. You know you've missed me, dear. By the way, red is your color. It brings out those shockingly green eyes and offsets your lovely auburn locks. Absolutely fabulous. That dress is to die for." He made a sweeping motion over her body.

Detective Kerry almost looked flustered, but she held out her hand in a motion to stop him.

Lance wasn't done. "And need I remind you that without our help you wouldn't have closed your last case?"

They had been introduced when Lance had been wrongfully accused of a murder. The two of them hadn't exactly hit off. Then again, I didn't get the sense that Detective Kerry warmed to many people. Her steely exterior made it clear that she had no interest in making friends. Yet I was starting to wonder if her armor was cracking. Between dancing and laughing with Thomas earlier at the wedding and her attitude with Lance now, maybe there was a chance that she would let her guard down.

Thomas gave Lance a warning look.

"You need to see this." Thomas handed her the iPad.

Detective Kerry read it twice and then stared at me. What had Megan written?

She gave Thomas the iPad back. "Let me go talk to her." With that, she thrust open the door and immediately slammed it shut.

"Thomas, what's going on? What did Megan say?" I asked.

He held out the iPad. "Read it for yourself."

Lance leaned over my shoulder as I read the note that Megan had written: "Jules Capshaw in danger! Drink not for me. Talk to kitchen staff—stat. Poison in glass. Or bottle."

"What?" I asked. "That doesn't make sense. I filled

the glasses myself. I would have noticed if there was poison in one of them."

Thomas shook his head from side to side. "Would you though? Think about it. It could have been a drop. Maybe a trace of powder. The doctor doesn't think that there was enough poison to actually kill a person. I don't know if that was intentional. Maybe someone was trying to send a message. Or maybe our perpetrator made a mistake and didn't estimate the amount they would need for a lethal dose."

"I guess," I said, swallowing twice. My throat felt tight, or was that just psychological?

"But how would they have known that Juliet was going to drink the poison? That seems way too risky," Lance added. "Impossible, if you think about it. There were hundreds of guests in attendance. Unless someone specifically handed her a drink."

"True." Thomas looked thoughtful. "I guess we should start by interrogating the kitchen staff. They are all temporary workers, right? How long will they be on-site?"

"I don't know. It depends on how long the guests stay. I would think at least for another hour or so." I looked around for a clock in the narrow hallway.

Detective Kerry emerged from Megan's room with a stoic half smile. She smoothed the bodice of her dress. "I don't know. I'm leaning toward believing the victim. It sounds like we could have a case of the wrong drink in the wrong hands here."

"Really?" I gulped.

She gave me an almost sympathetic nod. "Too soon to jump to any conclusions yet. No need to panic."

Easy enough for her to say; she wasn't the person who had nearly been poisoned.

Thomas filled her in on what she'd missed. "I guess we should head back to Uva, right?" he said.

She nodded. "The victim appears to be stable. I don't think she's in any immediate danger. We can have the nursing staff rotate into the room throughout the evening, but I don't think it's necessary to have police presence here tonight."

Thomas stepped back to let Detective Kerry walk in front of him. They started down the hall when Lance threw his hands in the air and yelled, "Wait!"

We all froze.

"I can't believe I didn't think of this earlier. This is huge! Critical. I have a major clue in this case."

Detective Kerry folded her arms across her chest. "And are you intending to share it?"

Lance tilted his head toward the ceiling, pressed his heels together to form a V, and then proceeded to close his eyes, extended his arms, and touched one finger and then the next to his nose. "Ta-da!" he announced, standing straight again.

"Is there a reason that you're demonstrating you're not inebriated?" Detective Kerry said with a sneer.

"Yes!" Lance clapped twice. "I'm completely sober."

"And?"

"And the wine that Juliet brought outside for us never touched my lips."

I gasped.

Lance nodded. "Exactly. You didn't drink any of it, Juliet. I didn't drink it, I simply wanted the glass as a prop. You know, I have to maintain a certain social standing for my fans. But I didn't drink tonight. Not a single drop. That must mean that Clarissa didn't drink any either. Leaving poor Megan in a hospital bed as the only sad soul who drank the tainted vino."

Detective Kerry and Thomas shared a look. "That is something," she conceded. "Where is the bottle and the other glasses?"

I bit my bottom lip. "I set the tray down on the grass when Megan got sick. The bottle was in the kitchen. It's probably in the recycling with the rest of the wine bottles. Although, when we left they were already starting to pick up. It could be anywhere."

"Then it looks like we're doing some Dumpster diving," Kerry said to Thomas.

Lance inhaled. "Oh, do let us tag along. Pretty please."

Thomas nodded. "Yeah, we need you both to show us exactly where you were. What about Clarissa? Do either of you know anything about her?"

"She's married to Roger, my architect, and she's head of the arts council. I don't know much more about her, other than for some reason she isn't a fan of mine."

"That can't be true. What's not to love about Ashland's pastry goddess?" Thomas said with a half smile. "Did she react to the incident? Did you notice anything out of the ordinary? And, are you sure she didn't drink anything?"

I shook my head. "I don't know. I wasn't paying attention. She took a glass, but maybe she never took a drink."

"Then I guess we should find her first," Thomas said, motioning us toward the exit.

Lance walked in stride with Detective Kerry. "Do tell, Lady in Red, will you be scrounging through the trash in this? Because, if so, I'm going to need to film it for posterity."

Detective Kerry smiled. A genuine smile that gave her face a lightness I'd never seen. Her green eyes glimmered. "You'll just have to wait and see."

Lance whipped his head around and dropped his jaw. He grinned in eager excitement and mouthed, "O—M—G!"

Chapter Fourteen

A handful of guests lingered over slices of cake when we returned to Uva. Otherwise, the vineyard was quiet except for the Ashland Springs crew. They stacked chairs and tore down tables. Carlos and Ramiro were in the mix, carrying trays loaded with empty plates and glasses into the kitchen.

Thomas whipped out his flashlight. "Hold up, everyone," he called, holding the light beneath his chin which gave his face an odd glow. He looked more like he was telling a ghost story around a campfire than trying to lock down a crime scene. "Police! We need everyone to stop what you're doing and stay exactly where you are."

A murmur sounded through the staff. Thomas turned to Detective Kerry. His eyes moved from her head to her ankles. "I'll start going through the wine bottles and dishes if you want to interrogate the remaining guests and the crew."

She nodded to me and Lance. "What about these two? Apparently, this one wants to go Dumpster diving." Was I mistaken or did she wink at Lance.

"We'll help him look for the wine bottle," Lance said, yanking my arm and pulling me toward the deck.

"Ouch." I rubbed my shoulder. "That hurt."

"Not worse than being sidelined by the femme-fatale detective," Lance replied. "I would have absolutely died to see her dig through the trash in that runway dress, but apparently your boy toy Thomas came to her rescue."

"True." I thought for a moment. "Wait, how will we know which bottle it is? They all look the same."

Lance let out an exasperated sigh. "This is no time to be a voice of reason. For starters, we'll look at the scene of the crime, and from there who knows? Maybe it will be obvious that one of the bottles was tampered with, or maybe one of them will have a skull and crossbones on it."

"Unlikely," Thomas said. "But it's worth a shot."

We stopped at the spot where I had abandoned the tray. "This is it," I said to Thomas, scanning the grass. There was no sign of the tray or wine bottle.

Thomas ran the beam of his flashlight in parallel lines, sweeping across the grass. Most of the tables in the area had already been flattened and stacked for the delivery truck to pick up in the morning. "Nothing."

"It was a long shot, wasn't it?" I asked.

He clicked the light on and off a couple times. "Yeah. I think our best bet is to collect every wine bottle as evidence. We can put them in my squad car and I'll take them to the lab in Medford."

"Every wine bottle?" Lance repeated. "How big is your squad car? Did you see how much wine was consumed? This was an evening of merriment and people certainly got merry."

Thomas wasn't deterred. "Then I guess we'll fill the car." He shined the flashlight on the steps so that we could see where we were going.

"Actually, we only need the white wine bottles," I said, following them up the steps onto the deck. The serving dishes, linens, and tables had all been put away. The deck now felt spacious.

"Let's get to it." Thomas held the door open for me. He repeated instructions for the three staff members on kitchen cleanup to step away from their tasks. "Jules, do you have gloves? If not, I have some in the car. I don't want either of you to touch anything without gloves on."

I walked to the far cabinet to get a box of gloves. Thomas directed Lance and me to sort through the boxes of empty wine bottles waiting to be recycled. Then he examined the dirty glasses sitting next to the sink.

"I never pegged you as a Dumpster diver, darling." Lance tried to keep the mood light as we shuffled through the wine bottles.

"And I never thought I would be looking for a poisoned bottle at my mom's wedding."

He placed a bottle into the box. "Touché. Touché."

"How did you leave things with Leo?"

"He's meeting me at Torte tomorrow morning with his little legion of minions."

"Do you really think that Megan could be working for him too?"

Lance held a bottle up to the light before putting it in the box. "I thought I saw something on the lip of the bottle but it's just a crack. I'm not sure, but when she's released tomorrow I'm going to have a chat with her.

Something isn't right. I can't put my finger on what exactly, but I feel it in my theater bones."

"Your theater bones?"

"Darling, it's late. We're sorting trash. My father has died and you were almost poisoned. Cut me some slack. Yes, I'm a master at crafting cunning one-liners, but I can't always be at my best."

I tried to think of a funny retort, but I felt the same. The kitchen had been cleaned and Chef Garrison's staff had boxed up the leftovers. Garlands and vases were piled on one of the tables. Twinkle lights and paper lanterns had been taken down. Napkins and linens sat in baskets, awaiting a trip to the dry cleaner. A few hours ago, this space was alive with food and flavor. Now it smelled like bleach. I knew that feeling nostalgic after a wedding was normal, but what had happened to Megan added a layer of bleakness to the already strange mood.

Once we had sorted the bottles and taken them to Thomas's car, we waited for further instructions. Carlos and Ramiro must have finished being questioned by Detective Kerry because they came inside. Ramiro looked shaken.

"Julieta, what is this about?" Carlos didn't waste any time. He marched over to us and put his hands on his hips. "This is not right. Why are the police asking so many questions? Where have you been? I have been looking for you for at least one hour. Were you with the police? I don't understand."

I started to respond, but Lance held out a hand to stop me. He curled his index finger, motioning Carlos and Ramiro closer. "There's been a *poisoning*." He emphasized the word "poison."

"Someone slipped poison into the wine."

Carlos reached for one of the bottles.

"Uh, uh, uh." Lance swatted his hand away. "Don't touch. The evidence the police need might be in one of these bottles."

"I do not understand," Carlos repeated, looking to me. "Who would do such a thing?"

"We don't know," I replied, internally willing Lance not to say anything about the fact that the poison might have been intended for me.

"The woman earlier." Carlos tapped a finger to his temple. "This is why the ambulance came. She drank the poison."

"Just a little," I assured him. "She's going to be okay."

"Julieta, why did you not say anything?" Carlos looked injured.

"I . . ." I couldn't think of what to say. I felt terrible watching Carlos stare at me with a pained expression on his face. I was also acutely aware of Ramiro's presence. I didn't want him to worry.

Lance rescued me. "The police asked us not to say anything. Well, more like told us that we weren't allowed to say anything. Don't be upset with Juliet. They asked us to come to the hospital to speak with the victim. Juliet poured the wine and was right there when it happened, so they needed her official statement." He sounded legitimate. I hoped that Carlos would buy his story.

"This is terrible. Terrible. Why would someone bring poison to a wedding? This makes no sense." Carlos paced from one side of the room to the other.

He was right. I still couldn't fathom what had happened. The only thing I kept coming back to was that there had to be a connection between Lance's investigation into Leo and the Brown Family Group and Megan's poisoning. The wine couldn't have been meant for me, could it? It was too much of a coincidence that the PI Lance had hired was the person who drank the tainted wine.

Detective Kerry came inside. She walked over and whispered something in Thomas's ear. They both scanned the kitchen. What were they looking for?

I glanced out the windows. The outside lights flooded the deck. Someone moved in the shadows near the railing. I squinted to get a better look. It was Adam.

"Hey!" I waved Thomas over. "See that guy out there?"

Thomas and Detective Kerry both turned in the direction I was pointing.

"Have you talked to him?"

Detective Kerry flipped through her spiral notebook. "That's Adam Tucker. He works for the temp agency you used to hire for tonight's event."

"I know. Did you talk to him?"

She pursed her lips. "This is not my first rodeo. Of course I spoke with him."

"No, that's not what I meant." Why did I always manage to irritate her? "I saw him and Megan fighting behind the speakers in the barn."

"They were?" Thomas asked.

"Yeah." I nodded. "I don't know what they were arguing about, but Megan was obviously angry. I got the sense she didn't want him here."

Detective Kerry jotted something down in her notebook.

"I saw him at Torte too."

Carlos, who was still pacing around the kitchen, caught my eye and shot me a look of concern.

Lance chimed in. "Yes, yes. Juliet is right. He's quite shady. Lurking around the plaza. Hiding behind bushes and trees. I'm sure he's been following me."

"Care to expand?" She rested the tip of her pen on the paper and waited for us to say more.

"He's been everywhere," Lance replied. "At the theater. At Torte, like Jules mentioned. Everywhere."

"I remember him because he was wearing biker gear. He stood out. He was dressed from head to toe in black leather. He hung out at the espresso bar for a while, but didn't interact with anyone. Megan was there at the same time. She was meeting with Clarissa. At the time, I thought it was weird because he was definitely watching her. The minute she left, he followed her."

"Are you sure, Jules?" Thomas asked.

"Positive." I nodded.

Carlos had removed a napkin from one of the baskets and was twisting it into a tight spiral. "I do not like the sound of this. This is not good. A stranger following Lance and Julieta around town."

Thomas gave him a solid thumbs-up. "I agree. Sounds like we better talk to him again," he said to Detective Kerry.

"Already on my way." Kerry's heels clicked on the floor.

"Do you think he tried to kill Megan?" Lance asked, after they were out of earshot.

I shrugged. "I'm not sure, but when I saw him here I tried to ask him about coming to Torte. He claimed that Chef Garrison told him to come check out the bake-shop."

"Maybe he disappeared after he put this poison in the wine," Carlos added.

Lance patted his shoulder. "That's the spirit. Yes, exactly what your delightful husband said."

"But why would he come back?" I thought aloud.

Ramiro scuffed his shoes on the floor. I felt terrible for involving him in this. "That could be his disguise. Is that the right word?"

"Disguise for what?" Carlos asked.

"I saw it in a movie once. I do not think 'disguise' is the word I am looking for, but in the movie the criminal pretended to be a worker to—how do you say it? Blend in?"

"Sí, sí!" Carlos clapped him on the back. "To blend in. Yes, this is a good theory."

"It's not a bad idea," Lance agreed. "Let's imagine that Adam, our mystery man, knows Megan. She's a PI, so perhaps she's been tracking him. Maybe he's wanted for something else. But he's one step ahead of her. He knows that she's working a case here in Ashland and he gets hired as a temporary worker to follow her. He had access to the kitchen, right?"

"Right." I nodded.

"So, he easily could have been in and out throughout the night," Lance continued. He was gaining steam as he worked out his theory. "It was dark. People were drinking. He could have snuck up behind Megan and dropped something into her drink. Then he vanished.

Maybe he took shelter in the grapevines for a while. He waited until the police and everyone left and returned to his position. If you think about it, it might have raised more concern if he didn't finish his shift. I'm assuming that Chef Garrison makes his employees check in and out?"

"Probably." I could check with him in the morning.

"Right. So once he knew that the coast was clear he blended back in with the rest of the cleanup crew and no one would be the wiser. If it hadn't been for our astute Juliet, he would have grabbed his paycheck and been out of here."

Lance's idea had some merit. I wondered if Adam was even his real name. Maybe he had used a fake name to get the position. It was late and Thomas and Detective Kerry had told us we could leave. I wasn't sure why Adam and Megan had been fighting, but I knew one thing: in the morning, I was going to box up a care package of pastries and go back to the hospital to see what I could find out.

Chapter Fifteen

I wasn't sure what to do with myself when I woke the next morning. Usually, in times of stress I immerse myself in baking. I've found that my problems fade away, or at least are put in perspective, when I'm up to my elbows in bread dough. But baking would have to wait. Unless Roger and his team had pulled off a miracle yesterday, the bakeshop would still be in the throes of construction. If I couldn't bake, at least I could see how much progress they had made.

I pulled on a pair of capris, an ivory V-neck, and my tennis shoes. Then I twisted my hair into a long braid, and snuck past Carlos and Ramiro. Sunday mornings were usually quiet on the plaza and today was no different. I didn't pass another soul on my short walk to Torte. The plaza felt different today. It was as if Ashland knew that two of her most beloved residents were missing. Mom and the Professor were probably flying somewhere over the North Atlantic. They had promised they would text when they landed. The flight from Portland to Greece was almost fifteen hours, so I didn't expect to hear from them for a while.

The sign on Torte's front door read: CLOSED FOR RE-MODELING. COME SEE US FOR A COFFEE AND A SELEC-TION OF SUMMER TARTS WHEN WE REOPEN ON MONDAY.

I hoped that Roger hadn't oversold how quickly they could get the new kitchen set up. Every day that we were closed was a day of lost revenue. I realized that I was holding my breath when I unlocked the door and stepped inside.

The dining room tables and chairs had been stacked against the window booths. Thick opaque plastic barricaded the coffee bar and kitchen from the front. I assumed that the crew had taped the plastic in place in an attempt to contain the dust. Even with the effort a thin layer of dust covered the floor. My tennis shoes left imprints in the residue as I walked toward the back. We were going to have to give Torte a full wipe-down once construction was finished.

In order to get a peek at the demoed kitchen I had to lift the edge of the plastic to sneak underneath it. What greeted me on the other side was a happy surprise. The ovens and the big equipment were gone. Where cupboards had hung from the walls there was blank space. The island that had resided in the middle of the room had been disassembled. Roger had asked us whether we wanted to sell it or try it in the new space. After much debate, we opted to hold on to it for a while. Mom proposed salvaging it and using it to store plastic lids, stir spoons, napkins, cream and sugar, and the other coffee supplies. It had been the first piece of furniture that she and my dad had purchased for Torte, and held sentimental value. I liked the idea of repurposing it.

The kitchen felt huge. I couldn't believe how much

space we were going to have to work with. Some of the square footage would be taken away with the new set of stairs that would be put in, but we would easily double the size of the current pastry case and espresso bar. I had a feeling that Andy was going to freak out when he saw what would soon be his new digs. Not that I could blame him. My worries were unfounded. Roger had come through on his promise. Now I had to go see the basement.

I ducked back under the plastic and headed outside. The basement steps had seen use. Dusty footprints led the way below. I unlocked the door and went inside. Where was the light switch? I was going to have to familiarize myself with the layout. Darkness surrounded me as I fumbled along the wall, feeling for the switch. My fingers finally slid over the plastic cover, and I flipped on the lights.

The first part of the basement looked untouched. I walked down the short hallway that opened in front of the wood-burning stove and moved into the kitchen. There the ovens, dishwasher, industrial mixers, and other equipment had been placed in their new home. Instead of a stationary island like the one upstairs, we had opted for two rolling stainless steel workstations with white quartz countertops. The wheels on both stations could be locked down so that if one of us was piping royal icing onto sugar cookies or doing delicate design work we didn't have to worry about the cart moving. When we had a big project, though, we could move the carts anywhere in the kitchen for extra space.

From the looks of it, Roger and his crew might be done with phase one of the renovation. Fingers crossed.

If they were finished, maybe Carlos and I could take the kitchen for a test run later. The thought of baking by his side made my heart flutter.

I ran my hand along the cold, gleaming countertop. We had done it. A few months ago, the task had felt insurmountable. Now we were almost to the finish line. I couldn't believe it. An equal mix of excitement and trepidation ran through me. Change would bring new energy and infuse life into Torte, but it also meant that our small team and easy rhythm would be shaken up. I just hoped I hadn't made a mistake.

Focus, Jules, I told myself, walking toward the ovens. I was about to turn on the oven to see if it was working when I heard footsteps upstairs.

I froze.

Were those footsteps?

Sure enough, thudding steps reverberated above.

Someone was inside Torte.

Had I locked the door when I left?

A crash sounded, like something had been knocked over. Who was up there? And what were they doing?

Without thinking I sprinted for the door, I took the steps two at a time and burst into Torte.

"Who's here?" I yelled. Then a sinking feeling hit my stomach. It might not have been the wisest idea to confront whoever was in the bakeshop on my own. I probably should have called Thomas or at least given this more thought. Could this be connected to what happened last night? Or was it simply a prowler taking advantage of seeing an open door?

Another crash sounded. It came from the kitchen.

I stood in the doorway and considered my options.

The plaza was lifeless. The only sound outside was the gentle flow of the Lithia bubblers. I glanced in both directions, but there wasn't so much as a slight breeze. Even the travelers who often busked near the information kiosk hadn't yet risen.

If I confronted whoever was in the kitchen alone I ran the risk of them harming me and no one knowing. At least not for the next couple of hours. If I went to get help, they could get away.

"Jules? Is that you?" a man's voice called.

My teeth unclenched. Okay, whoever was in here knew me. That was a good sign, right?

The flap of plastic flipped up and Roger stepped from the kitchen into the dining room. He was dressed in a pair of expensive khakis, hiking boots, and a long-sleeved shirt with a puffy vest over it.

"Roger, whew. It's you. You scared me." I moved away from the door.

"Sorry. I didn't mean to startle you. I didn't think anyone would be here this early." He held the plastic up and Clarissa appeared from the other side. "We were off for our Sunday-morning walk. We always take a long stroll through the park before church, and I wanted to stop in and see how much farther the construction crew got yesterday. I had to leave for the wedding. When I left they were in the process of tearing down the cabinets. It looks like they got that done."

I exhaled. My nerves must be frayed. Why had I jumped to the conclusion that there was an intruder at Torte? Then again it was early. Not as early as my normal baking hours, but church wouldn't start for at least another hour or two. Could Roger be lying?

"I know. I'm impressed," I replied. "I was just downstairs and it looks like everything is already hooked up and running."

Clarissa stood next to her husband's side. She wore a strappy summer dress, covered by a knee-length jacket and tennis shoes. I guessed that her church shoes were in the handbag on her arm.

"That was the plan. You should be able to fire up the ovens this morning," Roger said.

"Great." I wondered if they were picking up on my unease.

Roger looked to Clarissa. "Well, we won't keep you. I'll return after church. The crew should be here by about nine to keep working on demo. We'll move the island to storage until we're ready for it. I'm having the guys take the cabinets and hardware to the ReStore store up in Medford. Once we get everything moved out they will take out the walk-in fridge and then we should be ready to cut through below and start building the staircase."

"Wow. I'm so impressed by how quickly everything has come together." I turned to Clarissa. "Your husband is a miracle worker."

She gave me a curt nod. "So I've heard."

They started toward the front door.

"Hey, before you go. I wanted to ask you about last night," I said to Clarissa.

"What an event," Roger said with enthusiasm. "I can't remember the last time we danced like that, can you, Clarissa?"

Clarissa shook her head.

I didn't remember them dancing. That must have been after I left. "I think it turned out well," I agreed.

"But I wanted to ask you about the wine. Remember when I brought out glasses for you and Lance and Megan?"

"Yes, what about it?" Clarissa snapped. She adjusted her purse strap.

"The police think that Megan's wine was spiked with poison," I said, paying careful attention to Clarissa's re-action. "They've sent the bottles to the lab in Medford to be tested. We'll know for sure later, but they were ask-ing me and Lance about it last night. Neither Lance nor I drank the wine. You were the only other person who could have drunk from the same bottle. Did you drink your glass?"

Clarissa looked surprised. "Yes. I drank the entire glass."

"And you didn't have a reaction? You didn't get sick or anything?"

She shook her head. "Not in the slightest. I feel won-derful."

Roger stared at his wife. "The wine you drank might have been poisoned? What are you two talking about? I missed all of this."

I explained what had happened. How had Roger missed the ambulance?

Clarissa reached into her handbag and removed a tube of pale pink lipstick. She applied it to her lips as she spoke. "That is simply terrible, but if Megan's drink was spiked it must not have been the entire bottle of wine because I'm fine."

"That's good. I'm very glad to hear that you didn't experience any ill effects." I changed the subject. "I didn't know that the Brown Group was going to donate a very generous sum to the arts council."

Roger snapped his head around. "What?"

"It's nothing. I floated an idea out there to Sarah, who apparently holds the purse strings for the company." She made a dismissive motion with her hand. "Who knows if anything will come of it."

"But—" Roger didn't finish his train of thought, because Clarissa placed her lipstick back in her purse and tapped her narrow wrist.

"Sorry, we must be off."

They left for their morning walk. I was stumped. We had been so sure last night that the poison had been in the bottle. The fact that Clarissa drank her entire glass of wine changed everything. That meant that whoever poisoned the wine had to have been close by. Did that mean it was more likely that Adam was the culprit? Could he have snuck up behind Megan while we were talking? The waitstaff was circulating throughout the night. It was certainly possible. But wouldn't Megan have noticed?

I sighed. The good news was that if the poison had been in her glass that meant that I probably hadn't been the target. That was a slight relief. I guess I would have to wait and see what Thomas learned from the lab. In the meantime, I was going back downstairs to get my hands sticky and christen the new kitchen.

Chapter Sixteen

This time I locked Torte's front door and secured the basement. I felt an eager sense of anticipation as I punched in the temp and watched the oven turn bright orange. Of course, finding baking supplies was going to be challenging. I walked over to the new built-in fridge. The team had transferred our cold and frozen items into the fridge. I gathered berries, buttermilk, eggs, and butter. I creamed butter and sugar together until it was smooth and yellow. Then I mixed in buttermilk. Substituting regular milk with buttermilk or sour cream is one of my favorite chef tips. Tangy buttermilk or sour cream deepens the flavor profile of traditional cake batter and gives it a subtle tanginess.

It was surprising how quickly I fell into a rhythm in my new "mixing zone." Since Mom and I had provided input in the design, the kitchen's flow was intuitive. Once we had unpacked and organized our supplies from upstairs, I could tell that the new space was going to streamline our production.

Roger had suggested baking zones based on our feedback. There was a designated rolling zone with extra-wide countertops for pie crust, cookie dough, and fondant. A mixing zone with neat rows of our mixers. A decorating zone offered additional lighting and pull-out drawers to store our tools for sugar art and piping. Lastly, next to the wood-burning oven there was the warming zone with huge rolling carts where loaves of our home-made bread could rise while awaiting their turn in the oven.

If only Mom could be here to help me christen the new kitchen, I thought, shifting the mixer to low as I cracked in eggs. The batter whipped into a lovely golden color. After incorporating flour, baking soda, salt, and a touch of cinnamon, I folded in the berries by hand, careful not to damage the delicate purple, juicy beauties. Once I had spread the batter into a greased pan, I got to work on the crumble for the top of the coffee cake. I forked butter, brown sugar, oats, cinnamon, nutmeg, and allspice together and sprinkled it generously over the top. Then I slid my coffee cake into the oven.

With the coffee cake baking, I dug our French press out of one of the boxes and started a tea kettle boiling. I found a stash of our espresso beans and ground them. The smell was intoxicating. We sourced our beans from a local roaster. The heady coffee scent quickly filled the kitchen.

While I waited for the water to boil, I began unpacking boxes of spices—cardamom, chili powder, and curry. I smiled to myself as I realized that Andy had packed the spice boxes alphabetically. His technique would make unpacking a breeze. We typically stored spices used in our savory baking in one cupboard and spices for sweet baking in another. That way we didn't run the risk of cumin or crushed red pepper flakes accidentally mixing into our sweet bread.

The teakettle let out a shrill whistle. I jumped and nearly shattered a jar of whole vanilla beans. French press is one of my favorite leisurely morning treats. The process is simple but requires patience. The key to brewing a full-bodied cup of French press is the amount of contact the grinds have with the water. No one wants a bitter, grainy cup of coffee. Typically, the end result of a perfectly brewed French press is deeper, stronger, and in my opinion more delicious coffee. Andy had taught me to skim the grounds at the top of the press before plunging it. This assures that none of the fine particles will end up in the bottom of your cup. I poured half of the hot water evenly over the grounds and waited for it to "bloom." This is the process of the coffee oils mixing with the water. A crust of grounds began to form. I stirred them thoroughly and then added the rest of the water. Then I let the grounds sit for five minutes before plunging them.

The aroma was incredible. It was almost impossible to wait, but I knew that it would be worth it. When five minutes hit, I slowly pressed the plunger down, poured myself a cup and savored it. The dark roast was perfectly balanced with a bright nutty finish. I circled the kitchen to survey my work and map out what to do next. The cupboards had modern sliding racks that would allow for easy access. I organized savory spices in the cabinets next to the stove and spices we used most often in baking, like cinnamon and nutmeg, in the cupboards near the mixing zone.

I wanted Steph and Bethany's help in organizing the decorating zone. Roger's crew had labeled every box from upstairs and placed it in its zone. Yet another touch of his professionalism. No detail had been spared. Assuming the next phase of renovations continued as smoothly, I would definitely be writing Roger a glowing letter of recommendation.

The scent of my berry coffee cake made my mouth water. I tossed three empty spice boxes on the floor and went to check on it. It had baked to a bubbling brown color with purple berries bursting to the surface and creating a gorgeous crisp. I removed it from the oven. The smell was so heavenly that it was hard to resist cutting myself a taste. I set it on the counter to cool and unpacked the last four spice boxes.

A knock on the basement door startled me. After my earlier run-in with Roger and Clarissa I was on edge. Fortunately, I heard Lance's singsong voice calling, "Juliet, open up!"

I walked over to let him in. "Lance, this is getting to be a habit," I said, opening the door.

"What, darling?" He glanced behind him up the stairwell before coming inside.

"You. Up this early. What happened to your beauty sleep? Didn't you once tell me that you never wake before you've had eight hours of contented rest?"

He waved me off with an exasperated sigh. "Yes, but not when we're on a case."

"On a case?" I raised an eyebrow.

"What is that smell?" He brushed past me and made a beeline for the kitchen.

I followed after him. "French press coffee and triple

berry coffee cake. It should be cool. Do you want a slice? Have you had coffee yet?"

"Is that even a question?" He leaned against the island. He was wearing a pair of tailored black shorts, black loafers, and a polo shirt. If I didn't know better I would think he was about to go boating.

"The question is, can I find plates and utensils?"

Lance helped me search for the boxes labeled "flat-ware." Once we found them, I cut us each a slice of the coffee cake and poured Lance a cup of French press.

"Okay, so let's get serious," Lance said, stabbing his fork into his coffee cake. "We have two orders of business this morning. First, we have to go see if we can get Megan alone. Second, I want you to be there when I meet with Leo and his delinquents."

"Delinquents?"

"You know what I mean. That shady, albeit well-dressed lawyer, Jarvis, and our tacky little assistant, Sarah." Lance stared at me over the rim of his coffee mug.

I wasn't sure that I would describe either Jarvis or Sarah as delinquents.

"Fine," Lance said. "I can tell by your signature stare that 'delinquents' is the wrong choice of word. You know what I'm getting at, darling. Something is amiss with my father's death and you and I are going to get to the bottom of it."

I wanted to help Lance, but I looked at the piles of boxes. There was much work to be done at Torte and then there was the fact that Carlos and Ramiro were in town and I had promised to take them on a tour of Southern Oregon. I hesitated. "Lance, I want to, but I don't know how much time I'm going to have."

His fork clanged on his plate. "Then there's no time to waste. Make haste, darling. Let's go."

"Right now?"

"Yes, right now." He pointed to the berry coffee cake. "Slice up a hearty piece of that and put it in a box. I do believe that your magical pastry is just what we need to sweet-talk our way in for an early-morning visit."

It was futile to try and argue with Lance, and I had to admit that I was more than curious to talk to Megan. I boxed up a slice of coffee cake and we left together.

The hospital was a short walk from downtown. Lance and I discussed potential theories and I told him that Clarissa had drunk the wine last night.

"How vexing," Lance replied with distaste as we passed a popular breakfast spot with outdoor seating that looked out onto Ashland's golden hills. "That ruins our best theory. When will Thomas have the results back from the lab?"

I shrugged. "I don't know. He said that he was taking the bottles to Medford this morning, but I have no idea how long the process is. There are quite a few bottles to test."

"We should have had him gather the wineglasses too."

"But how? There were hundreds of glasses in circulation last night and the kitchen crew was constantly running the dishwasher."

Lance stopped to pick up a piece of trash on the

sidewalk. "What you're saying is that odds are good we won't know where the poison originated."

"Probably."

We arrived at the hospital. The reception area was empty except for a couple of patients waiting to be seen. Lance swept into the room as if he was about to introduce a new play on the Elizabethan stage. He took the hand of the woman sitting at the reception desk and kissed the back of it. "Good morning, my friend Juliet and I are here to see our dear, dear friend Megan."

The young woman blushed at Lance's dramatic greeting. "What's her last name and room number?"

Lance relayed the information. The receptionist punched something into the computer and then frowned. "I'm sorry, but you can't see her."

I started to move away from the desk. I had figured that we were probably too early for visiting hours. Lance grabbed my wrist. "We understand that it's early, but you see, our dear friend Megan had quite a nasty accident last night. We were here with the police and she begged—absolutely begged—Juliet to bake her something special. She said that a slice of pastry would be the only way she could possibly start to feel better."

He was laying it on thick, and shockingly the receptionist smiled and nodded attentively. "So you see, we absolutely must deliver her this box of healing sweets."

The receptionist tapped her computer screen. "It's not that I won't let you in to see her. I would, but she's not here."

"What?" Lance's voice boomed in the quiet room. A patient with a pack of ice resting on her arm turned in our direction. "What do you mean she's not here? Check again. She must be here. We just saw her last night. Late last night."

The receptionist checked her screen again. She rotated it for us to see. "It says right here that she was discharged and left."

"When?"

"About an hour ago."

"Where did she go?"

The receptionist shrugged. "She left on her own. I have no idea."

Lance snatched the box of coffee cake from my hands and gave it to her. "Megan's loss is your gain. Thank you for your help. Let us offer you this as a token of our appreciation."

She took the box and smiled broadly. "It smells wonderful. Thanks."

With that Lance yanked me outside. "She left?"

I was equally surprised. Megan could barely speak last night and it sounded as if the doctors had intended to keep her until they confirmed what kind of poison she had consumed. "I know. It's weird."

"It's not just weird, darling. It's worrisome." Lance reached into his pocket and removed his phone.

"Who are you calling?"

"Megan." He placed the call, tapping his toe on the pavement repeatedly while waiting for her to pick up. "No answer," he said with his hand over the phone, before leaving a message begging Megan to call him immediately.

"Her office is in Medford, right?" I asked.

He nodded.

"Do you think there's a chance she went there? What

if she has information on whoever tried to poison her? If I were a PI that's the first place I would go. Unless she's feeling terrible, in which case I would go home and go to bed."

Lance stuffed his phone back in his pocket. He linked his arm through mine. "This is why we make a perfect team. I like the way you think. Let's go."

"To Medford?" I asked.

Lance was dragging me down the street. "Yes, of course. We'll stop by my place and get my car. It's only a ten-minute drive."

I wanted to go with him. The fact that Megan had been released from the hospital gave me an uneasy feeling. I looked at my watch. It was still early. Carlos and Ramiro would likely be asleep at least for another hour or so. "Okay, but I need to be back before too long," I said to Lance.

He paid no attention and broke into a sprint. "Yes, yes. I know you don't want to miss out on a minute with that delicious husband of yours. Trust me, I wouldn't want to either. I'll have you back and in his arms in no time."

We ran the rest of the way to Lance's house. By the time we got there I was gasping for breath and dewy with sweat.

"Hop in," Lance said, when we made it to his car.

He sped out of Ashland and onto I-5. Thankfully, the village sat in early slumber. Otherwise, I would have been terrified that he would mow down a pedestrian. "Lance, slow down. We don't have to fly there," I cautioned as he pressed the gas pedal.

"I have a bad feeling about this, Juliet. We need to

get there quickly. In fact, why don't you call that puppy-dog police detective and tell him we're en route to Medford." Lance liked to tease me about Thomas holding a torch for me.

"Do you think that's a good idea? Maybe we should wait until we get to her office and see if she's even there."

Lance kept his eyes glued to the road. "Suit yourself."

It only took eight minutes to get to Megan's office, which was located in a nondescript strip mall on the outskirts of town with a tattoo shop on one side and a bail bond office on the other.

"This is it." Lance jumped out of the car.

"I can't picture you opting to hire Megan in a place like this," I said, stepping over what looked like the remains of a half-eaten hamburger that was teeming with flies.

"She's the best. Sometimes the best doesn't come in a pretty package."

We approached Megan's office. The door was open partway. Lance knocked twice. "Anyone home?"

No answer.

"Megan, it's your favorite client," Lance called.

No response.

He looked to me and then kicked the door open with his foot. We stepped inside. The interior office wasn't much of an improvement from the exterior. I squinted in the dull light reflecting from a 1970s brass light fixture. There was an oversized oak desk, a burnt-orange couch, bookshelves, and dented filing cabinets.

"She's not here," I said to Lance who had walked to the other side of the desk.

His pupils grew huge. "I hate to say it, Juliet, but I told you so." He motioned for me to come closer.

I had a bad feeling as I moved closer to the desk.

Lance pointed to the floor where Megan's body was sprawled on the green shag carpet. He tried not to gag. "Call the police."

Chapter Seventeen

I blinked rapidly. Was this really happening? Megan was definitely dead. Her face was a garish blue. Had she succumbed to the effects of the poison she consumed last night or had the killer followed her here? The thought made my knees weak. I grabbed the edge of the desk to steady myself.

Lance stepped around her body and walked back to the desk. He wrapped a silk handkerchief around his hand, removed a pencil from a canister on the desk, and used it to flip through a stack of files.

"What are you doing?" I hissed.

"Looking for evidence. This is our only chance before the police come."

"Are you crazy? You can't touch anything." I scanned the office. It hadn't been updated since the 1970s. Dark, fake-wood paneling covered every wall. Thick vomit-green shag carpet lined the floor. There were bookshelves stuffed with dusty paperback true-crime novels and private-investigation manuals. A cheap cabinet housed binoculars, walkie-talkies, and camera equipment.

He held the pencil with the tips of his fingers. "Why do you think I wrapped this?"

"That's not what I mean, Lance. We shouldn't touch anything. This is a crime scene." Megan's desk was tidy, minus a stack of old takeout containers and plastic silverware.

"And I am a client. Megan might have damning evidence in this stack of paperwork. This is our one chance," he repeated, and continued to look through the stack. After a minute, he stopped and used the handkerchief to remove one of the files from the stack. "Aha!"

"What?"

Lance motioned me over. "Get your phone."

The sound of sirens wailed in the distance. I wavered.

"Hurry, we don't have much time."

I intentionally kept my eyes focused on Lance as I made my way past Megan's body. I couldn't believe she was dead. There was a faint hint of stale cigarettes in the dingy office. I wondered if Megan had been a smoker or if the fake-wood paneling had absorbed years of smoke.

Lance lifted the edge of the file folder with the handkerchief. "Look, these are Megan's notes on Leo and his henchman lawyer, Jarvis. Get your phone. Take a few pictures—quick. We can look at them later."

For some reason, I followed Lance's demands and snapped pictures. Within minutes the sirens were right outside the door. Lance shoved the folder back in the stack and we both returned to the door.

Everything was a blur from that point on. The Medford police and EMS workers attended to Megan's body. Lance and I hung around outside until Thomas arrived on the scene. He was accompanied by Detective Kerry who was not pleased to see us.

"You two, again?" She shook her head in disbelief. "Do you have a police scanner or something?" Her narrow heels dug into the shag carpet.

Lance stepped forward. His shoulders arched with pride. "Actually, Juliet and I discovered the body. You should be thanking us."

"Thanking you?" She looked to Thomas for support.

Thomas shrugged. "I'll take care of them if you want to check in with the Medford first responders."

"Look, I get that Ashland is a small town. I'm learning that about the police force." She and Thomas shared a look. He nodded.

Kerry continued. "We work in conjunction with one another. In fact, we sent a team of our guys to Talent last night to help with a domestic situation. We all play nice, but this is out of hand. You're on the scene of a homicide in Medford. This is not our jurisdiction. Our friends in Medford aren't going to share details of the case if we have civilians disturbing the crime scene." Detective Kerry swept her auburn hair into a bun, and gave us a hard stare. Then she walked over to the lead Medford detective.

"She's right. You know? You guys are going to end up in trouble if you keep pulling stunts like this," Thomas said once Detective Kerry was far enough away.

"Stunts?" Lance sounded injured. "Thomas, how can you say such a thing? Juliet and I were concerned about Megan. We went to the hospital to deliver her a delectable box of Jules's pastry earlier and learned that she had vanished."

I almost interjected that she hadn't exactly vanished. The receptionist had told us that she had been discharged.

Lance was undeterred. "We knew immediately that something must have been wrong. This must have some connection to my father's murder. You can't blame us. We're trying to help, and I'm not exactly of sound mind and body at the moment."

Thomas tapped the badge pinned to his chest. "And you didn't consider calling me beforehand?"

"There was simply no time. We were already en route." He nodded to me to back him up.

I tried to smile, but I felt terrible. Thomas and Detective Kerry were right. Lance had swept me into his drama once again. I didn't want to do anything that might jeopardize the police investigation.

"In any event," Lance continued with a flick of his wrist. "When we arrived here at Megan's we found her in this horrific state." He paused and shielded his eyes. In any other circumstance, I would have figured that he was being intentionally dramatic, but I knew that finding Megan had shaken him too, despite his outward appearance. "We called the police immediately and have stood guard ever since."

Except for when we rifled through her files, I thought to myself.

Thomas noted something on his iPad. "Look, you guys should head back to Ashland. Thanks for calling me, but you need to get out of here. I'll try to fill you in later if I can." With that he turned and headed inside Megan's office.

Lance and I returned to his car. "You know what this

means, don't you?" he asked as he steered toward Ashland.

"No. What?"

"Whoever spiked Megan's drink last night must have intended the poison for her. When they failed they returned to finish the job. Which means we don't have to lose any sleep over worrying that a killer is after you, darling."

He had a good point. A sense of relief flooded my body, followed closely by a wave of guilt. I felt terrible for Megan.

"And, we now have potential evidence in your phone. Open up the pictures you took and let's see what Megan found out about that villainous brother of mine."

I tugged my phone from my pocket and began scrolling through the photos. I had to zoom in to read Megan's notes. Every page had been typed with official dates and times. She had been a meticulous note keeper. I wondered if that came with the job. She was probably used to recording every detail when providing surveillance for her clients. Reading through her notes made me feel even worse. She didn't deserve to die.

"Well, darling, don't be stingy. What does it say?"

"I'm looking," I said. "Megan was tailing Leo and Jarvis." She had broken down her notes into four sections: subjective, objective, assessment, and plan. In the margin on a few of the pages she had jotted down things to follow up with. Most of the pages were straightforward. It looked as if she had pulled financial records of the Brown Family Group, interviewed employees, and spent over ten hours following Leo. There were notes about his movements each day and photos of him interacting with a variety of people I didn't recognize. When I got to the last page, there was a small note in the margin that read: "Assessment—Jarvis. Disbarred in Nevada. Pull state records."

I must have gasped because Lance veered off the highway. The warning strips rumbled under our tires.

"Sorry," Lance said, twisting the wheel to steer us back into the center of the lane. "But you can't gasp while I'm driving sixty miles an hour."

"Did I gasp?"

"Yes," Lance snapped. "Stop stalling. What did you read that made you suck in air like that?"

"It could be nothing," I replied, flipping back to the page. "Megan made a note that Jarvis had been disbarred in Nevada. It looks like she was planning to pull the records."

"Or maybe she already did."

"What do you mean?"

"I mean, darling, what if she dug into his shady past, discovered that he'd been disbarred, and he found out? That would be motive for murder. I told you there was a connection with my father's death."

"Yeah, but he wasn't anywhere near Megan when she drank the wine last night. Leo dragged him away, remember?"

"How do we know that? There were over three hundred people milling around. It's completely possible that Jarvis—or anyone for that matter—could have snuck close by us, spiked Megan's wine, and then slunk away without anyone being the wiser."

He had a point. It wasn't as if we had had tight security at the reception. That was the opposite of Mom and the Professor's goal of having an open and welcoming party where everyone in town had been invited.

"Think about it. Jarvis could be our killer." Lance's voice became more animated as he began to string a theory together. "I asked Megan to look into my family's holdings. She learned that things aren't on the up and up with Jarvis. Maybe she had tangible proof that he killed my father. He figured that out and realized that he had to get his hands on Megan's evidence. Maybe he's not even certified to practice law here in Oregon. That would ruin him, right?"

I nodded.

"Let's say he snuck over to where we were chatting and slipped the poison into Megan's drink. Maybe he waited around for a while. He probably saw the paramedics arrive and realized that he hadn't administered a lethal dose so he went to the hospital to finish the job. When he arrived at the hospital, Megan's room was surrounded by cops. He knew it wasn't worth the risk so he took off and waited for her at her office. When she was released he delivered the final blow."

As much as I hated to admit it, Lance's theory was plausible.

"You had better get on the phone with Thomas," Lance urged. "Jarvis could be making his getaway as we speak."

"But Lance, we don't have any evidence, or anything connecting Jarvis to either crime."

Lance kept one hand on the steering wheel. The other made a tsking motion in the air. "Details, darling. Details. That's what the police are for."

"Exactly." I stared out the window as Lance took the

turn to Ashland. Then I texted Thomas the pictures I had taken of Megan's files. I knew he wouldn't be happy with us snooping. Odds were good that Thomas and Detective Kerry would find the file anyway, but I didn't want to withhold anything from him.

In the distance, sunlight brushed the forested hillside of Grizzly Peak. Sturdy evergreens stretched out as far as my eye could see. As always, I was struck by Ashland's beauty, while at the same time distraught over Megan's death. We didn't know enough yet to conclude whether Jarvis's being disbarred had any connection to the case. However, what I did know was that we had a new suspect in the case—a murder case.

Chapter Eighteen

Lance dropped me at Torte. I wondered if Carlos and Ramiro were up and stirring yet. Sunday morning had brought slow risers out to Torte's plaza. The first signs of life emerged in the form of couples strolling hand in hand drinking iced coffees on their way to brunch.

I wasn't sure what to do next. Should I dive back into organization or was there anything else I could do with the case? I was about to make my way downstairs when I noticed two men talking near the entrance to the Calle Guanajuato, a cobblestone path that paralleled Ashland Creek. Every weekend from April through November the creekside path hosts the Lithia Artisans Market. Photographers, jewelry makers, and potters were setting up open-air tents to display their wares. The market is a popular spot for tourists to purchase one-of-a-kind keepsakes.

Was it my imagination, or was that Jarvis and Adam? What could the two of them be doing together? Yet another coincidence. The story of my life as of late.

The two men walked with purpose past the vendor

tents and crossed a footbridge. Then they disappeared into a wooded area on the opposite side of the creek.

Without thinking, I raced after them. When I made it to the footbridge, I spotted them arguing next to a metal sculpture. If they turned around they would see me right away. I was too exposed out in the open, so I ducked behind an empty vendor tent. From my vantage point I couldn't make out either of their faces. One man was dressed in black leather. He looked to be about the same build as Adam. The other wore a suit and held a briefcase. I had to get closer.

I stayed low and made my way toward the far end of the pathway where the creek flowed beneath the foot-bridge. The problem was going to be how to get within earshot without either of them noticing me. I decided my best bet was to approach them from the opposite side of the creek. I crouched as I crossed the sidewalk over the bridge onto the other side. Then I darted between giant sequoia trees until I was directly across from them. The trail was densely packed with pine needles and dry leaves. I could hear a group of travelers strumming on guitars and bongos somewhere nearby. The sound of their music drifted up from Ashland Creek.

Upon closer inspection, I saw that it was definitely Jarvis and Adam, but I couldn't hear a word. The rush-ing creek below, swollen with snowmelt from the Sis-kiyou Mountains, provided a sound barrier. I cupped my hand over my right ear to try to amplify the sound. It didn't work. Whatever Jarvis and Adam were discuss-ing looked serious.

Should I call Thomas? Would they hear me? Thomas and Detective Kerry had been looking for Adam since last night. I wondered if they'd had a chance to speak with him. He certainly wasn't trying to blend in in his biker gear. Jarvis thrust a manila envelope into Adam's hands and walked away.

What was going on? My heart thumped with nervous excitement. Whatever the two of them had been discussing and whatever Jarvis had just handed Adam must have a connection to Megan. She was their only commonality as far as I knew.

Adam ripped open the envelope. He scanned the paperwork. Then he ripped the papers to shreds, stuffed them in a nearby garbage can, and stomped off in the opposite direction. Without thinking, I sprinted back to the other side of the creek. I had to get the paperwork.

I yanked the lid off the garbage can and plugged my nose. This is what it's come to, Jules? I thought as I removed the shredded strips of paper. I glanced around to make sure no one was watching and then shoved the lid back on top of the can and hurried to the bakeshop.

I called Thomas before doing anything else. In the past, I'd made some mistakes trying to take on criminals on my own, and I had learned from those experiences.

"Thomas, come to Torte as soon as you can. I think I have something that might be important to the case." I left the message on his voicemail.

Taking the torn papers to one of the front booths, I left them on the dusty table and went to find some tape. I locked the door on my way to the office. Again, there was no harm in being overly cautious. After all there was a killer on the loose.

Once I found tape, I began trying to piece the papers back together. It took longer than I thought it might.

Adam had ripped each page in quarters and then in two-inch strips. Once I figured out the pattern, I followed the tear lines and began to puzzle everything together.

The result was a crumpled tape-covered mess, but I could easily read the document. What Jarvis had handed Adam was a restraining order. The order, signed by a judge in Medford, banned Adam from having any interactions with Megan. He wasn't allowed within two hundred feet of her. I read through the rest of the terms, including the fine and potential punishment of jailtime should Adam violate the order. Sadly, Megan wouldn't have to worry about that any longer.

Adam must have killed her. He had been on-site last night and had the opportunity to spike her drink. The fact that she had taken out a restraining order against him would likely give the police the motive they needed to arrest him.

I stared at the mangled paper. Poor Megan. Why had she needed to take out a restraining order against him? How had they known each other? I thought back to our first meeting right here at Torte. Megan had seemed jumpy when she'd spotted Adam hanging around the coffee bar. I felt terrible. I should have noticed. I should have taken action. She might still be here now.

A soft knock shook me from my thoughts.

Thomas stood outside Torte's front windows accompanied by Detective Kerry. I went to let them in.

"Whoa, the place looks different." Thomas held the door open for Detective Kerry. "What's behind the plastic?"

"Demo." I ran my finger along the pastry case, creating a trail in the dust. "The plastic is supposed to contain the dust."

To my surprise Detective Kerry gave me a sympathetic nod. "My dad worked in construction. I assure you this is really clean compared to some of the job sites I've seen."

"Thanks for the reassurance. That's good to hear." I directed them to the booth. "I think you guys are going to want to see what I found."

I intentionally handed the ripped restraining order to Detective Kerry.

Her face was passive as she read the document. "We're going to need you to explain how you came to be in possession of this. This could be a crucial piece of evidence for the DA's case if it turns out Jarvis is guilty."

I explained how I had seen Jarvis and Adam arguing and went to see if I could get a closer listen.

"You were eavesdropping?" Detective Kerry suggested. However, her tone was different than it had been in the past.

"Not exactly."

"And then you were rifling through the garbage?" she said with the faintest smile. "One night of Dumpster diving and suddenly it's a trend."

Thomas took close-up photos of the tattered restraining order with his phone. "See, this could be something we use in the police app. Jules, once we get the app up and running you could shoot me a text with a photo of this. We are trendsetters. We're going to be the first police station in Southern Oregon with an app, and you're a Dumpster-diving trendsetter, Kerry."

"Let's hope not." She folded her arms across her thin torso. "Back to what you witnessed."

"Right." I nodded. "I couldn't hear what they were saying, but I could tell from their body language that neither of them was happy with the other. Then Jarvis handed Adam the manila envelope and he ripped it up. I'm sure I should have called you first and waited, but what if someone walked by with a full cup of coffee? Everything in the garbage can would have been ruined."

Thomas punched a number into his cell. "I'm going to take this outside."

Detective Kerry nodded. "Can you take me to the spot where you found this? We are going to need to search the area."

"Sure, but I didn't see Adam or Jarvis drop anything else."

Her lips shrunk together in a thin line when she frowned. "Thinking that you've recovered evidence and utilizing police procedure to actually collect said evidence are two very different things."

"Got it." I led her to the cobblestone pathway and showed her where I had hidden it, as well as the garbage can where Adam had tossed the restraining order. She motioned for me to give her space and then proceeded to do exactly what I had done. The only thing in the garbage can had been the shredded restraining order. Ashland city maintenance crews swept the streets every morning, long before the tourist crowd began to think about rising. By the time visitors to our fair city were up and taking leisurely strolls through the plaza, the hanging baskets along Main Street had been watered, litter had been picked up, and the sidewalks washed down.

Detective Kerry waved to Thomas who had ended his call. "We're going to need a team to sweep this entire area," she said, pointing from one end of the cobblestone path to the other.

"Is that necessary?" Thomas asked.

"Absolutely." She didn't waffle in her response. "Send a team. You and I need to track down Adam immediately."

Thomas started to say something more, but Detective Kerry cut him off. "Which way did he go?" she asked me.

"That way." I pointed toward the bridge.

"Let's go." She was already halfway to the bridge.

"Thanks, Jules." Thomas shot me a smile. "Good work. You're becoming a real detective. That was quick thinking."

I felt my cheeks warm at the compliment. "Thanks."

"Hurry up!" Detective Kerry called. How she managed to run in three-inch heels and a pencil skirt was a mystery to me.

Thomas winked. "Duty calls." He hiked up his shorts and raced after her.

They sprinted away. I wasn't sure whether relief or guilt would win out. I felt relieved that we knew who had killed Megan, and equally responsible. Why hadn't I paid more attention? She had clearly been afraid for her life, so much so that she had gone to court for help and protection. I should have done more. I should have reached out to her. I could have done something. Isn't that what community is supposed to do? Rally around to support one another during times of crisis. Megan had been without a community and now she was dead.

I sighed and returned to Torte. Megan's death was a glaring reminder of how important our personal connections are. All the more reason to ensure that Torte would always be a safe and welcoming space for anyone who stepped inside our front doors.

I wished that Mom was here. As if on cue my phone buzzed with a text from her, letting me know that they had landed and were on their way to the hotel. A picture came through of her and the Professor posing in front of a Greek statue at the airport. I smiled and tucked my phone in my pocket. At least they were happy and none the wiser about any of the drama that had unfolded since they left.

My mind tried to make sense of what had transpired thus far. Was Adam a past client of Megan's? Or maybe an old boyfriend who couldn't let her go? Both of those possibilities seemed plausible. What didn't make sense was why Megan went to Jarvis for the restraining order. She was investigating him—well, technically, maybe not *him* but the Brown Family Group. Wouldn't it have been a conflict of interest? Maybe that's how desperate she'd been for help. I sighed again. The only comforting thought was that it had to be much less likely that the poison had been intended for me.

Before long Carlos and Ramiro appeared. They had showered and looked fresh and ready to tackle a day of sightseeing. I tried to push thoughts of Megan's death from my head as we loaded into Mom's van. Showing Ramiro my favorite childhood getaway, Lake of the

Woods Resort, a remote alpine lake tucked into the mountains, helped quiet my concerns. Carlos and I had spent an impromptu weekend at the high alpine lake. He had arranged a surprise visit in an attempt to explain why he had kept quiet about Ramiro for so many years. A blizzard had struck, stranding us without power at the remote lodge. I didn't realize it at the time, but that weekend had been a turning point in our relationship. The fact that Carlos had traveled thousands of miles and crossed oceans to find me in Oregon's faraway Cascade Mountains was symbolic of the distance he was willing to go to save our marriage. Being back on the same road reminded me of how far we had come. I caught his eye and smiled. He reached over and gently caressed my hand.

The winding route along dozens of twists and turns up Dead Indian Road gave me a chance to chat with Ramiro. He told us about his school in Spain, his friends, his soccer club, and how much he loved to surf. He even opened up about his mother and the extended family of uncles, aunts, and cousins that he had grown up with. "It is like your family at Torte. We laugh. We fight. We eat. It is always lively. Never boring, right, Papa?"

Carlos tossed him a grin. "Sí, sí."

"You must come visit. They would love to meet you," he said, mimicking Carlos's speech pattern. Their inflection and tone were so similar, I had a feeling that if I was speaking to them on the phone I wouldn't be able to tell the difference between them.

"That would be fun," I said with a smile, cranking the wheel hard to the left as we rounded a corner past the high grasslands dotted with grazing cattle.

"No, no, you must." He tapped Carlos on the shoulder. "Sí, Papa, don't you think she must come see Spain?"

Carlos was less enthused. "She has seen Spain many times on our travels."

"But not *our* Spain," Ramiro insisted.

Carlos nodded. "Sí, this is true."

He didn't chime in as he usually might. I had a feeling this was due to his tentative relationship with Ramiro's mother's family. She had kept Carlos from knowing his son. When she learned that she was pregnant, she left and never told Carlos. It wasn't until years later that she reached out to him to inform him that he had a son. She claimed that it was because her family wouldn't approve. Carlos forgave her because he wanted a relationship with Ramiro. I was proud of him for that, but knew that there was a piece of him who was still uncomfortable around her family. Bringing me into the mix would only complicate things.

I let it go and enjoyed an afternoon at the lake. Ramiro swam out to a dock about a quarter mile from the rocky shore and proceeded to show off his diving abilities. He would wave at Carlos and me to get our attention and then belly flop into the frigid lake or do a perfect backflip off the side. He quickly found a group of boys about his age and ended up in the middle of a raucous water fight.

Carlos and I sat in bright red Adirondack chairs in the shade of a towering evergreen tree. I kicked off my sandals and dug my toes into the warm, pebbly beach. I unpacked a picnic blanket, a bottle of lemonade with candied lemon slices, and generous helpings of my berry coffee cake.

He clinked his plastic glass to mine. "Cheers, Julieta, to a successful wedding. Last night was magnificent."

"Except for the poisoning," I said, suddenly realizing that Carlos didn't know about Megan. I filled him in on Lance's and my excursion to Medford, and explained that Thomas and Detective Kerry were on the hunt for Adam at the moment.

"This is no good, Julieta. You should not have been in the middle of this. It is dangerous." Carlos frowned. He ran a slice of lemon along the rim of his glass. "I do not understand why this always happens. It is not right. You must leave this to the police."

Maybe it was the stress of the wedding, or missing Mom. It could have been a compilation of the remodel and expansion, the reality that I had just discovered a dead body, and having Carlos and Ramiro here in the new life that I had carved out for myself. Whatever the reason, I broke down. A lump formed in the back of my throat. I tried to hold my emotions inside. I could feel my cheeks begin to burn. I couldn't keep it in. Tears flowed like the wine at the reception last night. I sobbed openly.

Carlos's face clouded. He scooted his chair next to mine. Placing his hand on my shoulder, he stared at me with concern. "*Mi querida,* I am sorry. I did not mean to scold you. I worry about you, that is all."

"It's not that. It's everything." I had a hard time catching my breath between my sobs.

He massaged my arm. "I see. It is good. You must cry. You said good-bye to your mother last night and now you found a body. I understand."

His words made me cry harder. What was wrong

with me? This was two meltdowns in the span of a couple days. I knew that weddings made people cry, but I didn't expect to be a basket case.

Carlos folded the napkin that had come with his lemonade. He dabbed my cheek. "Julieta, it is good. You let this emotion flow like the waters in front of us."

His ability to embrace his emotions had been one of the reasons that I'd fallen in love with him. And it was one of the reasons I was also finding it impossible to let him go.

Chapter Nineteen

The afternoon at the lake was exactly what I needed to restore my spirits. One of my favorite quotes was by the Danish writer Isak Dinesen. After my dad died, Thomas brought me a basket of bath salts and a card with a quote by Dinesen that read: "The cure for anything is salt water: sweat, tears, or the sea." That had been true for me. The sea had been a place of healing. Lake of the Woods wasn't salt water, but the act of sitting by its shores and allowing the cool water to lap against my feet made my nerves settle.

I enjoyed watching Ramiro swim. His smile lit up his entire face as he raced down the dock and splashed into the cold alpine water with the boys. When he finally took a break, and plopped on the rocky shore next to me and Carlos, I noticed the sun's angle had shifted.

"You must be famished," I said. "It's after six. We should get you some dinner."

Ramiro shook water from his hair. "She is just like Mama," he said to Carlos. "Why do mothers always want us to eat?" He winked.

I thought of Mom. She was constantly reminding me to eat, maybe it was genetic. "Should we pack up?"

"Sí." Carlos stood and offered me his hand.

"We could go out for dinner, or if you want there are tons of leftovers from the wedding back at my place." Secretly, I hoped that they would say leftovers. The thought of going to dinner and facing the entire town was overwhelming.

Carlos tugged on his shirt. "Let's stay in tonight."

Thank goodness. To be honest, I was exhausted after last night's festivities. The thought of a cozy night with just Carlos and Ramiro sounded like a dream.

Ramiro jumped in the shower when we arrived at my apartment. Carlos helped me set out the spread from the wedding and opened a bottle of wine. As I unpacked box after box of leftovers I knew we had made the right choice to stay in. There were grilled chicken kebabs with lovely blackened tomatoes and red peppers, smashed garlic potatoes, pasta salad, flank steaks, and enough cheese, veggies, and dips to feed a small army.

The three of us laughed and ate and laughed some more. They fed off each other with stories of their adventures in the Spanish countryside. Like the time they rented a Jeep to drive up into the hills for a two-day hike. They left before dawn in order to beat the heat.

"Papa drove so fast I thought I might fall out," Ramiro said, clutching his chair and tipping it side to side. "He was like a maniac."

"Tell me about it," I agreed. Carlos had a need for speed. Whenever we were in port I would say a little prayer before getting into the car with him. He was a good driver, but tended to view speed limits as suggestions not requirements. "I still have scars on my hands from clutching the door handle super tight when driving with your dad." I held out my hand. Indeed there was one scar that ran the length of my palm.

Ramiro stared at my hand and then looked to his father. "That is a terrible cut."

I laughed. "No, I'm teasing. That isn't from driving with this speed demon, here." I didn't elaborate on how I'd come to have gotten the scar. It happened not long after I returned to Ashland and came face-to-face with a crazed, knife-wielding killer. It didn't hurt anymore, but it was a reminder of how close I'd come to danger in the past.

"This is not fair. I cannot defend myself against the two of you." Carlos mocked us with a look of despair.

"No, no, let me finish my story," Ramiro insisted, popping a piece of cheese in his mouth. "We are flying up the one-lane highway, so fast that I think I cannot even breathe and then we stopped suddenly." He lurched his body forward to demonstrate. "If I had not been holding on I would have fallen out of the Jeep for sure."

"You were wearing a seat belt," Carlos said in his best dad tone.

Ramiro waved off his dad. "We stopped so quickly that the Jeep it rocks back and forth and I scream at Papa asking what is wrong. He points to the ground in front of us and there is a turtle in the road."

"A turtle?" I looked to Carlos.

Carlos shrugged.

"Sí, a turtle." Ramiro's voice cracked. "A turtle was crossing the road. Papa raced from the car, picked it up, and set it on the other side. We nearly flipped the Jeep to rescue a turtle."

"Is that true? You have a soft spot for turtles?" I teased Carlos. "Good thing we didn't decide to put turtle soup on the wedding menu."

"You make fun, but if you had seen the poor thing you would have done the same. I could not leave it in the middle of the road. Or run it over." Carlos cupped his hands together. "It was only like this size. It must have been a baby."

"Sí, and he almost killed his only son to save a baby turtle." Ramiro laughed.

Carlos tossed a carrot at him.

The story of the turtle didn't surprise me. Carlos had a soft spot for animals. On the ship, we would sometimes sneak away for evening walks together on the pool deck. He used to call to the birds. There was one banana bird with a bright yellow underbelly that would land on the railing and let Carlos feed him scraps of bread from his hand. Once at port on a small island off the Italian coast we met a stray dog while meandering through an outdoor market. Carlos seriously considered whether there was any possible way he could sneak the mangy dog onto the ship. Of course there wasn't, so he paid a local villager handsomely to look after the dog. He was a lover of all creatures. Animals were naturally attracted to him.

I sat back and listened as they tried to outdo one another with stories. We had quickly fallen into an easy rhythm. I could almost picture the three of us around the dinner table every evening, with Ramiro giving us updates from school and Carlos and I sharing our tales from a busy day at Torte. Could this be my new life? I hadn't been able to fathom the idea of Carlos settling into Ashland so much so that I had never allowed myself to even consider it. I found myself reconsidering. Could the three of us be happy together?

The sound of footsteps thudding up the stairs shook me from the moment. Next a hand pounded on the front door. Carlos went to see who was here.

It was Thomas. His face was flushed. "Sorry to barge in, but I have an update."

"Come in, come in." Carlos extended his arm and wrapped Thomas in what Andy calls a "bro hug." "We have food, my friend. Would you like to eat? You must join us."

There had been tension between the two of them in the past, but tonight I sensed a shift. Thomas stared longingly at the boxes of food on the small table. Without another word, Carlos pushed him to his vacated seat and went to get a plate in the kitchen. He piled it high with leftovers, set it in front of Thomas, and then patted his shoulder. "Eat, eat."

Thomas gave me a sheepish smile as he popped a meatball in his mouth. "You know me and food. I can't ever say no."

"Sí, this is a good man," Carlos said, pulling up an extra chair that had been tucked in the corner.

"But I didn't come for food. I have some important information on the case." Thomas wiped his hands on a cloth napkin.

With this news Carlos's face hardened.

"We caught Adam." Thomas looked at me. "Thanks to you. He didn't get far. Detective Kerry caught up to him. I don't know how she can run that fast in heels. I was gasping for air just trying to keep pace with her."

"Sí, I think she is a strong woman," Carlos interjected. He gave me a knowing look.

What did he mean by that? I waited for Thomas to continue.

"Adam confessed that he and Megan used to date, but he claimed the restraining order was just a ruse."

"A ruse?" Carlos asked.

Thomas nodded. "He said that the two of them broke up about a year ago, but that they were still friends."

"Why would she get a restraining order?" I interrupted.

"I'm getting to that." Thomas shook his head.

Carlos gave him a matching look. "She is so impatient sometimes, no?"

"Yeah." Thomas reached for a hunk of bread and dipped it in velvety hummus. "Adam says that after he and Megan broke up she hired him to work for her."

"What?"

"Yep. He says that when they dated he would tag along on stakeouts and stuff and he learned the ropes. She sometimes needed an extra set of hands so they teamed up."

"Do you believe him?" I asked.

Thomas sighed. "I'm not sure. This is when I really wish the Professor was here. Detective Kerry doesn't believe him, but there's something about the guy that seems sincere. I don't know if it's a gut reaction, which Kerry tells me should never be used in police work."

"This is not true," Carlos interjected. "We must always trust our instincts in the kitchen—in everything, yes?"

"Thanks, man," Thomas said. "We're checking his story. If Megan was really working with him you would think there would be a paper trail, notes, payroll, that sort of thing. Although he says that she paid him under the table so I don't know if we'll be able to find anything to corroborate his story."

I took a sip of wine. "What did he say he was doing for her?"

"That's the thing. He says that she was pretending that he was stalking her. In fact, they staged a couple of public fights. He called her cell phone constantly to have a record of the calls. She wanted it to look like he was after her and dangerous."

"Why?"

"Because she needed an excuse to go to Jarvis. She was investigating Jarvis, but she knew that he was smart. She figured he would realize right away that Lance had hired her, so she created an elaborate plan. She came clean to Jarvis almost immediately about Lance and his investigation into his family's fortune, then she came up with a sob story about being harassed by her ex. She begged Jarvis for his help. That way they would stay in contact and she could continue digging into the Brown Family Group without Jarvis being any the wiser."

"That's brilliant," I said.

"Sí." Carlos nodded. Ramiro who had been quiet the entire time even chimed in. "It's like a movie I saw. A con is doing the conning."

"Right." Thomas spread butter on a slice of bread. "If it's true, of course."

"And you think it might be?" I twisted my ponytail. My skin felt grimy from sunscreen.

He wavered. "I don't know. Like I said, if the Professor were here . . ."

Carlos held up a finger. "But remember, like I said, you must trust your instincts. Do not worry what the Professor would say. You have learned from him for many years now, no?"

Thomas nodded.

"Sí, so in here." He tapped his chest. "You know. You must trust this."

I appreciated that Carlos was encouraging Thomas.

"Yeah, my gut says he's telling the truth. He says that Megan was close to uncovering some serious information about Jarvis." Thomas dabbed the corner of his mouth with the napkin.

"Like the fact that he was disbarred in Nevada," I added.

"Yeah. Maybe. Or maybe something else." Thomas frowned and stared at me. "Adam told us something else. Something much more disturbing, which is another reason I wanted to come over here right away."

"What?" I scooted my chair away from the table and crossed my legs.

"He said that he was there right before Megan drank the poison. And that he saw who spiked the drink."

"Who was it?" I didn't like the way his eyes had narrowed.

"He claims that he saw Clarissa slip something into the glass of wine."

"Clarissa? Why would she want to poison Megan?" I asked.

He scowled. "According to Adam she wasn't trying to poison Megan. She was trying to poison *you*."

Chapter Twenty

"Me?" I gulped. "Why would Clarissa want to poison me?"

Thomas furrowed his brow. "No idea, but Adam insists that he witnessed the entire thing. Says he'll take a polygraph. Swear under oath, blah, blah, blah."

Carlos puffed out his chest. "Who is this Clarissa, Julieta?"

I swallowed. "She's the wife of my architect."

"And did you feud?"

"Did we feud? No. I barely know her. I mean, I will say that she's been pretty icy every time we've interacted but I think that's just her personality."

Carlos and Thomas shared a look.

Thomas brushed some crumbs from his hands and stood. "We're going to follow up on it. I'll keep you posted, but in the meantime, I would recommend keeping your distance from Clarissa and Roger. At least until we can see if there's any validity to Adam's claim."

"How am I supposed to keep my distance from Roger? He's working on Torte, almost around the clock right now."

"Good point. I want you to bring Carlos or someone with you when you interact with him, and do not mention anything about the investigation. It's probably nothing, but we can't take any chances. Especially since a woman has been murdered."

"Do you think there's some kind of a connection with Torte?" I tried to think back through every conversation I had had with Roger. Unless I was missing something, our relationship had been smooth. The entire renovation process had been seamless thus far. Roger and I had never had a disagreement. He had commented on more than one occasion about how easy it had been working with Mom and me.

Thomas walked toward the front door. "It's too soon to say. Like I said, just keep an eye out and be extra cautious until I can get you an update, okay?" His eyes were filled with concern.

Carlos stood and shook Thomas's hand. "Thank you for this information. Ramiro and I will not leave Julieta's side. I will promise you that." They shared a look of solidarity.

"Good." Thomas gave me a nod and walked outside.

Carlos returned to the table. "This is not good. I do not understand why this Clarissa would want to harm you."

"I don't either. Honestly, I'm not used to people not liking me." I paused. "Except for maybe Richard Lord."

"The baboon." Carlos chuckled. "Sí, he is of no worry. He is, how do you say it? Full of hot air."

"Right." I noticed Ramiro fiddling with his napkin. I didn't want to worry him. "I bet that Adam is lying to try and shift suspicion to someone else. Clarissa might not want to hang out with me, but there's no way she would try to poison me. She's the head of the arts council and well respected in town. I can't picture her ruining her reputation. And what would be her motivation?"

Carlos raised one dark eyebrow. "Maybe she is jealous. You have been spending time with her husband, no?"

"For work. My relationship with Roger has been strictly professional. He's at least twenty years older than me."

"This is my point, Julieta. You are a beautiful, young woman. What wife would want her husband spending so much time with you? And then you make him a delicious pastry—ah. I see the possibility now."

"You're kidding, right?" I couldn't believe Carlos would even suggest that Clarissa would have a reason to worry about me and her husband.

"No. I'm serious. A woman in love—protecting her marriage—she could be fierce. She could be deadly." He loosened his leather belt and gave me a knowing look.

"Carlos." I motioned to Ramiro who nodded in agreement with his dad. "Come on, this is *me* we're talking about. I promise you that Roger has no interest in me beyond talking about Sheetrock and flooring."

"I understand that, but I am saying that his wife might not. Thomas is right. Ramiro and I will be your guardians."

I tried to protest, but Carlos began picking up our dinner dishes and went to the kitchen to make us espressos. On rare occasions when we both had a break in food service on the ship, we would meet in the lounge for Spanish coffees. The rich, boozy drink was one of

Carlos's specialties. His philosophy was that anytime was a good time for coffee, and a spiked coffee was that much better.

"Do you want me to add a touch of spice to your espresso?" he asked with a sultry wink.

"No, thank you. I'm fine." I wanted to keep my head as clear as possible. I was fairly confident that Adam must be lying, but was there a chance that the poison had been meant for me? I shuddered at the thought.

Not long after we finished our espressos and slices of wedding cake, Ramiro began to yawn. "We should get you to bed," I said.

He grinned and stretched. "Too much swimming."

"That will do it. As will the mountain air." I smiled. "I'm tired too." In truth, between Carlos's strong espresso and the newest information on the case I was wide awake. I had already formulated a plan in my head. As soon as Carlos and Ramiro were asleep, I was going to meet Lance. I went to my bedroom and shot him a quick text: *Meet at Puck's in thirty minutes?*

He replied immediately with: *YES!*

Getting past Carlos and Ramiro wasn't a problem. They were both out immediately. I couldn't believe that either of them could crash so quickly after a shot of espresso. Then I had to remind myself that they were still adjusting to West Coast time. I made my way to Puck's Pub where Lance was already waiting with a martini in hand. The pub was themed like an old-world tavern with warm wood accents and giant keg barrels for tables.

"Darling, what took you so long? It's been ages." He tipped his martini.

"It's been ten minutes."

He brushed me off and escorted me to a high bar table near the back of the pub. "Do tell, what is the latest?"

I filled him in on what I had just learned from Thomas.

"A woman scorned. How very Shakespearean." Lance threw his hand to his forehead.

"How is Clarissa a woman scorned? Nothing has happened between Roger and me, nor will it ever."

"But she doesn't know that."

"Now you sound like Carlos."

"Listen to that dreamy husband of yours, Juliet." Lance paused when a waiter stopped by our table to ask if I wanted anything to drink.

"Just a water, thanks."

Lance scoffed. "Boring. You should have a martini. It will help loosen you up."

"No way." I assured the waiter that I only wanted a glass of water. "Weren't you the one saying that you weren't drinking to keep your head clear?"

"Details. Details." Lance fiddled with his twist of lemon. "They do make a mean martini here. It's ice-cold, with my favorite gin. Perfection."

"Do you really think that Clarissa has it out for me?"

He drummed his long fingers on the top of the distressed-wood table. "I think we have to consider that it's a possibility. Clarissa isn't the warmest woman in town, but she did seem to take a particular dislike to you. Then again, she's quite revered in the art community."

"Exactly. What would her motivation be?"

Lance stared hard at me. "Let's see. Envy. The lines dotting her once flawless face, widening hips, graying roots. Shall I continue?"

"Please don't."

"Well, in that case, let me tell you what I've learned while you've been soaking up the sun today." For effect, he took a long sip of his drink. "I went and I had a tête-à-tête with Sarah, the office manager, about Jarvis."

"And?"

"Patience, darling. Patience." Lance waved the waiter over to order a second martini. "According to Sarah, my brother hired Jarvis about a month ago. He hasn't been with the Brown Family Group for long. I find it quite interesting that right about the time that my father took a turn for the worse, my brother happened to hire his new 'lawyer' and, believe me, I use that term loosely."

"You think there's a connection?"

"I know it." Lance handed the waiter his empty drink glass. "Megan agreed. She said that the first thing the two of those goons did was have a private meeting with my father. She was sure that's when his will was changed, which is elder abuse by the way. There is no way he was of sound mind or body when he signed the new paperwork. You can tell by his signature. I don't think he could even hold the pen. There's no way it's going to hold up in court. Believe me, I'll sue."

"Right." I felt a headache coming on. "I guess it's good news that this backs you up."

"True, but it doesn't change the fact that my father is dead and I'm convinced my brother helped push him off the cliff, so to speak."

Lance's fresh martini arrived in a frosty glass. "You

and I need to talk and see what we can get out of him. And Adam. Did Thomas tell you if they are keeping him downtown or up in Medford?"

I shook my head. "He didn't say."

"Well, then the minute I finish my drink, let's take a little walk, shall we?" With that Lance knocked back his drink.

"Are you going to be able to walk?" I asked. If I had had two martinis that fast I would barely be able to stand, let alone walk.

"With you at my side, of course." Lance looped his arm through mine and we headed for the police station, which was nothing more than a small office on the corner of the plaza. Lance quivered when we knocked on the front door.

"What's wrong?"

"Memories. Bad memories."

I knew he was referencing the time he had to spend locked up in the supply closet when he had been a suspect in a murder investigation.

No one answered, which must have meant that Thomas or Detective Kerry had booked Adam in the main jail in Medford.

"Oh well, it was worth a shot."

"Darling, we're not done. We're just getting started. The night is young."

I glanced at my watch; it was after eleven. "It's not exactly young."

He tugged me in the opposite direction. "Let's go get my car and take another quick jaunt up to Medford."

"Lance, you can't drive. You just chugged two martinis."

"Oh please, I didn't chug them, and you can drive."

"What are we going to do in Medford?"

"A little snooping." He practically dragged me across the plaza. We hoofed up Pioneer Street. I could hear the chorus swelling to a crescendo from the outdoor show at the Elizabethan theater. They must have been about to reach the final song. The music swelled and the audience began to applaud.

Lance stopped on the sidewalk in front of the bricks and cupped one hand over his ear. "The bass player is off again."

"What?" I stopped and listened. The music sounded masterful to my untrained ear.

"Right there." Lance tapped his free hand in the air to the beat. "I'm going to have a word with the conductor first thing tomorrow. I've told him at least a dozen times that he's been late, which is throwing the entire company off." He yanked me up the hill to his waiting car and opened the driver's side for me.

"Where am I going?" I asked, sliding behind the wheel. I wasn't sure why I was allowing Lance to direct me, but I knew that my adrenaline was running too high to sleep. I might as well see if I could learn anything more about Megan's death.

"Megan's office."

"But what about the police? They probably have it roped off."

"A technicality. That's never stopped us in the past."

He was right, but this felt different. Snooping in a dead woman's office wouldn't look good for either of us. What I really needed was a hot shower and a good night's sleep, but adrenaline pulsed through me as we drove north toward Medford again. When we arrived at the strip mall, police tape stretched in front of the door. "See, I told you."

Lance didn't listen. He was out of the car in one fluid motion and strolling straight for the door. He lifted the edge of the yellow caution tape and motioned for me to go inside.

"Why do I have to go first?"

"Ladies are always first." He smirked.

I ducked under the tape. The door was unlocked. Had it only been this morning that we'd found Megan's body? I tried to calm the unsettled feeling growing in my stomach. This was a bad idea. What were we doing?

"What are we looking for?" I whispered to Lance.

He removed a flashlight from his pocket. "Evidence, darling. Evidence." He ran the light along the ugly shag carpet in a zigzagging pattern.

The chances of us finding something were slim. The police had scoured every square inch of the dingy office. Fingerprint-powder residue coated Megan's desk and filing cabinet. It smelled musty and the scent of cigarettes was more pronounced than it had been the last time we were here. I was about to drag Lance back outside when light flooded the room.

Someone was here. The car's headlights burst through the front window.

"Duck!" Lance shouted.

We both dropped to our knees.

"Who's here?" I asked.

"No idea," Lance hissed.

My heart thudded. Was it the police? If Detective Kerry caught us snooping she would lock us both up for sure. Or could it be Megan's killer? Neither of us had a weapon. This was a stupid idea.

The sound of the car door slamming made me flinch.

The next thing I knew the door burst open and Lance threw me to the ground and fell over my body, like a shield.

Chapter Twenty-one

Lance was usually skittish in situations like this, but to my amazement he whispered, "Stay down." Then he leaped to his feet, grabbed a ruler from Megan's desk, and jumped in front of me. "Who's here? You better back off. I have a weapon."

I couldn't stay down. I sat up just in time to see Lance's flashlight illuminate Adam's face. What was he doing here?

Adam blinked rapidly. He held his hand out to block Lance's flashlight. "What are *you* doing here?" A file folder was tucked under his free arm.

Lance aimed the beam of light directly into Adam's eyes. "I'm not kidding. Don't take a single step closer."

"Who are you?" Adam continued to shield his eyes.

"Your worst nightmare," Lance said in a tone that was laced with vigor. I'd never seen him like this. "You move a pinkie toe closer to us and you'll regret it."

I was impressed. Lance weighed half of what Adam did. If Adam wanted to, he could probably knock Lance off his feet with a single push.

Adam held out the file folder to shield his face from

the light. "Look, I don't know who you are but you shouldn't be here. This is a crime scene, and private property. Nobody's supposed be in here."

"We shouldn't be here, ha!" Lance made a stabbing motion with the ruler. "I said back up."

"I don't know who you are, but this is my property. Private property and I want you out now." Adam folded one hand into a tight fist.

"Look," I said, moving between the two of them. "Let's all calm down. Lance, this is Adam." I shot Lance a look, to try and convey that engaging in a physical battle with the muscular biker wasn't a wise idea.

"Yeah, I got that," Lance said to me. "What I want to know is what you're doing here." He kept the ruler out in front of him. "I happen to know that you were accused of murder. We were just with the police and know that you were stalking Megan, and most likely tried to poison my friend Juliet. Why? We don't know. But one quick call to the dependable Ashland police department and I'm sure you'll be locked behind bars, so please do go ahead and inform us as to why you could possibly think that you have a right to be in your victim's office."

My pulse slowed slightly, and the rational side of my brain kicked in. "Yeah, how are you here? Didn't Thomas arrest you?"

Adam threw his hands out again. "Jeez, can you stop with the light?"

Lance moved the flashlight a half inch off his face.

"They let me go." Adam cracked his neck.

"What?" I couldn't believe that Thomas and Detective Kerry would let the main suspect in a murder case go.

Adam kept his hands in the air. "Look, I'm going to turn on the overhead light. Put the flashlight down." He reached toward the door and flipped on the light.

Now it was my turn to adjust to the fluorescent glare. With the lights on it was even more evident that the police had done a thorough sweep of Megan's office. Yellow evidence markers had been placed on the bookshelves and filing cabinets. There was fingerprint-dust residue on the desk. Stacks of files had been arranged with color-coded notes.

"You guys have it all wrong. I loved Megan. I loved her." Adam's voice deepened as he spoke. He held up one hand to reveal black ink on each finger. "The police checked me out. I told them everything I know because I want the person who did this to her to pay."

"According to what we've heard you were stalking her," Lance said with conviction. "Perhaps you loved her too much. Did she find someone new? You couldn't handle seeing her with her new lover. If you couldn't have her, no one could. Am I right? It's a classic tragedy told again and again on stages throughout the world."

Leave it to Lance to find a way to weave in the theater in a moment like this.

"No. That's not it. Not even close." Adam walked toward the desk.

Lance waved his ruler like a sword.

"What are you going to do with that? Measure me?" Adam ignored Lance's threatening stance. He sat down at the desk and opened the top drawer. "You don't get it. Megan and I have known each other for almost twenty years. It's true that we broke up, but Megan was my best friend. I've been trying to convince her to give me another shot." He set the file folder down and removed a photo from the drawer and stared at it.

"Sounds like textbook stalking to me," Lance said with a snap of his wrist.

Adam ran his finger along the glass frame. "No, that was for a job. It was my idea. Megan was investigating that lawyer, Jarvis O. Sandberg." He said the name in a mock-pompous tone. "The guy said he was some hotshot corporate lawyer from New York, but he wasn't. Megan learned that he had practiced in Vegas before being hired by the Brown Family Group. She didn't trust him, thought he was a sleaze, but she knew that he was smart."

"That's a dangerous combination," I said out loud.

"Right. That's why we decided to play him. She was trying to get inside his office and the company's headquarters, but couldn't figure out an angle. I brought her a bunch of peach roses for her birthday a few weeks ago and the idea hit me—have her go undercover. You know, come clean. Tell Jarvis that you hired her to look into the family," he said to Lance. "Then she told the dude that she couldn't find any dirt on the Browns. The plan was simple. I was supposed to follow her to his office and hang around the window outside. She pointed me out to him and told him that I was her ex. She played it perfectly. She came outside shaking and cowering behind Jarvis. He told me to get off the property immediately. I pretended like I was going to punch him, shouted a bunch of profanity at them, and promised Megan that she hadn't heard the last of me. Then I waited in my car until she left."

I understood why Thomas had said that he believed Adam. He sounded sincere.

"It started out great. Megan begged Jarvis for his help. She knew that she'd have to document the 'stalking' incidents, and we staged a couple more public fights. I went everywhere she did, which was great because I was her second set of eyes. I saw everyone coming and going from the Brown Family Group headquarters. Jarvis helped her get the restraining order and Megan had access and an excuse to stop by the offices on multiple occasions. Each time she did, she found a way to do some digging. She was on to something." He paused. I watched as he clutched the photo in his stained fingers. Unless he was an actor of OSF's caliber I was sure that he was telling the truth. He had loved her.

"Why were you and Jarvis fighting earlier?" I asked. "I saw you two down by the creek."

Adam placed the picture on his lap. "Yeah, that's right. I wanted the restraining order. I knew it was going to look bad with the cops. Who's going to believe my story?"

Lance cleared his throat.

"And I wanted a chance to see him face-to-face. I don't know what's going on over at the Brown Family Group, but that guy is corrupt for sure. Megan told me that she'd learned something new. We were going to talk after the wedding, but then . . ." He couldn't finish.

"Do you think that Jarvis killed her?" I asked.

He tried to compose himself. "I don't know. Maybe. She had to be on to something. I warned her that something shady was going down. I was worried about her. I've never been worried before, but I had a bad feeling about this case. There were too many weird connections. Like you and that woman Clarissa."

My heart dropped. "What do you mean?"

"She's the one who put something in your wine," he said, giving me a hard stare.

Lance stepped closer to me. "We heard that's the story you've given the police. Quite convenient to throw suspicion away from yourself, wouldn't you say?"

Adam shook his head. "No. It's not convenient. It's the truth. Clarissa hired Megan to tail you. She thinks you're having an affair with her husband."

"She hired Megan?" I repeated Adam's words as if saying them again would help them make sense.

"Yep. I told the police. I saw it all that night. Megan wanted me there. She was working the case. She told me to get hired as a temp and keep my eyes open." He pushed up the sleeves on his leather jacket.

"Did she tell you what or who you were supposed to be watching?" Lance asked.

"No. She just said that the two of you were going together and she was sure that she was close to having enough evidence on the seedy Brown Family Group to go to the police. Said it all came down to money. Big money. There is a bunch of cash missing. Like in the millions. She wanted me there. That's all she said. The fact that she didn't say more is one of the reasons I was so worried. Megan was one tough woman, but I think she wanted me there for protection. I hung as close by her as I possibly could without getting noticed."

"And you saw Clarissa?" I asked.

He nodded. "Uh-huh. I was outside when you came up with the bottle of wine. I was only a few feet away. Like I said, Megan had me spooked, so I stayed in close range. The four of you were talking and I watched

Clarissa put something in the glass and hand it to you. You refused and Megan took the drink. The next thing I knew she was on the ground. Then everything happened so fast."

"You're sure?" I turned to Lance.

Lance raised his eyebrows and whispered, "I told you so."

Adam moved the picture from his lap. Then he picked up the file folder he had come in with. He stood and handed it to me. "Positive. The file is here."

I stared at the label which read: "Juliet Capshaw." Adam had been telling the truth. Clarissa had hired Megan to follow me. And worse, she had tried to poison me.

Chapter Twenty-two

"Take a look at that. You want proof. There's your proof," Adam said. "I swiped it. It was a stupid, rash move. I told the police they could find it here, but I had to get back here now to return it before they get here."

"You stole evidence from a crime scene?" Lance asked in a holier-than-thou tone. We were hardly in a position to judge Adam.

"Yeah, but like I said, I brought it back."

Lance leaned over my shoulder as I leafed through notes about my daily routine and photos of me crossing in front of the Lithia fountains and chatting with customers at Torte. I felt sick to my stomach. What a violation of my privacy. I couldn't believe that Megan had been tailing me. That must have been why she and Clarissa met at Torte and why I'd seen her hanging around the plaza. It had nothing to do with Lance's family and everything to do with me.

"You know, Megan didn't think there was anything going on, if it makes you feel any better." Adam cracked his knuckles.

"It doesn't. Not really." I sighed.

Lance snatched the file from my hands. He clicked off a dozen photos on his phone and then handed it back to Adam. "Why didn't you just give this to the police? You should return it right now." He glanced at me. "Better yet, why don't I call Thomas? He needs to have a little chat with Clarissa immediately."

I was too stunned to speak.

Lance stepped outside to call Thomas.

Adam tried to console me. "Look, I know it's weird to see yourself like that, but Megan was discreet."

"Discreet in watching my every move." I quivered.

"It was her job." Adam picked up the picture again.

"I don't understand what happened the night she was poisoned. You disappeared right after she fell to the ground. Why were you and Megan fighting? I saw you in the barn before she drank the wine." There were some holes in his story.

"We weren't fighting. She didn't want me to blow her cover. That's all." He massaged his goatee.

"But why didn't you tell the police that you saw Clarissa spike the wine?" I pressed.

"I did tell the police. I came out that night when Megan was in the hospital to tell the police. I mean, I tried to. My first concern was for her, but I knew I had to stay in the shadows. I watched to make sure she was going to be okay. I waited until the ambulance arrived. Then I went to the hospital to check on her, but they wouldn't let me in. I knew that the cops would think that I had done it. My plan backfired. Megan had filed a restraining order against me and I knew that would be the first thing that would show up in their investigation. I also knew that it was going to be impossible to get back into this office once the police were involved, so I came out here. Megan had said that she was close to having enough tangible proof in the Brown investigation to go to the police and I wanted to get my hands on it before they did."

"So you were here?" The hairs on my arms stood up. Was Adam a masterful liar? Maybe I had misread him? Something didn't add up. Was he implying that the police knew about the restraining order? Megan was killed in this very spot. Had he hidden under her desk and waited for her to return?

He must have noticed the look of trepidation on my face. "Yes, but not for long. I did *not* kill Megan. I looked through the files quickly, but I wanted to get back to the hospital to see how she was doing. When I got back, the police were gone so I snuck into her room. She told me that Jarvis had just drawn up the papers for the restraining order but hadn't submitted them yet. She asked me to go to the Brown Family Group headquarters first thing in the morning and snag a copy of the restraining order. She also wanted me to search his office again. I wanted to stay with her, but she made me promise. I should have stayed with her." His head dropped.

"Did you go to the Brown Family Group?" I asked.

"I did. I found a way into Jarvis's office."

"You mean you broke in?"

"In the field we like to call it 'finding a way.' "

"Okay, and?"

"And nothing. It was clean. Too clean. Like weirdly clean. Tons of shredded files jamming up the paper shredder. That kind of thing. I got there too late." He paused. "Maybe if I had had more time I would have found something. But Leo's personal assistant—or whatever she is—Sarah, caught me."

"She did?"

"Yeah. Said she had some filing to do, and told me to get out or she would call the cops. I didn't want to risk it, so I took off. There was no sign of the restraining order. I couldn't find a single document that might incriminate Jarvis or Leo. Nothing. It was a waste of time, and time I should have been at Megan's side. If I had been there she would still be alive." He broke down. The big biker guy coughed and sputtered out tears.

"You don't know that."

"I do. I should have stayed with her at the hospital. I should never have left. I can't believe she's gone." He clenched his right hand into a fist and pounded it into his left hand. "I went back to the hospital that morning— early. She was already gone. I don't know why. She must have been after something. She must have hidden evidence or something here. We made a pact not to communicate via phone in the short term. She couldn't exactly get a restraining order filed if there was a record of her calling me. I did get a call from a pay phone that morning, but she didn't leave a message. She was always careful. When I learned that she'd been discharged from the hospital I came here to find the place swarming with police and the ambulance, and then overheard that Megan was dead. I've been laying low and trying to piece together who killed her ever since." He buried his face in his hands.

Between his reaction and the file of Megan's notes on me, I believed him. Why Clarissa had tried to poison me was another matter.

Within a few minutes the front of the office lit up with red and blue police lights. Thomas and Detective Kerry arrived. Lance led them inside. "Show them the file," he said to Adam. I noticed he was still holding the ruler. It had become his prop.

Adam handed over the file.

Detective Kerry's green eyes fumed with anger. "Enough, you guys. This has to stop. We don't have jurisdiction to seize evidence." She turned to Thomas. "Call the Medford lead."

Thomas gave her a thumbs-up, and made the call.

Detective Kerry's scowl stayed in place as she studied the photos and notes. "This woman thinks you were having an affair with him?" She held up a photo of Roger.

"Woman of a certain age," Lance said in a snarky tone.

"Men of a certain age," Detective Kerry shot back.

Lance flicked the ruler like a wand. "Touché, dearest. Touché."

"Let's go," Detective Kerry said to Thomas, tucking the file under her arm. "We need to get to Medford headquarters."

Thomas gave me a parting glance. "Are you okay, Jules?"

"I'm fine," I lied. "But before you go, do you both think that Clarissa is connected to Megan's murder?"

Detective Kerry put a hand on her narrow waist. "You can rest assured that we're going to track every possible connection we can find. Regardless, this is attempted murder."

My stomach swirled. Clarissa had actually tried to

murder me. I couldn't believe it. Why? Was Carlos right? Was she jealous of me? I racked my brain to try and think of any signal I could have accidentally given that might have made her think I was interested in Roger. Nothing came to mind.

For the first time, Detective Kerry's eyes softened. "I understand this is disturbing. I need to warn you that we're likely going to need you to be actively involved in the case. You won't need to press charges. Assuming we can compile enough evidence, the state will do that."

Thomas nodded. "In criminal matters like this, the prosecution will review our file and determine the next steps."

The room began to sway. Lance grabbed my arm to steady me.

This couldn't really be happening, could it? Clarissa, a woman who was practically a stranger, had tried to kill me and in the process an innocent victim had ended up dead.

Chapter Twenty-three

I drove home in a daze. Even Lance was uncharacteristically quiet on the drive. When we made it to the plaza, he placed a hand on my knee. "Don't worry, Thomas and Detective Kerry will make sure that Clarissa is locked up for a long time to come. Of that, I'm sure."

"It's not that. It's the entire thing. Why would she think that I was having an affair with her husband? And hire a PI?"

Lance exhaled. "It is a tad extreme."

"And then what? Megan told her there was nothing between Roger and me and she didn't believe her? So she decided to try and kill me?" I could hear a shrill tone creeping into my voice. If Clarissa had been unhinged enough to poison a drink, could she have snapped? Maybe she was angry that Megan didn't find any evidence of an affair. What if that pushed her over the edge and she killed Megan in retaliation?

"It appears that way."

"Do you think she killed Megan too?"

"She is the most likely suspect, with one glaring issue."

"What, motive?"

"Exactly." Lance tapped the dashboard. "Darling, it's late and you've had quite an ordeal today. Go home. Get some beauty sleep. I'll make a few calls in the morning. As we know, Clarissa is engaged in the art community. Maybe we should look into any fund-raising connections with the Brown Family Group. What if she's pocketed some of that cash? There could be dozens of connections that we haven't considered. Let me do a bit of digging and we'll reconvene tomorrow."

"Okay." I got out of the car. Lance hugged me tight.

"I don't know what I would do without you." His voice was thick with emotion.

"Me too." I kissed his cheek.

He walked me to my apartment and waited to make sure that I got inside safely. I was lucky to have him as a friend. Inside Carlos and Ramiro were still snoozing, completely oblivious to the drama that had unfolded. I wished I could doze off into a dreamlike state. However, sleep was futile. I tossed and turned for a few hours, playing out every scenario in my mind. I must have missed something. There had to be a clue I had over-looked. Was Lance right? Could Clarissa have been embezzling money from the arts foundation? The Pro-fessor always said that money was a top motive for murder.

Sometime after four I gave up the fight and tugged on a pair of jeans and a T-shirt. With Carlos and Ramiro happily dozing I made my way to Torte. Ashland was like a ghost town at the early hour. The air held a slight chill. Or maybe it was just me.

I unlocked the front door and surveyed the progress.

Roger and his team had managed to put the dining room back in functioning order. The temporary coffee counter and pastry case had been installed and the kitchen had been resealed with thick plastic. There were PARDON OUR DUST signs posted on the plastic and hanging on the windows, but otherwise it looked like we were ready to be back in business as soon as we gave the bakeshop a cleansing wipe-down.

The only challenge would be carting pastries and cakes from the basement, up the stairs outside, and then back into Torte until the new stairwell had been installed.

I locked the bakeshop and headed for the basement. I needed to bake. Nothing else could soothe my nerves like baking.

The basement was eerily quiet when I unlocked the door at the bottom of the stairs. I turned on the lights and plugged my phone into the speaker system. With classical music playing, I made myself a pot of coffee and started a batch of yeast rising. Soon, I was up to my elbows in sticky bread dough. The act of kneading and pounding the dough helped center me. We rotate daily bread specials. This morning I opted for a honey wheat with chunky walnuts and a black bread with chocolate and molasses. We would toast the honey wheat and slather it with almond butter, apricot preserves, and a touch of salt. The black bread would be used for our grilled cheese special with goat cheese, balsamic vinegar, and thin slices of Granny Smith apples.

Once I had kneaded each loaf into lovely pillows I found my scoring knife. Scoring bread is more than just for aesthetics. It allows the dough to expand in a controlled manner as it bakes. For the wheat bread, I used the edge of the razor-thin tool to cut stalks of wheat into the loaves. For the black bread, I carved dainty spirals and tulips. The creative art of scoring gave Torte's breads a distinctive, beautiful signature.

I lost track of time as I massaged sweet loaves into greased pans and set them on the warming racks.

I didn't even hear the door open or footsteps until a voice sounded behind me.

A man's voice shook me from my happy baking escape.

"Juliet."

I dropped a loaf on the floor and turned to find Roger staring at me. He looked as if he had had less sleep than me. His hair was messy and his shirt untucked from his jeans.

"Roger, you're here early." I glanced around for the clock, but we hadn't hung it up yet. It couldn't even be five yet.

"You probably heard the news." His eyes were bloodshot.

Should I be worried? I backed closer to the countertop. Which drawer had I put the knives in?

"About what?" I decided for the moment it would be best to pretend like I didn't know what he was talking about.

"About Clarissa."

"No, what?"

He stepped closer. I ran my hand along the cold, smooth countertop. How could I open the drawers without calling attention to myself? Maybe Thomas had been right. Maybe I was in danger. I should have woken Carlos and brought him with me.

I started doing math in my head. How long had he and Ramiro been asleep? When he woke up and discovered that I wasn't there, he would surely come looking for me, right? Is this how Megan had felt?

"Clarissa was arrested an hour ago," Roger said. His voice was flat and lifeless.

"For what?" Did he know that I knew? I wondered what Thomas and Detective Kerry had told him.

"For attempting to poison you."

I gulped. Roger's eyes were wild. "I can't believe it."

Should I respond? I scooted farther away toward the sink, fumbling around for the scoring knife. It wasn't that big, but it would do in a pinch.

"She's not well, Clarissa. I know that she didn't really want to hurt you. She's always had terrible jealousy issues. Her father left her mother for a much younger woman when Clarissa was in high school and she's never been able to let it go. We've had the same argument for years. I've told her time and time again that she's the only woman for me, but anytime I work with a female client, especially one who's younger like you." He paused and tried to smile. "Her jealousy flares up."

I wasn't sure that I was out of the woods yet, but Roger sounded dumbfounded and dejected, not like he was about to hurt me too. However, I continued to move toward the scoring knife.

"That's why she kept stopping by. She wanted to keep an eye on you. I told her that not only could you be our daughter, but you were obviously deeply in love with your husband."

Was it obvious that I still had feelings for Carlos?

"I thought I had convinced her that she had nothing to worry about. I showed her plans, I gave her a tour of the bakeshop, I invited her to come by as often as she wanted, but apparently that wasn't enough. The police say that she hired a private detective and that she put poison in your drink. I'm so sorry, Juliet."

My fear dissipated. Roger was clearly distraught.

"It's not your fault," I said, taking my hand off the drawer handle. My fingers shook a bit as I released my grip.

"It is. I should have gotten her help sooner." He placed his hands on his head. "I've suggested counseling to help her heal her past wounds, but I never insisted. I thought we could work through it together. I never imagined that she would do something so drastic."

"Roger, do you think that she had anything to do with Megan's death?"

He shook his head. "I don't think so, but I would have told you a day ago that there was no possibility that she would have tried to hurt you. She swore to the police that she wasn't trying to kill you. She just wanted to make you sick and send you a warning." He rubbed his temples. "My God, even saying that sounds terrible. But, honestly, I don't think she wanted you dead. I think she went a bit nuts, and thought if you were sick you wouldn't be at the bakeshop and I could finish the job and be done with Torte."

That made logical sense.

"And you don't know anything about her connection with the Brown Family Group?"

He bit his bottom lip. "No. Nothing. I talked to her about that after we saw you. Honestly, the arts council is her thing. I try to stay out of it, but I'm not a huge fan of the Brown Group. Personally, I'd like her to find other funding sources."

"Did she do any fund-raising with them?"

"Not that I know of. She claims that she was simply putting some feelers out, but I don't know what to think anymore."

"What about Megan? Could Megan have seen Clarissa put the poison in my drink? Maybe Clarissa got scared and went to confront Megan about it?"

Roger covered his mouth with his hand. "Do you think that could have happened? Is that why the police took her in?"

"I don't know. I'm just thinking out loud." On second thought, that didn't make any sense. Why would Megan have taken a drink from the poisoned glass?

The intoxicating smell of bread baking in the ovens was a strange juxtaposition to our conversation.

"I need to get to Medford right away, but I had a feeling you might be here early and I wanted to apologize. I can't believe that she could have wanted to hurt you and I refuse to believe that she could have killed Megan, but I guess we're going to have to wait and see what the police say."

"It's okay, Roger. I'm sorry about this too. You've been wonderful to work with, and if it matters, I won't press charges. I'll tell Thomas and Detective Kerry that. I want Clarissa to get help too."

"Thank you. That's very gracious and generous of you." He looked toward the door. "I should go. Please accept my apology."

"Of course."

He left and I took the first batch of golden bread from the oven. I wasn't sure what to believe, but I had a nagging feeling that I was missing something. Were there two separate cases at play? Instead of assuming that the poisoning and murder were connected, maybe it was time to consider that they weren't. And maybe it was also time to throw Lance's dad's murder into the mix. There were too many points of connection.

Chapter Twenty-four

I didn't have time to stew on anything other than Torte.
The crew arrived early for a morning debrief.

"You've got us locked in this dreary dungeon," Sterling teased. To my surprise, he had shed his usual gray hoodie and wore a tight black T-shirt and skinny jeans.

"Speak for yourself," Andy bantered. "We know who the boss loves best. I'm upstairs in front of those huge windows, while you'll be stuck here with cobwebs and spiders." He flipped his baseball hat backward.

I swiped a wooden spoon from a canister on the counter. "Show me one cobweb or spider."

Everyone laughed.

"The space is amazing, Jules." Sterling gave an appreciative nod to the new workstation.

"OMG! I agree," Bethany said, snapping pictures on her phone. "Our Instagram followers are going to eat this up."

"Eat this up, nice." Andy nudged her shoulder.

Bethany's cheeks flamed with color. She fluffed her bouncy curls. "I didn't even mean to say that, but I've been doing live stories every day of Torte's progress. I can't wait to show everyone the final reveal."

"And don't forget that you and Steph get to organize the decorating station however you see fit."

Stephanie nursed a coffee. "What's the plan? Where are we all going to be working? It's going to be kind of weird to be in two different spaces."

"I know. I think it's going to feel a little clunky for the short term until we put in the new stairs. Once those are in, it will be different but I don't think we'll feel quite as disconnected. You and Sterling will both be stationed in the dungeon." I made a goofy face. "Andy, you'll be upstairs at the coffee bar, of course. And Bethany, I'm hoping that you and I can kind of be floaters."

"Sure." She motioned for the four of us to squeeze together. "Let me get a shot of everyone before the madness begins."

We posed for the picture. "Before we start to divide and conquer I need everyone's help cleaning upstairs. There's a pretty thick layer of dust that needs to be wiped down. Oh, and I'm putting a HELP WANTED sign on the front door today," I continued. "If any of you have a friend or someone you would recommend, let me know. We're going to need coffee help for you, Andy, and more bakery help down here."

"I might know someone," Andy said. "I'll ask around."

We finished our walk-through, cleaned the upstairs, and then everyone headed to their stations. Stephanie was right. Having the two spaces disconnected felt strange. A wave of regret passed over me. I hoped I hadn't made a mistake. One of the things that I loved most about Torte was the cozy, welcoming feeling I got each time I walked through the front doors. That, and the lively energy among us. It was temporary, right? I thought as I sifted flour for a batch of Swedish tea cookies.

Connections, disconnections—that seemed to be the theme of my life of late. Megan's murder, the poisoning, Mom's marriage, my relationship with Carlos and Ramiro. It was as if invisible strings stretched between each of us, creating an intricate and complicated web.

My worry faded slightly once the kitchen was alive with the scent of chili verde soup, gooey grilled cheese on black bread, and boysenberry scones. I loaded a tray with tea cookies, scones, chocolate mint wafers, and mini cupcakes to take upstairs. Sterling was adding diced cilantro to the soup. "Hey, how solid is the plan for upstairs?" he asked, stirring the giant vat of bubbling soup.

"How solid?"

"Yeah. I mean is it set in stone?" He diced green chilis and added them to the soup, which was bubbling with white beans, chicken stock, shredded chicken, onions, garlic, and cumin. We would serve it with a dollop of sour cream, shredded jack cheese, and tortilla chips. I had a feeling it would sell out before the lunch rush was finished.

I leaned to breathe in a whiff of the fresh, summery soup. "It's done. They're going to get started on the stairs this week, maybe even today." I paused. Given that Roger's wife had been arrested I wondered if construction would stall. "Why? Do you have an idea or something?"

He dipped his pinkie into the soup to taste. "Kind of. The four of us were talking at the wedding about our favorite summer memories and one of mine was going to this bakery down on the beach in Santa Cruz. It reminds me of Torte, only more surfer, less Shakespeare." His grin made his brilliant blue eyes light up. "They made a bunch of traditional baked goods—cinnamon rolls, sticky buns—you know. But they also made their own ice cream. I've been seeing concretes—a frozen custard—around lately, and I don't know if there's space up there, but I thought it could be cool to add in ice cream. I'd love to learn how to make it with our spin. Carlos mentioned that he could teach me."

"Oh, he did, did he?" I gave Sterling a fake scowl. "What else has he told you?"

Sterling laughed. "Hey, what happens in the kitchen, stays in the kitchen."

If Mom were here she would have swatted him with a dish towel.

"What do you think?" Sterling set the spoon on the side of the stove. "Really fresh flavors like Meyer lemon and blueberry, strawberry rhubarb, honey lavender. You know, like Torte-style."

"That's a great idea. Let me check with Roger later to see if we can tweak the plan. I can't imagine that it would be that hard to make space for a cooler."

"Right, and we were all saying that it wouldn't have to be big. Maybe enough to hold five or six daily flavors at most. I bet it would sell really well, especially with the theater crowd."

"I'm sure it would." I picked up the tray to deliver upstairs. Ashland summers were hot, with average temperatures in the nineties. Offering customers a cold dish of hand-churned ice cream or custard was a slam dunk. I loved the fact that Sterling and the rest of the team were brainstorming ways to improve Torte. I was so lucky.

Carrying heavy trays of pastries, soup, and sandwiches was going to give my legs and arms a workout. I had to balance the tray and make sure I had solid footing. At least once we had an internal staircase we wouldn't have to navigate the busy sidewalk and the line out the front door. I had to heave the tray up over my shoulder to get it past customers waiting to order drinks and pastries. Inside it was business as usual, despite the plastic barrier and construction signs. A small line stretched from the temporary coffee bar toward the door. I squeezed between customers with the tray of pastries.

"What do you have there, Jules?" The owner of the chocolate shop around the corner eyed a boysenberry scone. I had gone to high school with her and she stopped by at least once a week with her decadent chocolate for us to use in baking. That was yet another thing I loved about living in my hometown. Not a day went by that I didn't bump into someone I knew from my childhood.

"Hot out of the oven." I offered up the tray. Everyone in line ooohed and aaahed.

Andy managed the line with ease. He moved to the beat of the music playing overhead as he scooped ice into glasses and poured thick, creamy espresso shots.

"How's it going so far?" I slid the tray of pastries into the case.

"Awesome." He handed a customer an iced coconut

cold brew. "Everyone's happy that we're caffeinating them again."

"Excellent. I'll be up to check in soon."

"If I need anything I'll just pound on the floor." Andy stomped his feet twice.

"Good plan." I ducked under the plastic to get to the office. I wanted to make some HELP WANTED signs. It was time to move forward and if our expansion was going to be a success we needed more hands on deck, so to speak. I posted the sign on the front door. Bethany had suggested posting to our social media as well. Hopefully, we'd find a perfect mix—a hard worker who was eager to learn and someone who blended in with the team.

As I left to go back downstairs, I spotted Lance sitting on a bench in the middle of the plaza. He was talking to his brother, Leo. Was Lance confronting Leo? Was he telling him that his lawyer was corrupt? I wanted to eavesdrop but there was no way of listening in on their conversation without being seen. So I opted for the next best solution—pastry.

I poured two cups of coffee and tucked a few tea cookies into a bag. Bribery in the form of sweets never hurt.

"Morning," I called, crossing the street. I offered them steaming cups of coffee. "I thought you might want your *usual*," I said to Lance.

He shot me a narrow stare. "Darling, how thoughtful of you."

Leo took the coffee.

"Tea cookie?" I held out the bag.

He snatched that too.

"Manners, dear brother, manners. We have a famed pastry chef in our presence and ripping a bag from her dainty and valuable hands is simply uncivilized."

"Whatever." Leo rolled his eyes. He stuffed a cookie in his mouth. "Thanks," he mumbled through a mouthful of crumbs.

They looked like the odd couple. The resemblance between them was undeniable, with their angular jawbones and tall, thin frames. But that's where their similarities ended. Leo wore a pair of heavy work boots, baggy jeans, and another flannel shirt. Lance had returned to his standard daily suit. Today's was deep gray with a lemon-yellow tie and polished shoes.

"Juliet, I was just discussing with my dear brother what you and I have unearthed."

"You were?" What was Lance doing?

"Indeed. I explained that the police have discovered that Jarvis O. Sandberg is a hack."

Leo stuffed another cookie in his mouth. He didn't appear bothered by this news.

"I'm advising my brother to rethink his position on the family trust. Otherwise, I shall have to take matters into my own hands and proceed with a lawsuit." Lance held his coffee under his nose. "Your new stepfather is the head of police; what were you saying the jail term is for elder abuse?"

I had no idea. "Uh . . ."

"Didn't you say twenty years? Or was it more?"

"I think," I started to reply, but Lance cut me off.

"More, yes, you're right. It was thirty, wasn't it?"

Leo's face was covered in powdered sugar and cookie crumbs. Lance sighed audibly. "Clean up," he said, removing a pressed handkerchief from his breast pocket and handing it to his brother.

"Let's drop it, okay?" Leo smeared the crumbs around his face with the silky cloth.

"Drop what?" Lance replied in a cheerful tone.

"Everything. It's over."

"What's over, dearest brother?"

Leo crumpled the handkerchief in his palm. "You win. You keep your portion of the trust, I keep mine, and we don't ever need to talk again as far as I'm concerned."

I couldn't tell if his words had actually hurt or if Lance was tapping into his acting reserves.

"Never speak again, when we've just rekindled our relationship? How tragic."

Leo looked to me. I threw my hands up. I didn't want any part of being in the middle of their family feud. "Look, you can drop the act. I know you don't care about me. Like I said, it's over. I've already fired Jarvis."

"A likely story." The sarcasm in Lance's voice cut deep.

"I did," he insisted. "I didn't want to hire him anyway. Sarah was the one who said he was the best. She knew him from before. I guess they used to work together or something. She said that he could get me the maximum amount of money. I know you don't believe me, but I want the Brown Family Group to live on into the next generation. We need cash flow."

"Sarah recommended Jarvis?" Lance said. I could tell that the same thought that was forming in my head was forming in his.

"Yeah." Leo munched another cookie. "She does all

that stuff. I'm not a numbers guy. I know the business, but Sarah manages the money and tax and legal stuff."

"How long has she been with the company?"

Leo shrugged. "A couple years, I guess. Believe it or not, I hired her as a personal nurse for Dad."

"She's a nurse?" Lance shared a look with me.

"Not exactly. I think she's a medical assistant or something like that. I was looking for a caregiver and she was the first person to respond to the ad. She and Dad hit it off right away."

I made a mental note not to hire the first person to respond to our ad at Torte—at least not without checking references.

Leo dabbed the wrinkled handkerchief on his chin. "She told me that for other clients she would help manage their accounts and do basic stuff like taking checks to the bank, mailings, and organization. She was there anyway so it all worked out."

"Or did it?" Lance asked.

"Huh?" Leo turned to his brother.

"Leo, listen to what you're saying. Did you hire her on the spot? Did you call references? Check out her story?"

"No. She had a couple letters of recommendation with her. They were good. What more did I need?"

"My God!" Lance threw one hand on his forehead. He set his coffee on the ground. "All this time I've thought that you killed Dad."

Leo's jaw dropped. "What? What are you talking about?"

Lance patted his brother's thigh. "You're not a killer, are you, Leo? You're just not a business guy. Of course."

He looked at me. "My brother isn't an evil mastermind. He's a logger, and a damn good one."

"What are you talking about?" Leo stared at me and then Lance.

"Are you thinking what I'm thinking?" Lance asked me.

I nodded. "Yes. Oh my gosh, why didn't we make the connection earlier? Your father, the trust, Megan."

Lance jumped to his feet and patted his brother on the back. "Exactly. We know who the killer is."

Chapter Twenty-five

"Juliet, how have we been so dense?" Lance's tone was incredulous. "Juliet, call Thomas. We need him here immediately."

I felt sorry for Leo. He looked like a confused child. Lance on the other hand assumed his role of elder brother with flourish.

"Don't dally, Juliet. Call the police," Lance commanded.

I called Thomas. He picked up on the second ring. "Hey, Jules. What's up?"

"Where are you?"

"At the station."

I glanced past the information kiosk in the center of the plaza to the blue awnings of the police station. "Come outside. We're by the fountains."

"Who?"

"Me and Lance and his brother. We know who killed Megan."

"What?"

"Just come outside." I clicked off the phone. A minute later, Thomas and Detective Kerry, who was in yet another crisp suit, raced over.

Kerry's face clouded the moment she saw us. "You guys have to stop doing this. Seriously. We're going to end up the laughingstock of the Rogue Valley if two civilians keep trying to solve our cases."

Thomas pulled out his iPad. "It's okay. I've got this."

Lance pressed his hands together. "Trust me, Detective, you are most certainly going to want to hear what we've uncovered."

Detective Kerry sighed. "I don't doubt it. You're wearing me down. You know that, don't you?"

Lance tapped her angular jaw. "Honey, you know it. But you're so lovely when you smile, and don't you worry, yours truly will hook you up with the best seats in the house for any show you want as a token of my appreciation for letting us tag along on a real investigation."

Kerry looked to Thomas for support. "It's a lost cause."

Lance knew that he had an audience and was ready to take the stage. Then he stopped and seemed to take notice of me. "Would you like to do the honors, Juliet, or should I?"

I swept my hand in front of me. "Go ahead."

"Let me give you a bit of background first. You see, my brother and I have not seen eye to eye for many years." He proceeded to give Thomas and Detective Kerry the condensed version of his past.

"What does this have to do with our investigation?" Detective Kerry asked when Lance paused.

"I was just getting to that part." Lance waved his index finger at her. I wondered if she was internally considering slapping a pair of handcuffs on him. "I knew that my father's death wasn't natural. Yes, he was ill, and yes, he didn't have much time left, but someone sped up the process. The Professor was considering possibilities before he left, but without any evidence his hands were tied."

Thomas made notes on his iPad.

"Now it's all clear. My brother hired Sarah as a personal assistant. She must have realized that she had won the jackpot. She realized that my brother, a brilliant logger"—Lance patted Leo's knee—"was not a businessman and she seized the opportunity. She craftily weaved her way into the company and everyone's good graces. Then she began making suggestions. Taking over small things at first. The mail, bank deposits, organizing files. She quickly become invaluable. And that, my friends, is when she really dug her heels in to craft her master plan. She had worked with Jarvis in the past and probably gave her old buddy a call. She was working a scam and needed help. If she could convince Leo to come after me then he would have total access over the Brown Family trust, and she would control the purse strings."

"This is a lot of speculation," Detective Kerry interjected.

"True. True," Lance acknowledged. "But hear me out. She was my father's primary caregiver. When I popped back into the picture she must have freaked out. My skill set is different from Leo's. She must have known she had a small window of opportunity. So, she convinced Leo to cut me out of the trust, forced my father to sign the new documents. But what she didn't count on was my renewed relationship with my father. When she realized that we had reconciled, she probably panicked. She had to kill him, because otherwise he would talk. If I asked him about cutting me from the trust he would have said that he hadn't been part of it."

Everything Lance was saying I was thinking internally. It was as if pieces of the puzzle were falling from the sky and landing in perfect place in front of us.

"She killed him. It must have been simple. Adding a dose of something to his IV, slipping him something in his nightly glass of milk. I don't know how she did it. I'll leave that to you two, but she's the killer."

Leo stood up. "Are you crazy? Sarah wouldn't do that."

"Are you sure about that?" Lance asked. "She had the means, she had the motive, she had the opportunity. If I'm not mistaken I do believe those are the three things that the police look for in a case like this."

"But why?" Leo asked.

"For the money, dear brother. She realized that you were hands-off. You have a singular—and might I add, extremely worthy—goal to grow the Brown Family business. But she knew that you weren't about to go over the financial statements line by line. It would be easy for her to start tucking away cash. Lots of cash."

"Yes, and for the time being no one noticed. You were happy to have Sarah manage the books for you, right?" I asked Leo.

He nodded. "Math isn't my thing."

"Exactly. I'm not blaming you. I'm just pointing out

that the company is worth millions. At some point someone would have realized that money was missing. You must have accountants, right?"

Leo rolled his eyes. "Yeah, big brother, I'm not an idiot. I have an accountant."

Lance nodded. "Of course. That's likely why she wanted Leo to hire Jarvis. She knew that Jarvis was dirty and could help her funnel money. Or maybe she planned to stash away as much cash as she could, knowing that eventually someone would raise a red flag. At that point, she would make her escape and disappear before anyone figured it out."

"But do you have proof?" Detective Kerry asked.

"No." Lance shook his head. "That's your job. There must be a paper trail. I'm guessing that Megan found it. She told Adam that she had enough evidence to go to the police."

"Right," I said, looking at Thomas. "And we kept thinking that the poisoning and Megan's death were related. What if they weren't? Clarissa has admitted to spiking the wine. Only she intended that for me. Not Megan. Sarah must have come after Megan."

Thomas typed rapidly. "They make a pretty good case," he said to Detective Kerry.

She sighed. "True. We came to the same conclusion about the two incidents."

I felt vindicated.

"Sounds like we need to make a trip to Medford," Thomas said, shutting off the iPad.

"Can we come along?" Lance clapped his hands together.

Detective Kerry held out her hands to stop him. "Absolutely not. If any of you so much as set one foot outside of Ashland city limits in the next hour I'll arrest you." Then she shot him a quick wink, revealing a dimple on her left cheek.

"Under house arrest again. No, thank you." Lance moaned. He turned to Leo. "That's fine. You go do your police thing. I owe my brother a hearty breakfast."

Leo still looked slightly shaken, but Lance wrapped an arm around his shoulder. "Let's go, brother. We have some catching up to do."

I couldn't help but smile as I watched them cross the street and head up Main Street. Yes, they were very different, but they were brothers and I hoped that this was the start of new friendship for them.

"You're good, Jules?" Thomas asked.

"Yeah, I'm fine." This time that wasn't a lie. I was glad to see a positive resolution between Lance and Leo and equally relieved that Clarissa wasn't the killer.

Detective Kerry shot me a final warning glance. This time her humor came through. "You are back to baking, got it? No more sleuthing around town."

I gave her a serious nod. "I've never heard sweeter words."

Thomas grinned. "Good, because we're going to be hungry for some of your raspberry Danish when we get back. Arresting a killer always makes me hungry."

"Don't let him tell you that," I said to Detective Kerry. "He's just always hungry."

A wide smile cracked through her angular face. "Yeah. I've noticed."

With that they left. I paused for a moment and surveyed the plaza. Hopefully, Thomas and Detective Kerry would have Sarah and maybe Jarvis in police custody soon. I was ready for life to return to normal and to immerse myself in Torte's new space.

Chapter Twenty-six

Later that afternoon, Thomas stopped by to inform me that they had found Sarah at the Brown Family Group headquarters. She hadn't confessed, but they had teams searching every square inch of the property, as well as Megan's office again. They would be pulling up bank statements for Sarah's personal accounts as well as the Brown Family trust. Jarvis had confessed that Sarah had him put together the paperwork to write Lance out of the trust. In exchange for a lenient sentence he had agreed to testify that Mr. Brown was not of sound mind or body when he signed the documents. Jarvis would never be allowed to practice law in the state of Oregon again.

In light of the new information the medical examiner would be reviewing Mr. Brown's autopsy report. "Good work, Jules," Thomas said, slurping a bowl of Sterling's chili verde soup. "You and Lance were a big help, but please don't tell Detective Kerry I said that. She'll kill me."

I chuckled. "How's it going working with her?"

Thomas swirled his spoon around the edge of the soup bowl. "You know, I can't believe that I'm going to say this, but not bad. She's actually pretty cool. I mean you have to get past the suit and the all-business attitude, but she's really funny."

"That's great." Was it my imagination or did Thomas's cheeks have a soft glow to them?

"What about you? How is it having Carlos and his son here?"

"It's kind of the same. I didn't expect them to fit in as well as they have."

"Everyone loves them," Thomas replied. Something had shifted between us. We were talking like friends. In the past, there had been a thin layer of tension between us when we spoke of Carlos. That was gone. I was glad to be able to speak openly with Thomas. He had been an integral part of my formative years and I valued his friendship.

"Do you think they'll stay?" he asked, taking a bite of sourdough bread.

"No. No." I shook my head. I hadn't allowed myself to even entertain the thought of them staying. I was already dreading having to say good-bye. "Ramiro's mother lives in Spain and he has school and . . ." I trailed off.

Thomas met my eyes. "I get it. But I just have to say that it's obvious that they both really love you, Jules. You deserve that."

"Thanks, so do you." I excused myself before I started to tear up. Thomas headed out to the plaza with a bag of Torte goodies. I took a moment to compose myself before going to check on how things were going downstairs.

In the basement, the team was blasting reggae music. Carlos and Ramiro were both in on the action.

"Are you guys going to break out in a conga line?" I teased.

Carlos beamed when he spotted me. "Julieta, we are christening the new kitchen." He shimmied his body to the beat of the music. "It is a dance party, sí?"

Even Steph couldn't resist moving her head in rhythm with the drums.

"Shouldn't you be working?" I tried to make my face look stern.

That made everyone laugh.

My phone buzzed. I pulled it from my pocket. The call was from Mom. She and the Professor wanted to FaceTime. "Shut off the music. Come say hi, everyone." I held up the phone. Mom and the Professor appeared on the screen. They were standing on a white sandy beach. The breeze made Mom's hair fly behind her.

"You're all together," she said with delight.

"Hey, Mrs. C., how's the beach?" Andy leaned over my shoulder.

"It's great. It's wonderful. We're having the best time, aren't we, Doug?"

The Professor's smile was equally wide. "The sea and the surf are good for the soul, and with my gorgeous bride by my side, who could ask for more?" He winked and waved hello.

"How's the renovation?" Mom asked.

"We'll show you." I handed the phone to Bethany and let her take Mom on a virtual tour of the new space.

"It's beautiful," Mom exclaimed as Bethany moved the phone from station to station.

"Not a word about anything else," I whispered to everyone as Bethany started to move back toward us.

Sterling nodded. Andy and Bethany shared a strange look. I guess I hadn't even realized that the team wasn't completely in the loop. That was probably for the best. My poor staff was going to think I was crazy.

Mom clapped. "It's so fun to see everyone and the new space. I can't wait to get back and see it in person."

"Not too fast, Mrs. C. You're on your honeymoon."

"Don't worry, Andy. I promise that Doug and I intend to soak up every minute of our time here." She blew us kisses. "We'll see you in a week."

Everyone waved a final good-bye before I hung up the phone. It was good to see her so happy. We returned to Carlos's dance party and organization. I couldn't believe how well everything had turned out, especially now that Megan's killer had been apprehended. I wasn't sure what was going to happen with Clarissa, but as I had told Roger I would do my best to convince whoever I needed to not to pursue charges as long as she committed to getting some professional help.

I was ready for Torte's next evolution and excited about what was ahead. Late in the afternoon, when everyone was focused on cleanup and prep for the next day, Carlos pulled me aside.

"Julieta, can we speak for a moment?"

"Sure." I tried to hold a brave face, but my stomach dropped.

We moved into the seating area and sat in two oversized chairs in front of the woodstove. There was no need to light a fire today, but I knew this would be a coveted spot in the winter months.

"I must ask you something, *mi querida,* but I want you not to respond right away. I want to ask you this today so that you have some time to think and to consider my proposal. Ramiro and I will be here for another three days, so you do not need to answer until it is time for us to go."

I gulped. Was he going to ask me to come back to the ship with him? We'd had this conversation a dozen times and my answer hadn't changed. As much as I missed Carlos, I didn't want to return to my old life.

"Okay."

He scooted his chair closer so that our knees were touching. "Ramiro and I have been so happy here with you and your wonderful team for these past few days."

"I know. Everyone has loved having you here."

"Everyone?" His eyes held a longing.

"Everyone," I said quietly.

"Sí, I have loved being so close with you again, Julieta, which is why I must ask if we might stay."

"Stay?" I couldn't believe what I was hearing. Carlos wanted to stay.

"Sí, I have asked the ship for leave. They have granted my request. It is temporary. They will hold a position for me for one year. No longer. If I do not choose to return in a year, then I must reapply or find a new job, but for one year they will allow me to go."

"Wow."

He nodded. "And I have spoken with Ramiro's mother. She does not want him to be so far away, but he has wanted to study in America. It is common in Spain to travel, to study abroad. She will miss him desperately, but she has said she will allow him to come and go to school here next year."

"She has?" I knew I was only repeating everything Carlos was saying but I was dumbfounded by this news.

"I do not want to pressure you. I want to be with you. More than ever, but I understand if you do not feel the same. I also understand why you have fallen so madly and deeply for Ashland. We love it too."

"But what would you do? Don't you think you would be bored?"

"Bored?" Carlos leaned back and frowned. "Me? Never. How could I be bored with you? And the wonderful townspeople and so much food?"

I chuckled.

His tone turned serious again. "This is one of the reasons I have invested in Uva. If you are willing to have us and give us a try—another chance—I will run the winery. I would love to cook and be among the grapes each day. I can smell the earth right now." He closed his eyes and inhaled.

"I would want to give you your space. I do not want to interfere at Torte, but I would help and Ramiro would too. He would love to work with Andy after his classes at school."

I wanted to pinch myself. Was this real? Was Carlos actually saying that he wanted to stay in Ashland and become part of my world here?

"It is a lot to ask, I know. That is why I want you to think about it. Would you give us a chance?"

I started to speak, but he held a finger up to my lips. "Not now, *mi querida*. You do not answer yet. You must sit with this idea and let it simmer, no?"

"Okay." I nodded.

He squeezed my hand. Then he pulled me to standing and planted a kiss on my forehead. "Come, we must join the others. I have promised them an ice-cream workshop tonight. We will make some fabulous fish and a salad and open some wine. It will be a party, sí?"

"Sí." I clasped his hand tight and we returned to the kitchen together. I didn't need time to think. I already knew my answer. Of course, I wanted Carlos and Ramiro to stay. I wasn't sure if Carlos really belonged in Ashland, but I was willing to give it a shot. How could I say no?

Recipes

Pie Fries

Ingredients:
- 2 premade pie crusts (you can make your own like Jules or for a quick, fun dessert buy refrigerated crusts)
- ½ cup butter
- ½ cup cinnamon and sugar
- 1 cup of raspberry jam
- *If desired, serve in fry containers from your local party store

Directions:
Roll out pie crust into a thin sheet. Use a pizza cutter to cut ½-inch strips. Melt butter. Brush each side of the strips with butter, then sprinkle with cinnamon and sugar. Place on a greased cookie sheet. Bake at 350 degrees for ten to twelve minutes. Serve immediately with raspberry-jam dipping sauce. For a fun party dessert serve pie fries in fry boxes with a side of "ketchup" aka raspberry jam.

Greek Chicken Sheet Pan Lunch

Ingredients:
    4 chicken breasts
    ½ cup olive oil
    16 oz fresh green beans
    3 lemons
    2 large onions
    8 cloves of garlic
    1 can diced fire-roasted tomatoes
    1 jar Kalamata olives
    1 teaspoon oregano
    1 teaspoon basil
    1 teaspoon salt
    1 teaspoon pepper

Directions:
Dice onions and garlic and add to a mixing bowl. Cut the chicken breasts into thin strips. Rinse green beans and toss with chicken, onions, and garlic. Drizzle with olive oil and mix together with tomatoes, oregano, basil, salt, and pepper. Slice one lemon and squeeze juice into mixture. Spread mixture onto a greased sheet pan. Quarter lemons and arrange on pan. Sprinkle in olives. Bake at 400 degrees for thirty minutes.

Chili Verde

Ingredients:
    1 pound dried white beans
    6 cups chicken broth
    3 cloves garlic
    2 onions
    2 cans diced green chilies

    2 teaspoons cumin
    1 teaspoon oregano
    1 teaspoon cloves
    1 teaspoon chili powder
    4 cups chopped chicken
    2–3 cups chicken broth

Directions:

In a large stockpot combine beans, six cups of chicken broth, diced garlic, and one chopped onion. Bring to a boil, cover, reduce heat, and simmer for two to three hours, or until the beans are tender. In a skillet sauté remaining chopped onion, green chili peppers, and spices. Add chopped chicken and remaining chicken broth. Add to the beans and simmer for one more hour.

Garnish with a dollop of sour cream and shredded cheddar cheese.

Grilled Black Bread Sandwiches

Ingredients:

    8 slices of molasses or chocolate black bread
    8 oz of goat cheese
    2 Granny Smith apples
    Balsamic vinegar
    ¼ cup butter

Directions:

Slice the Granny Smith apples. Spread a layer of goat cheese on each side of the bread. Layer in apple slices. Drizzle with balsamic vinegar. Melt 2 tablespoons of butter in a frying pan on medium heat. Grill sandwich on both sides until bread is crispy and cheese has melted (approximately two to three minutes each side).

Triple Berry Coffee Cake

Ingredients for cake:
- ½ cup butter
- ¾ cup sugar
- 1 egg
- ½ cup buttermilk
- 2 cups flour
- 2 teaspoons baking powder
- 1 teaspoon salt
- 1 teaspoon cinnamon
- 2 cups of a triple berry mixture—any berries in season will work. Jules uses blackberries, marionberries, and blueberries

Topping ingredients:
- ¼ cup butter
- ¼ cup oats
- ¼ cup brown sugar
- ½ teaspoon cinnamon
- ½ teaspoon nutmeg
- ½ teaspoon allspice

Directions:
Preheat oven to 350 degrees. Cream butter and sugar together in a mixing bowl. Add egg and buttermilk. Slowly incorporate flour, baking powder, salt, and cinnamon. Once mixture is smooth, fold in berries, careful not to damage the berries. Pour into a greased 8×8 pan. In a separate bowl, fork together butter, oats, brown sugar, and spices. Crumble over the top of the batter and bake for thirty minutes.

Coconut Cold Brew

Andy's take on a classic cold brew. Simple, creamy coconut perfection on a hot summer day.

Ingredients:
  1 cup good quality cold brew
  ½ cup coconut milk
  ¼ cup ice

Directions:
Fill chilled pint glass with ice. Pour one cup of good quality cold brew over ice. Pour in half cup of coconut milk and allow to sink to the bottom of the glass.

Read on for an excerpt from the
next installment in the Bakeshop mysteries

LIVE AND LET PIE

❧

Coming in January 2019 from St. Martin's
Paperbacks!

They say that you can't go back, that it's better to keep the past in the rear-view mirror. That may be true, but as of late it felt like my past was creeping into everything I touched. Not that it was necessarily a bad thing. It had started with my mom's gorgeous midsummer wedding. Seeing her marry her longtime love the Professor (Ashland's resident detective and Shakespeare scholar) had filled my heart with happiness and opened up memories of loss that I thought I had buried long ago. When my dad died in my formative years, it forever altered the course of my future. Mom and I had cocooned ourselves in, sharing the burden of grief, and pouring all our energies into Torte, our family bakeshop. We weren't merely mother and daughter. We were best friends. She was my rock, my confidante, and my steadfast supporter. She had nudged me (well, maybe more like forced me) to follow my dreams of attending culinary school. Without her gentle, yet firm guidance I might have never left my hometown of Ashland, Oregon. Now I had come full-circle. After years of traversing the seas on a luxury cruise ship I had returned to Ashland, and hadn't once glanced back.

The only problem was that my husband Carlos was still out to sea. Like Odysseus, he had been sailing vast oceans lured by the siren song of steel blue waters. Just a while ago, he had professed his desire to return to me and plant his feet on Ashland's sturdy ground. I was torn. As much as I missed Carlos, I wasn't convinced that he belonged on land. Some people are born to wander. I couldn't quite picture Carlos thriving in our small, tight-knit community. Wanderlust ran deep through his Spanish blood. He made fast friends at every port of call and thrived on the thrill of ever-changing adventures. Ashland was bucolic, quiet, and quaint. Not that we were without culture. In fact, quite the opposite. As home to the famed Oregon Shakespeare Festival our sun-drenched town nestled in the Siskiyou Mountains saw travelers from all over the globe, who came to take in a production of *Sleeping Beauty* under the stars or dine at one of dozens of award-winning restaurants. But there was a difference between catering to adventure seekers and actually seeking adventure. I wasn't sure what Carlos was going to decide, but I knew that Ashland was exactly where I was meant to be.

More importantly I was meant to be at an interview in less than ten minutes. I shook myself from my thoughts and laced my tennis shoes. I had run home to change in between the morning rush and lunch after splattering tempered chocolate all over myself. Kitchen flubs can happen to the best chefs. I had had my fair share of disasters over the years, but today's mess had more to do with lack of space.

Torte was undergoing a major expansion. We had recently remolded the basement which was now home to our baking operations. The next phase of our growth was underway and involved punching stairs through to the coffee bar and dining area above. Our contractor had run into a couple of challenges (one being that our architect's wife had been accused of attempting to poison me) that had set us back a few weeks. Dust and the constant sound of hammering and drilling don't exactly mix with the artisan pastries and coffees we serve at Torte. I couldn't wait for construction to wrap and to get back to the business of baking.

In the interim, I had been lining up interviews for potential new hires. We had always run a tight ship at Torte with a small but mighty staff. Our physical expansion and Mom's desire to cut back a bit meant that we needed to ramp up our team. I was excited about the possibility. Ashland is a college town, home of Southern Oregon University, so there was never a shortage of energetic and eager help, but I wanted to make sure whoever we hired would be a match. The wrong person could completely change the recipe we had created with our young and highly capable staff.

Sterling, a closet poet with soul-piercing eyes and a gentle heart, was responsible for the majority of our savory items—daily soups, grilled paninis, fresh chopped salads, and hearty pastas. Bethany and Stephanie were my pastry stars. They couldn't be more different in appearance or attitude. Steph's goth style and aloof attitude, paired with purple hair and a tendency to stare at her feet while speaking, gave off the impression that she didn't care. Nothing could be further from the truth.

Working with her had taught me never to judge a book by its cover. Stephanie was devoutly dedicated to the bakeshop and spent her spare time (when she wasn't studying for her coursework at SOU) watching baking tutorials on the Pastry Channel and poring through cookbooks. Bethany was bubbly and upbeat. Her cheery, positive attitude brought a lightness to the kitchen. Her baking skills were equally vibrant. She had a natural sense of how to balance sugary confections so that they didn't end up cloyingly sweet. Finishing out the team was Andy, our resident barista and all-around good guy. Andy's coffee creations had become a thing of legend. Locals and visitors lined up for his foamy lattes and flavor-infused cold brews.

The trick would be finding new staff with complimentary skills to our current crew. It was a big task, but I was up for the challenge.

Armed with a list of interview questions and a clean t-shirt, I left my apartment and headed for Torte. The minute I stepped outside my small apartment above Elevation, an outdoor store, the sounds of laughter and music greeted me. The plaza, Ashland's downtown core, was awash with colorful activity. Tourists loaded with shopping totes stopped to admire a window display at the jewelry shop where sparkling diamond-studded tiaras and crowns of rose gold reflected the sunlight. I chuckled at the banner above the glittery gems that read: Where Women Get in Trouble and Men Get out of Trouble.

One of the tourists pointed to the clever line as I walked past. "So true, honey," she said with a wink to one of her friends. "Let's go get into some trouble. I see a pair of platinum earrings that will make my husband's eyes spin."

I smiled as I continued on toward Torte, which sat at the far end of the block. Across the street, near the bubbling Lithia fountains, a musician blew on a didgeridoo. The trumpet-like sound echoed throughout the crowded streets. It was nearly impossible not to feel happy in Ashland. Maybe that was due to our Mediterranean climate, the long stretches of sun, the fact that mountains swept to the sky in every direction. The sepia-toned hills to the east and the dark green forests to the west. Or maybe it was due to our eclectic community of artists—drawn to the southernmost corner of Oregon for its picturesque vistas and star-cluttered skies. Ashland was a haven for creative types—writers, painters, sculptors, dancers, actors, visual artists, technology wizards all landed in our hamlet, meshing together seamlessly. And then there were the tourists. One of the reasons I was convinced that Ashland exuded such a laid-back and happy vibe was because at any given time vacationers filled our charming downtown streets, popping into shops and restaurants for an unhurried afternoon and lingering over late-night cocktails after the evening show.

Yep, you're one lucky woman, Jules, I said to myself as I arrived at Torte and pushed open the front door.

Inside, the familiar throng of hammering and the hum of the espresso machine greeted me. Our makeshift dining room consisted of crammed-together chairs and a handful of our dining tables. Usually the front of the bakeshop is open with bright, airy window booths, a collection of two- and four-person tables, our pastry counter, and coffee bar, but during construction we had temporarily reconfigured the space. It was snug, to say the very least.

The entire back half of the shop had been taped off with thick clear plastic. We had removed most of the tables, taken out the old pastry case, and set up a small counter in the short-term that housed our pastry trays and espresso machine.

Andy waved from behind the counter where he was pulling shots of dark, aromatic espresso. I breathed in the scent and said hello to a couple of regulars who were sitting within earshot of the coffee bar. "It's looking good in here, Jules," one of them said, raising an iced matcha latte. The green tea and foamy milk made for a lovely glass.

I glanced around the tight space. Every spare inch of countertop contained trays of cookies, hand pies, and crusty loaves of bread. The plastic tarp flapped in rhythm with the work crew's power tools. Customers squished into booths and tables, and light dusty footprints led from the front door to the construction zone. "Thanks, I think. Hopefully we're in the home stretch. It's . . . uh . . . cozy in here."

"No one cares." The woman pointed to her honey lavender scone. "As long as you keep making baked goods that taste like this, we'll eat out of garbage cans, won't we, Wendy?"

Her friend, Wendy, flashed me a thumbs-up as she took a bite of her pesto egg croissant sandwich.

"Let's hope it doesn't come to that." I grinned and left them to their breakfast. "How's it going?" I asked Andy.

He wore a red Southern Oregon University football

t-shirt, revealing tan, muscular forearms. Practice for the new season began in a few weeks, which meant that Andy would have to take off early for daily doubles. Yet another reason I needed to hire extra staff—stat. "Great, boss!" he yelled over the sound of a jackhammer. "Another quiet morning in coffee paradise."

"Right." I rolled my eyes.

Andy grinned. His impish attitude was one of the many things that endeared him to customers. Particularly with the teen and twenty-something set. There was often a long line at the espresso bar that I knew had as much to do with Andy's boyish good looks and charm as it did with his drool-worthy espresso concoctions. "Hey, there's a girl waiting for you downstairs. She's here early for an interview and I didn't know where else to put her." He motioned to the packed dining area.

At that moment Bethany came through the front door with a tray of lemon drop cupcakes just as two women were leaving. Bethany balanced the tray with one arm as the women ducked under the tray, narrowly avoiding a collision. Visions of lemony buttercream splatting on the floor and windows danced through my head.

"Nice reflexes." Andy applauded. "Skills."

A splotchy blush crept up Bethany's fair, freckled cheeks. I had suspected for a while that Bethany had developed feelings for Andy. I couldn't tell if he was oblivious to the fact that she turned bright red anytime she was around him, or if he simply wasn't interested and figured the kindest thing to do was to play dumb in order to spare her any embarrassment. "Thanks." She set the tray on the counter. "There's a girl waiting for you downstairs, Jules."

"Already told her. You're too late, Beth." Andy shot Bethany a wink and poured foam in the shape of a heart in one of our signature Torte mugs.

When my parents had opened the bakeshop three decades ago, they had wanted to create a gathering space where everyone who walked through the front door was treated like royalty. Torte's cherry red and teal walls, corrugated metal siding, and focus on handmade artisan coffees and pastries had done just that. Now it was my responsibility to make sure that we stayed true to their vision through the new changes and growth. My goal was to ensure that the Torte our customers knew and loved would feel the same. From our delicate Torte logo with its fleur de lys design to our fire engine red aprons and diner style coffee mugs, my mission was to keep the essence of the bakeshop strong and steady through our expanding square footage.

It was a lofty goal, but I was up for the task. Now if I could just find the perfect new staff members, everything would go according to plan.